PLANETSIDE

MICHAEL
MAMMAY

HARPER Voyager
An Imprint of HarperCollins*Publishers*

This is a work of fiction. Names, characters, places, and incidents are products of the author's imagination or are used fictitiously and are not to be construed as real. Any resemblance to actual events, locales, organizations, or persons, living or dead, is entirely coincidental.

First HarperVoyager mass market printing: August 2018

Print Edition ISBN: 978-0-06-269466-9
Digital Edition ISBN: 978-0-06-269467-6

Cover design by Guido Caroti
Cover art by Sebastien Hue
Front sales art © Alan Uster/Shutterstock, inc.

FIRST EDITION

18 19 20 21 22 QGM 10 9 8 7 6 5 4 3 2 1

For my mom, who was the first one to believe.

PLANETSIDE

CHAPTER ONE

I STEPPED OFF THE shuttle in a shitty mood. Three straight days on a crowded ship with two jumps and no booze would do that. Nothing good ever came from answering a communicator in the middle of the night. But when a friend calls, you pick it up. When that friend happens to be the second most powerful man in the military . . . well, he'd have found a way to get through anyway.

The buzzing crowd rushed past me in every direction, one out of ten in some kind of military uniform. Advertisements for armament and defense companies plastered every flat surface, all dazzling colors and lights. I ignored their messages and spotted a sign for ground transport. Slinging my bag over my shoulder, I waded into the river of humanity.

"Colonel Butler?" A lieutenant with a pressed uniform and a round Space Command patch on his sleeve stood at a respectful distance. Headquarters guy.

I glanced down at my name tag. "Yeah."

"Sir, Lieutenant Hardy—"

"General Serata's aide?" I asked.

"Yes, sir." His eyes widened in his dark face, his bearing slipping for a second. Aides usually had the same look about them. Stiff and official. Young. Hardy was no different. "How was your flight, sir?"

"It sucked." Ferra Three to Gamma Six was one of the shortest interplanetary flights going, but that didn't do much to recommend it. "How'd you find me?"

"The general said to look for the colonel wearing the Student Command patch, sir. It stands out here." He pointed to the triangular green-and-yellow patch on my shoulder, not so affectionately known as the Pyramid of Death.

"That's what he told you?"

Hardy cut his eyes away for a second. "Not exactly, sir."

I laughed. "What did he say?"

"He said find the angry, bald colonel with the STU-COM patch, sir."

I laughed again. Classic Serata. "Like that makes me easy to find. Half of us are bald, and we're *all* angry."

Hardy looked at me without reacting. "Our car is just a couple hundred meters. Can I take your bag, sir?"

"No, I've got it."

He paused and frowned, unsure what to do, but finally turned and led the way.

THE HOVER-CAR DRIVER dropped us off at SPACE-COM, in the reserved area. The big-time treatment. Serata was either in a real hurry to talk to me or buttering me up for something.

Probably both.

The building rose from the ground, huge, imposing steel and armo-glass, reflecting the reddish orange of the mid-morning sun. “Damn,” I said.

“You’ve never been here before, sir?”

“I always tried to avoid it.” I’d been in SPACECOM for thirty-seven straight years before my recent assignment to Student, twenty-four of those outside of cryo. Somehow I managed to stay in field units. Headquarters didn’t fit my style.

“You served with the general before, didn’t you, sir?”

I smiled. “That’s right.” Without a doubt Hardy had read my file, knew every assignment, but wanted to make conversation. I didn’t hold it against him. Serata and I served together three times, and they wrote books about at least two of them. Hardy wanted me to tell him a story about his boss. But that was *not* going to happen. I don’t tell those stories sober. “What’s the boss want to see me for?”

“I’m not sure, sir. He didn’t say.” It didn’t matter. Even if he knew, Hardy wouldn’t tell me. Not one of Serata’s guys. The man inspired near fanatical loyalty. I should know. Why else would I be walking in the front entrance of SPACECOM three days after getting his call?

We caught the command elevator, joining a skinny lieutenant colonel wearing infantry insignia. He nodded hello, glanced at my STUCOM patch, and then ignored me. Yeah. Fuck you too, buddy. I’d never met the man, but I knew him. Self-important Staff Guy.

"I need five minutes with the boss," Staff Guy said to Hardy. "I need to get his approval on this." He had a large tablet with a white-and-red Level 4 Classification screen tucked under his arm. He mashed the button for the top floor.

"Yes, sir," said Hardy. "He has a meeting now, but I'll get you in after lunch."

"This will only take a minute." Staff Guy stared me down, daring me to say something. I didn't bother. My days of dick-measuring contests passed a few years back.

We arrived on the top floor and Staff Guy walked quickly, making sure he got in front of us. He put his hand against the scanner and the door to the command suite binged, then whooshed open. Serata, a big beast of a man, waited in the outer office talking to his secretary.

"Sir, I need to get your approval—"

"Carl! Brother!" Serata cut Staff Guy off, pushing past him. He engulfed my hand in his massive paw and we shook and half hugged in the way that male friends do.

"Sir, I just need—"

"Later, Canforra," said Serata. "Come on, Carl."

I didn't look back at Staff Guy—Canforra. I didn't need to. I knew what his face looked like right then.

"Leave your bag with Hardy. He'll get you signed into the DVQ," said Serata. DVQ—distinguished visitor quarters. They had really rolled out the first-class treatment for me. I glanced around for any clues to why, but saw nothing. Serata ushered me into his office, then pulled the door closed. A real wooden door. Who had a wooden door?

"Damn, sir, nice place." Huge floor-to-ceiling windows dominated the room on two sides; a giant wooden desk that looked like it could seat a dozen for dinner sat at least ten meters away from me. Memorabilia from old commands decorated the other two walls, and a framed picture from a decade back drew my eyes. Serata stood in the middle, three of us to each side of him on a snowy hill. Only four of us had lived more than a year past that photo.

"Yeah, they treat me pretty good here." He sat behind his desk and leaned back, interlacing his fingers behind his head. He had close-cropped silver hair, annoyingly thick for a guy several years older than me. "It's good to see you, Carl."

"You too, sir."

"How's STUCOM treating you?"

I snorted. "I teach a few classes, escort VIPs around once in a while. Pretty taxing stuff. I'm not sure they know I'm gone. Good local booze, though."

"Ferra Three always did have good whiskey."

"I brought a bottle." I looked around. "Crap. Hardy took my bag."

Serata waved his hand. "We'll get it later. How's Sharon? She like it there?"

"Hates it. Too cold." My wife, Sharon, loved her warm weather.

"Yeah. Lizzie always hated it there too." He paused, finished with small talk, and the silence grew awkward.

"That Canforra guy, he's kind of an ass," I said.

Serata laughed. "Nah, he's good. He just thinks everything is an emergency. The galaxy won't implode if I don't sign the deployment order for another hour."

"Sending more troops forward?" Living at STU-COM, I stayed out of touch. I could have followed things if I made an effort.

I didn't.

"Just a brigade," he said. "It will give us some extra combat power until we rotate one back. Make a little push out at Cappa Three."

"That's not what you need me for, is it?" It seemed unlikely. He had better guys for that. Commanding a combat brigade didn't really match my skill set.

"No, I'd never ask you to do that." His tone made it clear that he'd ask me to do something else. He could order me, but he wouldn't. Not sure why I knew that. History, maybe. Instinct.

"You want to stick the knife in now, sir?" You didn't call someone out of semi-retirement and put him on an interplanetary flight to give him good news.

Serata put his feet up on his desk, almost too casual. "Investigation. We've got a missing lieutenant."

I stared at him for a moment. He couldn't have possibly needed me for something that simple. Then the other hammer dropped.

"The lieutenant's name is Mallot. As in *High Councilor* Mallot," he clarified. "I know you don't pay much attention to the news these days, but if you did, you'd have seen it."

"Oh. Shit."

"Yeah. Kid's gone MIA out of Cappa Base," he said.

"On the front. What's a councilor's kid doing out there? I mean, it's pretty quiet now, but still."

"Family tradition. Every son for four hundred years has served. A lot of daughters, too. Ever hear of Emily Eckstedt?"

"The Angel of Death? Yes, sir, everyone's heard of her."

"That was this kid's great-grandmother's sister."

"Wow. We sure this isn't simply a case of a kid not wanting to stand in line for comm time to call home? Happens all the time." A stupid question, but I needed the time to process things. Cappa Fucking Base.

"Come on, Carl. You know we've done everything we can. And you know I wouldn't ask you to go unless it was important. Not to Cappa. Not after—"

"That was a long time ago, sir. I'm over that now," I lied. "You want me to go to Cappa. How long a trip is that? Nine or ten months cryo each way? I'm supposed to retire in a year. That's why they put me out to pasture at STUCOM." I didn't want to do it, but it wouldn't be easy to turn down Serata. Not after everything we'd been through.

"I know it." Serata swung his feet down and walked to the window. Several low, boxy buildings lined the opposite side of a large, open square. "You can say no if you want. You've got as much cryo time as any colonel in the force. As much combat time, too. You've done your part."

I sighed. Telling me I could say no made it harder. Shit. "Sharon is going to pitch a fit. I'm already thirteen years younger than her because of all my time in cryo."

"So fifteen months of cryo pay, plus a bump in your retirement years. Buy her a treatment. They can take ten years off." Serata smiled.

"Fifteen months? It's farther than that," I said.

"I've got you on the XT-57 on the way out. Less than five months."

"Damn." I sat up in my chair. The Executive Transport 57 was the fastest transport in the military. There were maybe fifteen or twenty of them in the inventory, and they didn't use them for transporting random colonels. "This really *is* important."

"Yeah. We need you there fast, before everyone forgets what happened," he said.

"Makes sense. How long has his unit been there?" Again, I was asking questions, but my mind was churning. *He could get someone else. A simple mission. Lots of guys could do it . . .*

"Just under five months." Serata paused. "I've got something for Sharon, too. Maybe she won't be so pissed at me. To make it work, we'll need to transfer you to SPACECOM. We'll assign you to Fifth Space."

My breath caught. "Sir . . ."

"Yeah." He turned to face me. "It's important. But it's a good deal, too."

Fifth Space, based at Elenia Four. My first duty station. Sharon's home planet. Even if I hadn't planned to do it before, I couldn't pass that up. My wife would kill me. "Fifth Space has a slot?"

He drew his lips into a line and nodded. "They do now."

I swallowed, then nodded. "What do you need me to do, sir?"

"Just go out there, poke around, file a report. Lot of Special Ops there, plus a line brigade. I need someone who speaks their language, but understands the importance of what I'm dealing with back here. That's a pretty small subset."

"Yes, sir." Most guys on the front wouldn't give half a thought for a federation High Councilor. "How do you want the report to read?"

Serata laughed. "I knew I had the right guy." I wouldn't falsify a report. He knew that. But you could find a dozen truths in any situation. I had no problem telling the one that helped the team.

"The truth is, I don't know what I want." He sat on the edge of his mammoth desk.

I paused to think about it, but didn't find an answer. "I don't get it, sir. Why me then?"

"Because I have no idea what you're going to find. It might be clean, it might be messy. And I need someone who knows which it is when he sees it." He paused. "Here's the deal: This *has* to be clean. I don't care what you do, I don't care who you have to burn. High Councilor Mallot has enough sway that he practically owns our budget, and he's all over my ass. Find his kid, or find out what happened to him. This thing needs to be quick and tight. Airlock fucking tight."

I sat for a moment in silence. Serata pretended to

look out the window, giving me time without any pressure. "Shit, sir. I hope this kid knows how much trouble he's causing."

"He probably doesn't . . ." His voice tailed off like maybe he had something else to say, but decided against it. Odd. Serata never did anything by accident.

"I'll do it."

"Great. Important people will be watching this."

I stood. "It's good, sir. You know me."

Serata chuckled. "Yeah, I do. That's why I mentioned it."

I put my hands to my heart in a mock gesture of hurt. "I've got it, sir."

"Thanks, Carl."

"Yes, sir. Sharon will be ecstatic. Elenia Four, plus she gets rid of me for a year."

Serata smiled. "You want to call and tell her?"

"Hell no, sir. I'm saving this one until I get home."

CHAPTER TWO

I STEPPED OUT INTO the hangar orbiting above Elenia Four and the headquarters for Fifth Space Command twenty days after I walked out of Serata's office. People say you can't move your entire life from one planet to another in two weeks. Those people haven't had enough practice.

I'd settled Sharon in a rented house, far from any military base but close to her sister and her aging parents. By settled, I mean I left her with a couple hundred containers of stuff that she had to unpack, but she never liked me getting in the way of decorating.

That's what I told myself, anyway.

She didn't make the trip to see me off. We had grown past that stage of our life together. We'd done it before more than once, the teary farewell, so we didn't feel the need for a repeat performance. Easier to say our good-byes at home, in private. Always better, if you ask me, because people frowned on you getting naked in the hangar.

Instead I met up with Hardy, who I found somewhat lacking as a substitute. I hadn't wanted him on the trip, but Serata insisted. I'm a colonel. Colonels don't have aides, and I didn't need one, but the boss thought the kid had potential and wanted to give him a chance to go to the front. Serata liked the kid. That meant something. For starters, it probably meant Serata had tasked him to report back on me.

"Did you see the news, sir? There's a lot of talk about our mission." Hardy still wore pressed battle dress, ridiculous given our destination.

"I try to avoid it."

"I don't understand, sir. Don't you need to know what's going on?" He went to grab my baggage. Two bags and one box.

"I know the mission, Hardy. Anything else just clouds things up."

Hardy paused and looked at me. When I didn't explain, he grabbed the box, which clinked when it moved.

"Sir . . . what—"

"It's whiskey, Hardy. Very good Ferra Three Whiskey."

"Sir, we're not allowed to transport alcohol on a SPACECOM vehicle."

I stared at him. "What are they going to do? Make me retire? Wait, maybe they could send me to the front as punishment."

Hardy looked at me with that look people get when they aren't sure if I'm serious. "Sir, the pilots won't let you take it on."

"That's why the first bottle's for them," I said.

"Sir—"

"Look, Hardy, you're going to have to get used to something. I'm not General Serata. I do things . . . differently. I can get away with it, mostly because I'm not a general. I don't have the disposition for it. Or the hair." I paused. "Where was I?"

"The liquor, sir."

"Right. Hardy, if we get in trouble for the liquor, I will swear that I ordered you, against your will, to load it on board. That you protested vehemently, to no avail. Can we move forward now?"

"Yes, sir." He almost smiled. He might make it. If I had to have an aide, he'd need to have a sense of humor.

The XT-57 sat on a raised platform, a monster of a ship with a set of stairs leading up. Nobody would call it sleek, or sexy. More snub-nosed and blocky. Looks were deceiving, though: Shape didn't matter much in space, only thrust and mass. That's where the XT made money. She carried only six passengers and three crew, keeping the mass low. All engine and fuel cell. Ridiculously inefficient, unless you wanted to transport a colonel a long way in a hurry.

My boots clanked on the webbed iron stairs and a slight breeze hit me as I reached the door, the overpressure exiting the craft. When I walked in, the inside looked too small to be part of the same beast. It sparkled, as if someone had replaced the interior recently, and it smelled almost sterile. Nine horizontal cryo pods dominated the passenger compartment in rows of three. Of course, I don't know why we call it cryo. They haven't used cold technology for stasis in several hundred years. Tradition, I guess. Whatever they were called, the pods were bracketed by six big, black comfortable chairs, three down each wall. I shook hands with the pilot, copilot, and doctor. I followed the same routine every time I got on something that flew. Call it superstition if you want, but I'm still alive, so I don't care. Mostly the computer flew the ship, but they'd handle the duties inside of the solar system on takeoff before entering their own cryo pods. They couldn't fly as well as a computer, but I think it made people more comfortable to know they had a person in charge. I know it did for me. The doctor would see us all safely sedated, then put herself under as well. I didn't want to even think about how one would manage that.

"Sir, I've got your body armor, in case you want to try it on before we take off," said Hardy.

"Is it a large regular?" I could jam into a medium-sized vest if I had to, but I preferred a little room to move, and the pauldrons on the medium sometimes pinched my shoulders.

"Yes, sir."

"It'll fit." Then I glanced over. "Mother of planets, do you think you could have got something shinier?" The polymer breast plate practically glowed.

"It's brand new, sir."

"I can see that, Hardy. Don't worry, that won't stand out at all on the front." I felt bad after I said it. Hardy resembled a dog that got caught taking a dump where it shouldn't. Kid meant well. I pointed two lockers over to a worn set, the tan surface of the vest pockmarked, with a scar on the right side. "See, that's what armor should look like."

A man stood up out of the farthest chair. "That's mine, sir. Staff Sergeant McCann. Your PS." PS. Personal Security. Another argument I lost with Serata. Basically my bodyguard, which I didn't need for this trip. But if I had to have one, McCann looked the part. He stood at least six or seven centimeters shorter than me, but what he lacked in height he made up for in width. All shoulders and muscles, probably not a kilo of fat in his entire body.

"McCann. Can I call you Mac?"

"Yes, sir, I'd be glad if you did," he said.

"Nice to meet you, Mac. What in the galaxy are you drinking?" He had a liter-sized container holding something that looked like a cross between avocado and vomit.

"Protein shake, sir. You want one?"

I winced in disgust. "I'm going to pass, thanks."

"Gotta keep the weapons loaded, sir." Mac slapped one of his biceps, the size of another man's thigh.

"I prefer my weapons to have longer range." I pointed to the Bikoski 71 projectile rifle slung across his chest. Affectionately known as the Bitch. "You're carrying the Bikoski instead of a pulse?"

"Yes, sir." Mac smiled proudly. "I don't trust those pulse weapons. Get them wet and they go to shit."

"We shouldn't be getting wet where we're going," I said.

"You never know, sir. I've got this Bitch kitted out

with every smart projectile in the inventory. Explosive, armor piercing, guided . . ."

I liked the guy already. The pulse was sexier, lighter, and always a favorite on base where nobody shot anyone, but true grunts always wanted a Bitch. "You never know. Are you the general's spy, or is it Hardy?" I said it half joking, but dumping it into the conversation so bluntly got the effect across.

Mac shrugged. "Not me, sir. I've never met the general other than to say good morning when I passed him in the hall."

I nodded. "So Hardy, how often are you supposed to report in?"

"Sir, I . . . sir . . ." Hardy's face puckered, like he couldn't decide if he should talk and forgot to breathe.

I let the silence hang awkwardly.

"Got your sidearm when you're ready, sir," Mac said after a moment. He held out a Mark 24 pistol and I took it. More of a decoration than anything else. I checked the chamber to make sure it was empty. Habit. I tossed it in my locker with my bag. I'd get it when we came out of cryo.

Mac nodded at my box of liquor. "Is that from Ferra Three, sir?"

"It is. Fifteen years old."

Mac whistled. "I'm going to like serving with you, sir."

"I hope you do. What'd you do to get stuck with this assignment?"

"I volunteered, sir."

I looked at him more closely. "Really?"

"Yes, sir. They were asking around HQ for someone with experience, and I jumped at it."

"What did you do at headquarters?" I asked.

"Admin clerk, sir."

I stared harder, unable to tell if he was screwing with me or not. Everything about him screamed infantry. "You don't look like an admin . . ."

"I used to be infantry, sir. Switched over three years ago. Thought it would give me more time to spend with my wife."

I moved out of the way so Hardy could stow some gear. "Makes sense. How is that treating you?"

"We got divorced last year," he said.

I nodded solemnly. "Sorry to hear it."

"It's all good, sir." He smiled with half his mouth.

Our pilot poked her head out of the front compartment, short black hair over a golden face. She waited for me to make eye contact. "Sir, we did our checks before you boarded. Whenever you're ready, we'll get under way."

"Thanks. How long until we go cryo?"

"About a day, sir. We can't use the speed of the XT until we clear the fifth planet. Too much traffic."

"Fair enough," I said. "Let's strap in, team. Long trip ahead, no sense putting it off." I picked out one of the oversized seats and made myself comfortable. I fell asleep before we left the station.

CHAPTER THREE

COMING OUT OF stasis, I didn't wake up exactly. More like I faded in. My seventeenth time, but who's counting? They say you're awake for a couple hours, but you're not aware. They pull your breathing tube, then there's light, and your eyes start to work, but you don't process anything you see. I'm not sure what to compare it to, as it's unlike anything else I've ever done. I had one colleague compare it to finishing a twenty-kilometer run, combined with a hangover and vertigo.

In other words, it sucks.

I looked at the big clock on the wall, the one with the date in bright red digital numbers. Four months, nineteen days since I went under.

"Doc, I'm back," I said, my voice raspy from nonuse, my throat dry and sore from the tube I'd had shoved down it for months. I forced myself into a sitting position in my pod, letting some of the sticky orange mess slide down from my chest and shoulders.

"Colonel. Good to see you." She wore a white jumpsuit under a lab coat, her blonde hair pinned up in back, like she came out of the doctor catalogue. She'd have woken two days prior to prepare for the rest of us, so her hair wasn't matted to her head in goop the way mine was. What little hair I had.

She pressed a stethoscope to my chest and listened for a moment through my sticky stasis suit. "Sounds good. I'll get your shot."

"No shot," I said.

"Sir, it will help with the nausea."

"I don't need it." I started to lever my legs out of the pod, then decided I needed another minute. "All I need is some biscuits and gravy."

"Sir, you will really feel better—"

"I can't believe they don't teach you about biscuits and gravy in med school."

She put one hand on her hip and looked at me with annoyed doctor eyes.

"I'm not taking a shot." I wasn't kidding—biscuits and gravy really did work for me.

"As the mission medical officer, I could order you." She continued to glare at me, but I shrugged. She sighed. "You're really not taking the shot, sir?"

"Nope. Who else is up?"

"Just the pilots. I brought you out before the other two passengers, per your orders."

"Good. Bring Mac out next. I'm going to get out of this slime suit and get a shower. Then I'm going to find some biscuits and gravy."

I KNOCKED ON the door to the flight deck before I walked in, fresh in my gravy afterglow. The copilot hastily stashed his reader. Maybe he thought I didn't know the ship flew itself, or that I cared.

"How far out are we?" I asked. I could see the white sun of the Cappa system, far away through the front viewport. I'd never seen another like it up close, so bright even from a distance. I wasn't aware of another Class F star like it that supported life, but then again I didn't really study such things.

"Four days, eight hours," said the pilot. I should have learned her name before we went into stasis, but I didn't. I'm bad at things like that. "We have to go slow because of the traffic in the combat zone."

"Four days out? Why so far?" One to two days was normal.

"I'm not sure, sir. The computer brought us out." said the pilot. "It's all automated."

"Sure. Does this happen often?" I asked.

The pilot shrugged. "It happens, sir. Not often."

I shook my head slightly, and tried to refocus. "What's the commo delay back to SPACECOM?"

"Twenty-eight jumps, sir. Seventeen minutes, nineteen seconds," said the copilot. That sounded about right—you can only jump so far, and every jump means a relay station for your comms. More relay stations, more delay.

"Get me a line." I sat in the jump seat. My stomach was fine, but my legs hadn't fully recovered from the stasis.

The pilot handed me a small tablet. "Do you need a private space, sir?"

"No, there's nothing secret. I just need to give a status and see if there's new guidance."

I tapped out my message with my thumbs.

General Serata, sir, we're live, just over four days out from Cappa, no issues. Checking in for updated guidance.

"Anything else, sir?" asked the pilot.

"No. Just let me know when you get a response." I headed back to the passenger compartment so that I could screw with Hardy as he came out of stasis. His first time. I kind of owed it to him.

I GOT SERATA'S response less than forty-five minutes later. I didn't know the time at SPACECOM, but with nearly thirty-five minutes of delay for the messages, he'd answered quickly. I tried not to guess at what that meant when the copilot handed me a device.

"Did you read it?"

"No, sir. We knew it was for you when it came in, so we had it go straight to the guest reader." I'd have read it if I were him. I couldn't fly all the way out to the middle of nowhere carrying a relic of a colonel and not be curious. The copilot looked honest though, so I believed him.

Butler: Four days out? You're late. I expected to hear from you two days ago, and expected you to land tomorrow at the latest. Media is still sniffing around the investigation. It's died down some, but they won't let it go. I think someone on High Councilor Mallot's staff keeps bringing it up to keep it alive. Get there and get this thing done. Make sure it's tight. Serata.

I swore silently. My gut reaction shouted to send him a note back, telling him that I had no control over the length of the flight. But he knew that, and even if he didn't, he wouldn't want to hear the excuse. Serata wanted everything now, regardless of the original timeline he gave you. He always had. I appreciated the heads-up about the media, but as an investigating officer I had the magic armor: "I'm sorry, I can't comment due to an ongoing investigation." Not that I expected the media out at Cappa Base. Well, maybe a field reporter, working down on the front, beaming news of the war to the rest of the galaxy. But I wouldn't know—that was the kind of news I avoided back home.

CHAPTER FOUR

THE INSIDE OF the hangar at Cappa Base remained much the way I remembered it, steel and aluminum painted in that light green color that said, "This place is too military to be painted white." It looked like every hangar on every system base I'd ever flown into, with a high roof, polymer walls, and skid-free decking. I think one company had the contract for all of them, developed one model, then built it to scale depending on the requirement, invoking as little imagination as possible.

I purposely hadn't studied the new situation much. Just enough to refresh my memory. I wanted to go in with a clear head, and anything I read before cryo would have gone stale by the time we arrived anyway. That's the trick with war. If you're out for ninety days, you don't know anything. Things change. So many people forget that. By the time you get back to civilization, everything you knew was already obsolete.

I walked down the ramp of the XT and headed for the hangar exit toward the brigade headquarters, trusting Hardy to follow. He'd supervise getting our stuff off the ship. I heard Mac's footsteps, hurrying to catch up. He wouldn't say anything about me leaving him behind. He also wouldn't let me walk off alone, even on a friendly base a couple hundred thousand kilometers from the nearest enemy. I slowed to let him catch up. He had a job to do too.

"Colonel Butler?" A female voice. Definitely not Mac. I stopped and turned, waiting for the officer to close the last forty meters. She wore a shoulder rig for her pistol over her battle uniform. Broad shoulders, like a swimmer. She had brushed-copper skin, short, almost spiky dark hair, and no hat. No hats for anyone in an active hangar. I don't know why.

"Sir? I'm Major Alenda. On behalf of Colonel Stirling, I'd like to welcome you to Cappa Base."

"Nice to meet you, Alenda. You get stuck meeting me?" Stupid question, but I had to say something.

"The colonel asked me to meet you, sir. Colonel Stirling is planetside. He won't be back until late tonight."

An interesting turn. I didn't know Stirling except by his reputation. Fast mover, a solid line officer who probably had a future. He knew when I'd be arriving and chose to be off base. Maybe he meant that to send me a message. Or perhaps he simply had a war to run and no time to play games with an asshole from headquarters.

Probably a bit of both.

I shifted my weight from one foot to the other. "I don't want to start my investigation without talking to him first."

"Yes, sir. The colonel anticipated that. You're on his calendar right after breakfast tomorrow."

"If that fits. I don't want to be a bother." I followed the format of the lie. I insisted I didn't want to be a bother, even though we all knew that I would be. A colonel from outside nosing around could never *not* be a bother.

She seemed to get it. "If you want to follow me, sir, I'll show you to your quarters. My people will see to your bags." Three soldiers stood slightly out of earshot, waiting for orders.

"Great." I thought a silent prayer hoping they wouldn't break my whiskey. "Is Sergeant McCann staying near me?"

"Yes, sir," said Alenda.

Of course she'd made sure of that. "Lead on, then. So, what do you do here, Alenda?"

"I work in the intelligence shop, sir. Now I'm your liaison."

I stopped, and Alenda stopped with me without a hitch. "My *liaison*?"

"Yes, sir. Colonel Stirling wants me to assist you with your investigation. Set up meetings and interviews, get you whatever information you require from the command."

I hadn't expected that, but I guess it didn't deviate too much from the ordinary. Of course Stirling would want to speed my investigation along as quickly as possible. Having someone to keep an eye on me was just a bonus. "Interesting." I said it as much to provoke a response as anything else.

She smiled flatly, her lips thin, not taking the bait.

I nodded. "Okay. But if we're going to work together, we'll get along a lot better if we don't bullshit each other. We both know you work for Stirling, and we both know what that means."

Something flashed across her face for a moment, but calmed just as quickly. "Yes, sir. I work for Colonel Stirling, but I have no standing orders to report anything to do with the investigation."

"But that could change," I said.

"Yes, sir. My orders could change."

"Fair enough. What's your first name, Alenda?"

"Lexa, sir."

"Do you mind if I call you that?"

"Of course, sir. That would be fine. Lexa, or Lex."

"Lex. One syllable is always good." I'd try to remember to call her Lex, though the real reason I wanted her first name was so that I could pull her file later. If I had to have a spy, I wanted to know her history. I needed to get an idea of how much to trust her. Right now my gut said not much, but that reflected more on Stirling than her. He'd want a loyal person on that job. I'd have to work to break that down. Try to at least sway her to neutral, even if she'd never completely join my side.

Lex glanced down at the ground, then back up. "Sir, I know this isn't very professional to say, but . . ."

"Go ahead," I prompted.

"Sir, I just want to say . . . it's an honor to be working with you. I've read a lot of history—"

"Yeah, thanks," I said, cutting her off before it got

embarrassing. I forced a smile. "We'll see if you think it's an honor after a few days."

I knew my quarters before we entered, but I didn't tell Lex. She probably knew. They hadn't changed the distinguished visitor suite since I'd been here last. The rooms glistened in freshly polished polymer and fake leather that had looked good fifteen years ago. It consisted of a sitting room and office combination, a sofa and coffee table along the left wall, a desk and food area along the right. The far wall held a large computer station and above that a digital window showed a view of the distant planet from the outside of the station, so real-looking that I might have been staring out actual glass. In truth, no living quarters were anywhere near external walls, and the station had no windows. An open set of double doors past the food area led into a bedroom, complete with my own shower and toilet. I didn't mind the perk. As I grew older, I appreciated a toilet nearby at night more and more.

I waited for Lex to leave, stashed my shoulder bag, then picked up Mac and Hardy and headed for the mess hall. Plenty of time to set up my room later.

PEOPLE BUSTLED THROUGH the big room, in uniform and out, military personnel mixed with the defense contractors who kept the base running. I'd hit a peak hour for chow by the looks of it, and I stopped out of the line of traffic to scan the room. Heads turned when I came in, the effect of a strange colonel. Voices hushed around me and people went about their business a bit quicker than they might have otherwise.

I'd asked Mac and Hardy to hang behind so I could enter alone. I wanted to make myself accessible. Somewhere I'd find someone I knew, someone I'd worked with, but too many faces passed by to process, too much movement. I've never been good at remembering people anyway.

I made my way to the line and grabbed a tray. Even if I didn't find someone to talk to I could at least fill my stomach. I pointed at one of the two entrée choices, the one that looked the least like a gray hunk of fused crap, and the server slopped it onto my plate. At least they had fresh vegetables, probably grown on base or on a nearby agriculture ship.

I weaved through the long rectangular tables until I found one with some empty seats. I took a chair a couple of spots away from three non-coms who immediately stopped talking. One of them nodded to me, respectfully, and a few minutes later they left. So much for learning something through casual conversation. I gave a mental shrug and then went about shoveling my food in.

"Sir! I thought that was you." A master sergeant stood across the table, no plate. I flipped through my memory trying to place him. A cook. Goodell . . . no, Goddard. He hadn't been a master sergeant.

"Hey! Did you get promoted?" I let my eyes flick to his name tape to confirm my memory.

"Yes, sir, about a year ago."

"Nice. You're not cooking out here are you?" I glanced down at my plate.

He laughed. "No, sir. This is all contracted. I do

quality control. Make sure the meat is the right temperature, stuff like that."

"There's meat?"

He laughed again. "Come back tomorrow. We're having real chicken."

"No kidding?"

"Yes, sir. They raise them down on the planet now."

"Excellent," I said. "I look forward to it."

"What brings you out this way, sir? Are you taking the command?" Something in the way he said it made me suspicious. Like maybe he knew something, but wanted me to confirm it.

I shook my head, playing along. "Nothing like that. Just out here doing an investigation."

Goddard let out a low whistle. "So it's true."

"What's that?" I asked, feigning ignorance.

"Rumor has been going around about a bigwig coming from headquarters to check out the brigade. I'd heard your name mentioned."

I bit back a grimace. That wouldn't help my cause, if they'd pegged me as the outsider. Soldiers tended to stick together in the face of external pressure, and in this case, sticking together meant keeping their mouths shut. I wondered if the media caused it, or something more intentional.

Goddard spoke again after a moment. "They bring someone like you out here to poke around, it must be something good. Senior officer put his dick somewhere he shouldn't?"

I smiled. "I can officially neither confirm nor deny that. But no, nothing like that. MIA case."

Goddard narrowed his eyes a bit, as if deep in thought. “Not that kid in the news.”

“That’s the one,” I said.

“Damn, sir. I can’t believe they sent a colonel all the way out here for that.” He paused, leaving an obvious opening for me to comment.

I took a bite of mystery meat to stall for time. It made the lull in the conversation slightly less awkward and gave him the hint that I probably wouldn’t be answering anytime soon.

“I’ll let you get back to your meal, sir. Just wanted to say hi.” He kept his smile. Good guy.

I stood and shook his hand. “It’s good to see you again, Master Sergeant. I’ll be around.”

“You too, sir. Good to see you.” As he walked off, I couldn’t decide if he’d given me good news or bad.

CHAPTER FIVE

I WALKED FOR ABOUT four minutes through the mostly empty corridors of Cappa Base, trying to establish some landmarks in the windowless construction so I could get around without a map. I'd forgotten the uniformity of everything related to space life, with only colored symbols on the walls to mark my location. I could have lived without experiencing it again.

I showed up in Colonel Stirling's outer office ten minutes before the appointed time. A soldier offered me coffee, which I accepted. I managed one sip of the scalding beverage before Stirling came out to greet me. No waiting games. Good.

He was a short man, at least six or seven centimeters shorter than me, and I'm average height. Thin, too, but not in a weak way. More like a runner, or triathlete. He had his hair cut high and tight, accentuating his poster-worthy square jaw. "Welcome, Carl. Glad you made it. I'm Aaron."

I shifted my coffee to my left hand so I could shake

the one he offered. "Glad to be here." I felt okay lying, since he lied first.

"Come on in." He led me into his functional office, moderate sized and appropriate. Pictures of soldiers in action planetside decorated the walls along with unit accomplishments. Military texts and journals lined the single bookcase along with a few volumes on leadership. Nothing personal to Stirling other than the photo of his family on his desk. One wife, two boys. Standard commander accoutrements that tried to humanize him a little without giving anything away.

"You know why I'm here," I said.

Stirling gestured for me to take a seat on the fake-leather sofa. "I do. Lieutenant Mallot. Councilor's kid. Good man, from what I've heard. Good grunt."

"You never met him?"

He shook his head, took a sip of his coffee. "I don't know most of the LTs. Hell, I don't even know all the captains. I keep a book with the faces of the commanders, so I recognize them."

"Smart." With nearly forty companies, you had to study.

"You've done a preliminary investigation," I said.

He nodded. "We did. Of course. By the book. It's not worth much, though."

I waved my hand, dismissing it. "I just need the basics to help me get started. Where he went missing, who saw him last, enemy in the area, that kind of thing."

Stirling froze, his coffee cup halfway to his mouth, staring. I stopped moving too, his look arresting me.

"You didn't get the basics before you flew?"

"I didn't ask for them. I wanted to see it fresh when I got here, keep an open mind."

Stirling stood and paced to the wall behind his desk, his back toward me. He paused a moment, then turned and walked back. He planted his palms on his desk and leaned over. "He didn't disappear in combat. Not exactly."

Something in his tone, the way he shifted his eyes when he spoke, made me sit up in my chair. The hair on my arms tingled. I set my coffee cup down on the end table and took out my device, thumbing open a note page. "What happened?"

He blew air out between pursed lips and paused, considering his words. "I don't know."

It wasn't the answer I expected, but I didn't say anything. Stirling continued.

"His battalion had chopped his platoon over to the Special Ops guys. They got hit. Nobody in my outfit even knew about the fight until we got the call for medical evacuation. We couldn't bring the bird in immediately. Too much heat around the landing zone. The battalion pushed out half a company to secure the site. They got there, and Mallot's legs were chewed up. Looked like a potato mine, my guys said."

I winced. A potato mine was a Cappan creation, buried in the ground, with an organic case which made it almost impossible to detect. Not always deadly, but always bad. "I thought you said it wasn't combat related."

"I said the disappearance wasn't. He got on the MEDEVAC. My guys saw them put him on."

"So he disappeared after he arrived at the hospital?"

He shook his head. "He didn't arrive."

I stopped writing mid-sentence and almost dropped my stylus before I recovered and looked up to meet Stirling's eyes. "Where did he go?"

"That's the million-mark question." Stirling sat at his desk, looked down, and rubbed his temples. "He got on the bird. That's the last time anyone saw him."

"So where did the MEDEVAC go?"

"Its records say it came straight back here to base. But the hospital shows no record of him arriving."

I tapped a quick note, not because I wouldn't remember. I needed to take a moment to think. "Huh."

I might have needed more than a moment.

"It's bullshit." He pounded his fist on the desk.

The outburst felt a bit contrived, but I let it go without reacting. "What's the pilot of the MEDEVAC say?"

"He doesn't say anything. He's dead. The whole crew, three days later, hit during another pickup."

"Shit." I paused. "Is that common?"

"Unfortunately it's not *un*common. We've lost four in the last five months. The Cappan insurgents have been targeting them."

Targeting evacuation ships? I looked down at my notes, which didn't tell me much. It didn't matter. The ideas had started to bounce around in my head, and

I needed the excuse to consider my next question. "Three days later. You had to know he was missing before then."

"Of course we did. We tried to get in to see him. Not immediately. He needed surgery, we knew that. But within half a day."

"And?"

"And he wasn't there. Maybe another half day before someone elevated it to my level. It's all in the initial investigation. Statements, timelines, lack of cooperation from the hospital commander."

Stirling sounded bitter about the last part, and I observed him for several seconds. He met my eyes without wavering, but also without challenge. "He wouldn't let you see Mallot?" I asked.

"She. Colonel Mary Elliot. The hospital commander."

"She wouldn't let you see him?" I repeated.

"I told you—Mallot wasn't there. Was never there, from what we can tell. From what they tell us, nobody saw him." Stirling almost pushed himself out of his chair.

"So the lack of cooperation . . . the pilot . . . she wouldn't let you talk to him?"

"Right." He relaxed, slightly. "Elliot invoked her own authority. Said she'd question her people, get to the bottom of it."

"But she didn't."

Stirling sighed, his shoulders sagging slightly. "Not that I can tell. If she did . . . well, she doesn't answer to me."

"You're the base commander."

"I'm the base commander for *SPACECOM*," he said a little too quickly. "She reports directly to MEDCOM. And Karikov—he reports directly to Special Ops Command."

"I see." Karikov. I didn't know him, but I'd heard of him. Everyone had. A legend and a badass. "That's a pretty messed-up way to run a war."

Stirling pulled his lips into a flat line. "Yeah."

"Got it. Not what I expected, that's all." I sat silently, but Stirling allowed me the time to think. Serata hadn't mentioned the issues with command structure. He may not have known, but that seemed like a stretch.

"I've got a liaison officer for you. Major Alenda. She's got a copy of the initial report," Stirling said, after a bit.

"I met her." I assumed he knew that, but it didn't seem prudent to make a point of it.

"She's solid. Use her however she helps. You don't have to keep her in the loop if you don't want." He knew I'd consider her a spy. Stirling and I had the same basic background, the same experiences. We would generally know what the other thought simply because we had the same thought process. I'd have to watch that.

I nodded. "Thanks. I'll give her a chance. You have anyone I can use at the hospital?"

Stirling shook his head. "I'm afraid you're on your own on that one. Elliot and I aren't on great terms, as you might have guessed."

"Okay. Well that's probably where I need to start."

"Good luck," he said.

"Thanks. I'll keep you informed."

Stirling stood up and came around the desk, forcing a smile. I expected that he'd relax a bit, now that the interview was over, but the muscles in his neck and the tension in his handshake said otherwise. He met my eyes very deliberately. "Thanks, Carl. If there's anything you need from my command and you aren't getting it, you let me know. We want to be completely transparent, and cooperate fully with your investigation."

I nodded. He used the right words. He had no choice. Not cooperating would reflect poorly on his command. I wouldn't know until later if he really meant them or not, but for now, I'd play along. "Thanks, Aaron."

"I just want this wrapped up quick and tight."

"We all do." Quick and tight. Serata's words. Might have been a coincidence, but I doubted it.

CHAPTER SIX

MAJOR LEX ALENDA buzzed at my door at precisely 1300 standard time, exactly the time I asked her to be there. She held a tablet with a blue cover screen in her hand.

"Come on in, Lex." I stepped out of the way to make space for her to pass. "You can go if you want, Mac." He'd been sitting there for a couple hours acting as a sounding board. I didn't really need security in my room.

"Yes, sir," he said. "I'm going to hit the gym. I'll be back before you need to go anywhere."

Alenda held up the tablet she'd brought. "I have a copy of the report loaded for you, sir. And I've dropped it into your account on the network as well. Did you have any trouble accessing the system?"

"No, I got in, no problem. What do you normally do, Lex? You said Intel, but what capacity?"

"Intel fusion," she said. "Targeting, mostly."

"Nice. I did some years in targeting." I wasn't an intel officer, but I'd spent a lot of time with them. I liked them, mostly, although it made a weird choice for a liaison. I didn't really care, though. I needed to start establishing a relationship. I needed Alenda to see me as a person rather than as a colonel from headquarters. She'd work better for me that way, or I'd know that I couldn't use her at all. Either way.

"So you can tell me what's going on planetside?"

"Yes, sir," she said. "Or I can set up an ops brief. That might be better—get you the intel and the ops at the same time."

"Sure, set it up. I'll go through this today." I waved the tablet in the air. "I'll figure out whose statements stand and who I need to talk to. Fair warning: I'm going to want to talk to most everyone, I think. Go ahead, sit down."

Alenda went to the sofa and perched on the front edge of it, her legs directly in front of her.

"You can relax, Lex."

She scooted maybe four centimeters farther back onto the sofa, her shoulders still square, her back rigid.

"Where are you from?" I asked. Senior Officer 101. Get people to talk about where they're from to establish a personal connection.

"Nowhere, really, sir. I'm a military brat. We moved around with my father. I have a house now on Elenia Four, so I guess that's home."

"Elenia Four. My wife's there too. She's from there originally. She went back to live near her family."

A hint of a smile crossed her face. "It's a nice system. Great weather, and I like that the terraforming is complete, so the amino acids are right and it's pretty much self-sufficient. Something about getting your food fresh makes life better. I could see myself settling there someday."

"Yeah. I could see myself settling there too. And not just because my wife said she's never leaving again." I smiled. "So . . . you have any thoughts on where to start on this thing?"

She sagged back a little into the sofa. "Yes, sir. I read through the initial report. It's . . . well, it's not very useful. I don't know if people weren't talking or if the investigator didn't ask the right questions."

I nodded. "It's okay. I'll use it as a baseline, to see if people keep the same story."

"Yes, sir. A lot of the guys are planetside. Mallot's unit, most of the Spec Ops people. They come and go. I can work to get them rotated back here. At least the ones who work for us. Spec Ops, not so much."

"I'm not sure I want to start bringing folks up off the surface yet. We'll talk to who we can here, and figure the rest of it out. Did you set up the meeting with the hospital commander?"

Lex didn't answer immediately.

I raised my eyebrows. "Nothing?"

"They said they'd get back to me, sir."

"Do you think they will?"

"No, sir, I don't." She didn't hesitate. Stirling's rift with the medical command apparently ran deep.

"Can you draw me a strip map to the hospital? I can't remember exactly how to get there."

"I can lead you over there, sir. Or arrange transportation. It's a long walk."

I smiled. "Lex, you don't want to be in the middle of this."

She looked at me a bit harder at that, studying me. "What are you going to do, sir?" Her question held no insolence, just curiosity.

"I haven't figured it out yet. But I'll let you know after I do." *Maybe.*

She smiled. "Yes, sir. I'll get the Ops and Intel brief set. Is after dinner okay? How's the space lag hitting you?"

"After dinner is fine," I said. "I'm pretty beat down from the trip, but I want to power through. I'm going to spend the afternoon with this report, and I'll know more when I see you again."

"Yes, sir." She stood and let herself out, leaving me alone with the report.

THE INVESTIGATION DIDN'T disappoint. Or rather, it did disappoint, if I'd held out any hope that I'd get anything useful from it. I got a few names, which I put into my device. People who'd seen Mallot loaded on the MEDEVAC. The Spec Ops team leader hadn't filed a statement, which jumped out at me. It couldn't be an oversight. Guys like Stirling didn't miss things that simple. I'd need to check that. I had three screens of notes. Reminders.

It was a start.

The Ops and Intel brief provided a little more value.

It got me up to date on the war. We weren't winning, though we weren't losing, either, so not much had changed. Nothing ever changed on Cappa.

When humans discovered a new planet, it broke into two categories: Habitable and uninhabitable. If humans couldn't live there in some comfort, the mining companies came in and did their thing from orbit, but that was about it. Nobody really thought about those uninhabitable planets again. Out of sight, out of mind. If a planet unsuitable for humans had indigenous life that affected mining, we could simply destroy it from space with XB25s. Planet busters. As long as it didn't hurt the commercial value, nobody cared. Well, *somebody* cared. Just not enough to actually make a difference.

If humans could live there, a planet became a potential colony. That changed the entire calculus. People cared a lot more about places they could see. Places where they lived. That's where the military came in. We'd go in before the settlers and pacify the colony area. With our technological edge, that usually didn't take long. But some planets pacified easier than others.

We had to put boots on the ground. We couldn't rely on fighting from orbit because the cost to the ecosystem made that untenable to use on a large scale in most cases. So we fought. Animals, mostly. Plants, sometimes. We did whatever we needed to do to make the planet safe for settlement and industry. If we could preserve a native species, we tried, even if we had to relocate them to areas without humans. People demanded it. But in the end, the needs of humans took precedence. I'm not here to judge whether that's right or wrong. That's just how things went.

Until Cappa.

We'd have probably left the planet alone completely, except for the silver. So much technology used silver, and none of the substitutes worked nearly as well. It sold for fifteen times the price of gold, and Cappa Three had huge veins of it. With that kind of money involved, politicians tended to change their views on things.

If I come off as bitter about that, I'm not. Well, maybe a little. More tired than bitter. Tired of the bureaucratic bullshit, the messed-up command relationships, and the multiple agendas. We could have been done with the place years ago if we ever managed to get out of our own way.

No chance of that.

With that cheery thought, I pulled out a bottle of good imported whiskey and poured myself a drink into a fake glass tumbler. No real glass in the VIP suite. I drank it straight, finishing it in about five sips. I poured another. I needed to sleep. I expected the next day to be a long one.

CHAPTER SEVEN

I LEANED ON A polymer wall in the low light of the corridor outside the wide entrance to the hospital wing, half a hangover pressing on the backs of my eyes. Mac had come with me but hung back a step, blessedly silent on our walk over.

"You wait out here," I said.

"You sure, sir?"

"Yeah. I don't want you to shoot anybody." I half joked, but not totally. I had a feeling I might piss some people off. Even more than I usually do. I had no idea how they might react to that. Medical people saw the world differently from other soldiers. Better to keep Mac out of it.

Mac looked at me as if he wasn't sure I meant it.

"Hold my weapon." I unclipped my leg rig and handed him my pistol, holster and all. They'd make me disarm to go in the hospital anyway. Standard procedure. Probably something about having psych patients.

"I'll be right here," said Mac.

I walked through the hatch and up to the access

control point, and waved the badge that Alenda gave me. I had no idea if they'd honor it, but I counted on my rank to get me access regardless. Either way, it worked, and a bored corporal waved me through.

I passed through a second wide hatch and winced at the astringent smell. Why does every hospital have the same odor? It reeked of chemicals, not cleanliness, bringing back bad memories of previous hospital visits. I stopped for a moment and checked the direction signs on the white walls. I didn't want to pause for too long, because if I did, someone would inevitably try to help me find something. A military organization hated an unescorted colonel the way nature abhorred a vacuum. I randomly took the hallway to the right. It turned out to be a good decision, as thirty meters later I found what I wanted. A door that said STAFF ONLY.

I pressed the button, half expecting that it wouldn't let me in without a badge or biometric check. When it zipped open I walked through. I guess that meant I was staff. A dark-skinned female sergeant in a lab coat accosted me almost immediately.

"Sir, can I help you find something? Patients aren't allowed in this part of the facility." She narrowed her eyes at me, her dark brows pinching together, but didn't show any other overt hostility.

"I have a meeting with Colonel Elliot. Is her office back here?"

"Oh. Yes, sir. Down the hall, second right, then the office is on the left."

"Thank you, Sergeant." During the whole exchange,

I never stopped walking. I didn't want her to decide she needed to show me the way. People didn't expect colonels to lie to them, and I didn't want to disillusion a perfectly good young sergeant.

I found the office exactly where she said it would be and entered through the open door. A lieutenant sat at a metal desk perusing some sort of medical journal on a large reader. He looked up when I came in.

"Can I help you, sir?"

"I'm here to see Colonel Elliot." He glanced to the second door in the room, then back to me.

"Can I ask what this is about?" He looked toward a monitor that I assumed had a schedule that wouldn't show a meeting.

"I just need to talk to her," I said with a little wave of my hand, as if it were nothing. I kept walking to the door, pressed the button to open it, and went in, knocking on the frame after I'd stepped inside.

"Sir! You can't—" The lieutenant called from behind me, but his voice cut out when the door whooshed shut behind me.

Colonel Mary Elliot looked up from a report to find me smiling at her. If my arrival surprised her, she didn't let it show. I put her at mid-fifties maybe, her hair gracefully tinged with gray, lines tugging at the corners of her eyes and lips. She looked fit.

"Doctor Elliot?" I asked. The question had a purpose. Sometimes hospital commanders were administrators, not doctors. My greeting would tell me quickly.

"Yes," she said, her expression still lacking visible emotion.

"Hi. I'm Carl Butler. Just in from SPACECOM."

"Why are you here, Butler? We don't have a meeting." Direct and to the point. I liked it, despite the fact that it didn't help me.

"You see, Doc, I have this pain in my ankle."

Her eyes narrowed. No accounting for sense of humor. I got the feeling Elliot and I might not hit it off.

She stood. "How did you get in here?"

The door whooshed open behind me. "Ma'am, I'm so sorry." The lieutenant from the outer office finally made it.

She waved her hand, dismissing her assistant much in the same way I had on the way into her office.

"I walked in," I said, after the aide left. "You don't have very good security."

"I didn't think we needed it, this being a friendly base where people usually follow orders." She smiled one of those hateful fake smiles that my wife always gave to people she didn't like. Another man might have found it terrifying.

I'm not that bright. I shrugged.

"What can I do for you, Butler?" She walked around to the front of her desk and leaned back against it, half sitting on the edge, not offering her hand.

"I'm here doing an investigation. A lieutenant disappeared."

She continued to look at me, not offering anything.

"Mallot. Maybe you remember the case?" I prompted.

"Doesn't jump out at me." She gave me a half smile that didn't touch her eyes. "Perhaps if you'd made an appointment, I'd have been able to pull the records." Her body language said, *Go to hell.*

Her tone said, "Fuck you."

"Your people didn't want to give me a meeting. I didn't feel like waiting."

She kept eye contact. "They're doing their job protecting my time. We've had a lot of casualties lately, and I keep a surgery schedule along with my administrative duties."

"What's your area of specialty?" I tried to steer us back onto a course that might lead to something other than her throwing me out.

"Genetics and orthopedic robotics." Her demeanor didn't soften. I could have looked up that information on my own.

"Interesting specialty for a place like this."

"It's a command. We go where we're told," she said. "I'm sure you understand."

"Absolutely. We go where we're told. That's why I'm here. Can we just cut through the crap and get to it?"

She drew her lips into a thin line. "What do you want?"

"I want to talk to some of your people." I leaned back against the wall next to the door, assumed as non-confrontational a demeanor as I could. I didn't pose any risk. She could let me have access.

She didn't move. "Who do you need to see?"

"Anyone who had access to incoming evac patients

after twelve hundred on thirteen eleven 3943 and before oh six hundred on fourteen eleven 3943."

Her eyes narrowed again. "That's over a hundred people. It would take a day to figure out everyone on shift at that time. And that's almost five months ago. Some of them aren't even here anymore."

"Of course. I understand it's a big request. Obviously I'm happy to talk to those who are still here. And I can give you a couple days."

"That's big of you."

I knew right then she wasn't going to willingly help me out.

"Why don't you submit your questions? Leave them with Lieutenant Jacoby in the outer office. I'll have one of my officers work on the list, then question everyone involved. We'll get you a full report. We'll put a rush on it. Give us ten days." She gave me a flat smile hinting at self-satisfaction. Well played.

"I really think it would be better if I talked to people directly." I pushed myself up off of the wall, but didn't move forward. Just preparing to get thrown out.

"I'm sure you do," she said. "And I'm sure I don't care. SPACECOM has no authority here. But then, you know that already."

"Yes, I do. I was hoping we could do this the easy way."

She half grunted, half chuckled. "The easy way. That's what this is?"

"Yeah. We'll see how it goes." I walked forward and offered my hand. "Nice to meet you, Doctor."

"Nice to meet you too, Butler." She shook my hand, matching my pressure, a nice firm grip. Her eyes didn't leave mine.

"I'll be in touch," I said. "I can show myself out."

"I look forward to it." The door opened when I touched the hand pad. "And Butler?"

"Yeah?" I looked back over my shoulder.

"Stay the fuck out of my hospital."

I kept walking without answering. *Well, that went well.*

CHAPTER EIGHT

LEX AND HARDY met me soon after I got back to my office-room and I let Mac go to do his own thing for a bit. He'd materialize again if I decided to go anywhere.

Hardy offered me a take-out box from the mess hall. I hadn't realized lunch had passed. I hadn't spent that much time at the hospital, but it took almost thirty minutes to walk from one side of the base to the other. Cappa Base sported a maze of mixed hallways and levels, accented with large multi-level open areas with nothing above them but the shell of the base. In some places the roof reached so high that it almost felt like a real world. I guess that made people forget they lived on what amounted to a giant spacecraft, orbiting a planet. I'm sure psychologists had done studies.

I peeked inside the box Hardy gave me, then set it on my desk for later.

"How did it go at the hospital, sir?" Lex kept her face neutral, and I couldn't tell if she really wanted to know or already had a report and wanted confirmation.

I settled on the former and I smiled. "About like you'd think it would."

She pursed her lips. "So what now, sir?"

"Well, Elliot is a dead end." I paused. I'd already thought through my next move, but I needed to convince myself I had it right.

"I can reach out to some lower-level people there if you want, sir," she offered.

"Maybe." I walked over and filled a tumbler with water, stalling so I could think. "Even if you get anywhere, I think Elliot would squash it before it helped. I think I need some *high*-level interference." I hated to call on the boss, but Serata wanted the job done fast, and I didn't see another way.

"Yes, sir. Should I set up commo?"

"No, Hardy can do it. Take this down." Hardy had his device ready almost immediately. "Message to General Serata. Sir, ran into a roadblock with the hospital. Request you intervene at higher levels with MEDCOM to get me access to their personnel. The case is more complicated than anticipated, and I need their information. Respectfully, Butler."

"Got it sir," said Hardy.

"Read it back." He had it right, and I sent him off to transmit and told him to wait for a response. I could have sent the message from the terminal in my room, but it gave him something to do.

"What can I do, sir?" Lex meant well, I could see it in her face, but Stirling owned her career at this point, and forgetting that would be naïve. Still, I didn't hold it against her. A major had to listen to her boss.

"You have family back on Elenia Four?" I stalled for time while I thought about how much information to share.

"Yes, sir. My wife is there along with our twins."

I smiled. "Nice. How old are they?"

She returned the smile the way people do when they talk about their kids. "Four. A boy and a girl."

"That's a good age," I said. "What are their names?"

"Allen and Ella."

"Good names." I took a sip of my water, ready now. "See if you can set me up in operations. I want to look at the flights that day. Not just the record. I want to see the radar tracks. I want to see where every ship in the solar system went, and I want to compare it to where the records say they went."

"Yes, sir." She didn't even hesitate at the monstrous amount of data I asked for.

"Start the data pull at noon on thirteen eleven and run it forward for twelve hours. How long until I can see it, do you think?"

"Not sure, sir. But I'll find out and let you know. Shouldn't be long, though. I just need to clear it with the Ops chief, make sure she can spare the tech."

"Great. I'm going to eat my sandwich and then I'll head to the Ops deck."

She let herself out, and I sat down and forced myself to eat half a sandwich while I waited.

THE OPS DECK reminded me of every Ops deck everywhere: a three-story-high room somehow dark and light at the same time. Screens blared pictures and words to watching faces while forced air circulated, a little too cool for comfort. Despite the sense of activity, it was quiet, people communicating over small microphones, listening to headsets. A glance at the big screens up top told me the war remained calm for the moment, but even in the middle of an attack the Ops center would keep control. Veteran outfits didn't panic unless something truly unheard of happened, and even then, only for a moment.

I could almost imagine the night the councilor's kid got hit. They'd have received the name, maybe recognized it, swore . . . and then driven on with the mission.

I waved to the Ops chief, a lieutenant colonel, letting her know I'd entered her domain. Courtesy. We'd met the night prior, so I didn't feel the need to introduce myself again, but she needed to know I'd come in. I joined Lex by an operator seated in a rolling chair in front of two screens in a row of a dozen. Soldiers occupied half the seats, leaving plenty of places to sit.

"Sir, this is Sergeant Sandoval," said Lex. "He can pull up the data you need." A short, thin, dark-haired man stood, assuming a rough position of attention. Nervous. He probably didn't brief many colonels, especially from outside.

"Good to meet you, Sandoval. Relax." I offered him my hand and he took it with a weak grip. "How long have you been doing this?"

"Here, sir, or overall?"

I recognized his accent. "Both," I said. "You from Elenia Four?"

"Yes, sir." He smiled. "I got the accent good."

"My wife's from there." Any bit of common ground would help him relax.

"Really, sir? What part?"

"Near Lake Mobile."

"Oh, wow. I'm not too far from there. Five hundred klicks, maybe." Always funny how time spent among the stars can distort your idea of near and far. "As for your question, sir, I've been here about nine months. Been doing this job at some level for five years."

"You like it?"

"Yes, sir, it's okay. I liked it down at the ground level better," he said.

"We all do, I think. Why don't you show me what you've got here?" I gestured to his screen.

"Yes, sir. You can sit here, if you want." Sandoval pulled one of the other chairs over and slid slightly to the side so I could see. "This is a live feed."

"That's a ship?" I asked, pointing to a blue track moving slowly across the screen. I knew it was. I could read most of a radar feed, but I wanted to let him tell me. For a tech, they lived with their machine, knew its quirks as well as I knew my wife's. They loved it. You could hear the pride they took in their work. And if you showed respect, they'd work magic for you.

"Yes, sir. You can tell it's a small transport by the symbol, and if I hover over it, like this . . ." He toggled an arrow onto the slow-moving symbol. "It gives me all of the data. Speed, attitude, call sign, destination. And if I click on it, I can open up even more. Alternate frequencies, manifest . . ."

"That's excellent. This is exactly what I need." I didn't know he'd be able to pull a manifest. That could prove useful. "You can replay data from an earlier time?"

"Yes, sir. Everything for the last two years, give or take. Every month or so they pull the oldest month and ship it to the archives, so the machines don't bog down. What date do you need to look at?"

"Thirteen eleven, starting around twelve hundred hours."

"Too easy, sir. Give me a second." He clicked a few times and typed in some data. He could have called it up by voice, but most of the techs preferred to type. I never asked why.

Sandoval stared at the screen. He tapped some more keys, paused, then tapped some more, a little more strenuously. Universal tech language that something wasn't working.

"What's wrong?" I kept my tone even, not accusing, trying to act like a co-conspirator, not a boss.

"Sir . . . I don't know. The data's not there." He typed in something else and a series of tracks appeared on the screen, then he tried it again and got a different set of similar graphics.

"Is that it?" I asked.

"No, sir. This is three days after the date you wanted. Sixteen eleven. And before, I pulled up ten eleven. Three days prior to the date you wanted."

"So the data is missing?" My gut tightened and a chill rippled through my body that had nothing to do with refrigerated air.

Sandoval banged on some more keys and stared.

"It appears so, sir. The five days surrounding the day you want . . . they aren't here. Everything from those days is gone."

"You're sure?"

"Yes, sir." He banged some more keys. "Shit . . . Sorry, sir."

"No, it's okay. 'Shit' is appropriate. How often does this happen?"

Sandoval looked at me. "In my life? Never, sir."

"Huh. Interesting coincidence." I tried to keep the sarcasm out of my voice, but I doubt I succeeded. "Could we access it from another station? Somewhere else on base?"

"No, sir. It's not here. If it was anywhere in the system, I'd be able to get to it. Someone had to have deliberately removed those days."

"Any chance it was part of the routine removal?" I asked. "Like what you mentioned about the oldest month?"

He hesitated. "Maybe . . ."

"Okay. Well it was worth a shot." I was fuming on the inside, but didn't want Sandoval to know it. Word of this would get out. He'd tell someone. He'd have to. Inevitably someone senior to him would ask how I reacted. I didn't want to give them anything, especially not until I could figure out what else someone might have tampered with.

"Sorry, sir." He looked down at the floor, his shoulders sagging. I judged that he had no part in the sabotage.

Sabotage.

I'd already categorized it that way in my mind.

"No problem, Sandoval." I turned and headed toward the door, stopped, and turned back. "Hey, would they have a backup at SPACECOM?"

He thought about it. "I'm not sure, sir. I don't think so. I think they only have the archives."

"Okay. Tell you what, though: Drop a request when you get a chance, just to see."

"Yes, sir. Too easy. Anything else I can do?"

"No, I think I'm good . . . wait. You think someone deleted this, right?"

He nodded. "Yes, sir. I mean, not for sure, but that's all I can think of."

"Who could do that?"

He thought about it. "I don't know, sir. Nobody here on the floor. I can't do it. I can't change anything beyond adding manual information. Add, but not delete unless I was the one who added it. And even that's always flagged."

"Okay. Just wondering. Thanks a lot, Sandoval. You were a big help."

"Thanks, sir."

I left without waiting for Lex and headed back to my room. I needed to pound my head against a wall where nobody could see me. The stench around Mallot's disappearance was getting stronger. A high councilor's kid had disappeared into nowhere, and somebody wanted it covered up.

I SAT AT the table in my rooms, picking at the second half of the turkey sandwich. I hadn't been there nearly long enough to calm down when the door buzzed and Hardy came in, paper in hand.

"Give me some good news, Hardy." I stood up, unable to keep from moving around.

He looked at the paper and hesitated.

"Shit," I said. "Just tell me."

"It's not bad, sir. The general answered quickly, so he may need more time."

"Read it."

"Yes, sir. 'Butler: Acknowledged. Will work through MEDCOM soonest. Best case, expect delays. Start looking for another way. Serata.'

"That's word for word, sir."

I slapped a plastic tumbler off the desk and it clattered across the floor until it careened into the far wall and spun for a moment. *Start looking for another way.* Serata may as well have said, *Don't fucking count on it.*

"Sorry, sir."

"Hardy, if you ever come to me and tell me that you've got some bad news, I may curl up into a little ball and start whimpering. Because if this isn't bad, I don't want to know what bad is."

Hardy stood there silently. He probably didn't know what to say. It's not every day you watch a colonel lose his shit. Hell, I didn't know what to say . . .

"Fuck!"

I shook my head. Start looking for another way. No help from MEDCOM and someone sabotaging the data I needed. What other way was I supposed to find? I could try to talk to the Special Ops guys, but that held less promise than the dead ends I already had. Those guys didn't talk even on a good day.

"You can go, Hardy."

"Are you sure, sir?"

"Yeah. I'm sure. Go file your report back to the general and tell him I'm pissed."

"Sir . . ."

I took three deep breaths and lowered my voice to a normal register. "What?"

"Sir, I know what you think, but I don't report back to General Serata. I work for you."

I nodded. "Yeah. Okay." I believed him. He didn't have the guile to lie.

"Do you need anything else, sir?"

"What I need is a nap."

"Yes, sir." He left.

The pressure built behind my eyes again, and this time I couldn't blame it on a hangover. Part of me felt bad for taking out my frustration on Hardy. I'd apologize to him later.

CHAPTER NINE

I GOT UP OFF the sofa after ten minutes. No way could I sleep, and it seemed ridiculous to lie there awake. It was too early to start drinking. Somewhere in that short horizontal time, I'd made up my mind. I needed to know where I stood. Like in a poker game where you didn't know what anyone else had for a hand. Sometimes you had to make a bet, splash the pot, make everyone else react. Read their faces. There was only one place to start, one other player in the game worth a bet. I grabbed Mac and headed to see him.

I entered the hatch to Stirling's command suite and, seeing the door to his inner office open, I kept walking past his assistant and went in. The soldier barely looked up, and made no effort to stop me. They probably expected me after what I'd learned in Ops.

Stirling looked up from his monitor when I walked in. "Carl. How goes the investigation?"

I stopped about a pace in front of his desk and leaned over so our eyes rested at the same level. "What happened to the radar tracks from the day Mallot disappeared?"

I read his face, but got nothing from it. My question didn't surprise him at all.

He drew his lips into a thin line. "I have no idea."

"But you know what I'm talking about."

"I know what you're talking about because my Ops officer called me fifteen minutes ago and told me what you found. Or, rather, what you didn't find." He raised his voice a little, but not nearly as much as he could have, given my aggressive tone.

"So you have no idea who erased the data."

"I have no idea who erased the data."

"Have you seen it?" I asked.

"Probably."

"What the fuck is probably? You've seen it or you haven't."

"Probably, Carl, is an expression that means it's likely that I saw it." His tone hardened, grabbed a little bite. "I don't recall seeing it, but when a councilor's kid gets hit, they call the boss. That's me. They called me, and I went to the Ops floor. While I was there, they probably had the track of the MEDEVAC. So when I say *probably*, what I mean is probably."

"But you haven't seen it since then." I didn't back off from my tone. I wanted him riled up. Push the chips in the pot, see how he reacted.

"I haven't." He leaned back in his desk chair, increasing the space between us without really backing down, staring lasers at me.

I lowered my voice to a normal tone. "Why wasn't there mention of it in the initial report? You mind if

I sit?" I helped myself to a chair without waiting for an answer.

"I assume that the investigating officer didn't think to look at the radar tracks. It's not routine. I've never seen a report that included that kind of data, except for a crash."

I don't know which bothered me more, the fact that he was right or the fact that I couldn't get a read on him. He could have been lying, but he just as easily could have been telling the truth. If he was lying, he'd prepared well. Shit.

"Who has access?" I asked.

He crinkled his face. "Excuse me?"

"To the data. Who has access?" More confusion. "I'm not asking who erased it. I want to know who *could* have erased it."

"Ah." His shoulders relaxed, and he thought about it. "That's a good question. I don't know."

"Can you find out?"

He paused longer than he needed to, making me wait. "Sure. I'll get the computer techs on it. I'll find out who had access, and go one step farther. Maybe they can trace where the access came from. Where the person might have been."

"Thanks. Sorry." I tried to sound contrite. I wasn't remotely sorry, but I needed Stirling's assets and his cooperation. I'd made my bluff and he called it. No use throwing good money after bad.

"No problem, Carl. I want answers as much as you do. No luck over at the hospital today?"

"That, uh . . . yeah. That didn't go as well as it could have."

"Fucking MEDCOM." He said it like a man who doesn't swear much. Like he knew that he was supposed to swear about Medical Command, so he did. It rolled out of his mouth awkwardly, and I felt a little bad about the amateurish display.

I'm somewhat of an expert on profanity.

"Yeah. She might help, but I doubt it. I sent a message back to SPACECOM asking for them to intervene, but I'm not optimistic there, either."

"So what's next?" he asked.

I shrugged. "I don't know. Let's see what your computer techs can dredge up. It's been almost five months since the kid disappeared. One more day isn't going to matter."

He nodded. "I'll tell them to hurry."

I stood up. "Thanks. I appreciate it. I'm going to need a good break somewhere."

"You'll find it."

I walked out, wondering if he believed that.

I didn't.

CHAPTER TEN

MAJOR ALENDA SAT on my sofa the next morning. I leaned forward in the desk chair, eyes closed, head in my hands as my skull tried to give birth to the remnants of last night's drinking. Lex had called much too early to tell me that the computer techs had my answers. Apparently they worked all night on it. The tech answered one of my questions over the comm. *Who had access to erase the tracks? Nobody.*

Nobody on base could order that, not even Stirling. That cut through my hangover.

The command had to have originated back at SPACECOM headquarters. When I heard that, I decided I'd better get up and talk to the techs face-to-face. I took a pull from my coffee without opening my eyes and waited for the door to buzz.

The computer techs made a mismatched pair, one a skinny, pale, pasty young woman with traces of acne, the other a large black man with rippling arms and the shoulders of a weight lifter. The big guy spoke. "You wanted to see us, sir? About what we found?"

"Yeah. Take a seat." I gestured to the sofa, and Alenda slid to make room. The woman sat on the opposite end, leaving the big soldier to sit awkwardly in the middle.

"What did you find?" I purposely gave them an open-ended question so they'd have the freedom to tell me stuff I didn't think of. Always good business with techie types, since I didn't even know what to ask. I risked learning more about coding than I ever wanted to know—and with a hangover to boot—but one has to sacrifice for the mission sometimes.

"Nobody on base has the required access to delete the data you wanted, sir," said the big man.

"Right. You said that on the comm. So the order has to come from SPACECOM? They can do that through all the jump portals?"

"Well, they *could* do it that way, sir," said the big man, his hands fidgeting.

"But you don't think they did."

He shook his head, and his partner mirrored the motion. "No, sir. They'd never do it like that. Too easy to trace coming through all of those jumps."

I tried to puzzle it out through the fog of my headache. "Sandoval told me they make monthly backups and they fly someone out here."

The woman spoke when her partner hesitated. She had a deeper voice than I'd have expected from a woman her size. "Yes, sir. Every month. There's a tech on every transport that arrives, pre-scheduled."

"Why?" I asked. "I thought they could initiate it long distance."

"Security, sir," said the woman. "Manually transporting the data is way safer than sending it through all those links."

"I see." I hadn't known that, but I took her at her word. "So there have been at least four backups since the time in question, and any one of them could have erased the pertinent information along with the standard removal of a month."

"Yes, sir," said the big man. The female tech fidgeted like she was about to wet herself.

"You have something to add?"

"Sir . . ."

"Go ahead," I said. "You can say anything you have to say." She still looked nervous, but nothing she said could surprise me at that point.

"We ran a trace. We figured you'd want to know which of the four data dumps took away the file." Her face nearly burst with pride.

"Good work. And you found . . . ?"

"Sir . . . it was none of them." She almost bounced out of her seat. "Someone erased the data a week ago. The last person who did a backup, she left more than two weeks ago."

A week ago. Right about the time I dropped through the last portal and made comms with the base. At the same time I got delayed in space. Could be a coincidence. I got a little chill. Coincidences rarely turned out coincidental. "So then how did it happen?"

The two techs looked at each other. "We don't know, sir," said the big guy.

"But you're sure of the timing."

"Yes, sir," they said in unison.

"Okay. Let me think." I put my palms against my temples and massaged the pain. "What are the possibilities?"

The male answered. "We were debating that, sir. Me and Ganos." Ganos was the female soldier, according to her name tag.

"What are the possibilities?" I asked.

"Well, sir, SPACECOM could do it, but that doesn't make sense," said the male soldier. Parker. "The other option . . . well, it would be hard."

I looked up at that. "Because the system wouldn't allow access?"

Ganos bobbed her head up and down. "Exactly right, sir. Not unless they physically plugged in. Or did one hell of a hack."

"But it's possible?" I asked.

Ganos frowned. "Possible, but unlikely, sir. It's just . . . the idea that it was an outside hack is too far-fetched. Who would even do that?"

I had some theories on that, but I kept them to myself. I looked at the big man. Parker. "You don't think the Cappans could have done it, do you?"

"No way, sir. They've got computers down on the surface, but nothing that can reach up here."

"Yeah, that's what I thought." The dominant life form on Cappa was an intelligent species, more so than any other race humans had ever encountered, but they hadn't even reached off-planet travel technology. Network attacks were well beyond them. I didn't like the options that were left. "Okay, let me be clear. You said it wouldn't make sense . . . but is there any chance it was SPACECOM?"

Parker pursed his lips. "No, sir. I don't think so."

"Okay. Expand on that for me." I fought the urge to stand. These two might have the break I needed. Computer types wouldn't feel political pressure. They were naturally immune. Or oblivious. I gave what they said a lot of credence.

He shifted in his seat a bit. "There's no record, sir. A delete command from SPACECOM . . . well, they're authorized to do that."

"Right—"

"But then," he said, not realizing he was cutting off a colonel, "if it was them, why would they hide it? They'd be *allowed* to do it. Yet someone went in and obliterated any hint that they were there."

"Obliterated?" I raised my eyebrows. "Pretend that I don't know anything about how computers work. What's that mean in your world?"

"Cyber-bombed it, sir," said Ganos, still bouncing a little. "Deleted the data, then deleted the fact that they deleted it, and then deleted that deletion. A million times over."

"So that's bad." I did stand up this time. I needed to pace, to think. Ganos leaned forward, her fists clenched in her lap. She had something else to say, and it was good news. "You can trace it," I said. It wasn't a question.

"Yes, sir." Her self-satisfied smirk told me she meant it. "Parker and I have a five-mark bet."

"So what do you need from me? How can I help?" I asked.

"Time, sir," said Parker. "We can trace it. But we need a day. Maybe two. And a bunch of computer power."

I looked at Alenda. "Get them anything they need."

"Yes, sir." She didn't hesitate. Good.

"Ganos, Parker. If anyone at all tries to stop you . . . if anyone even hints that you shouldn't be doing what you're doing, you come tell me immediately."

"Yes, sir," they said simultaneously.

"Come find me as soon as you have an answer. I don't care what time it is. You guys are awesome."

"Thanks, sir," said Parker. They got up to go, and for the first time I believed that someone might actually help me move forward. That belief would probably be short-lived, but still. Any win was a good one.

Lex got up to follow them out, but I called her back. "I mean it. Make sure nobody interferes with them."

"Roger, sir."

"That includes Colonel Stirling. And anyone else, even if they outrank you."

"Yes, sir. I'll do my best." Her voice hitched almost imperceptibly.

"Lex. Listen very closely. If someone tells you to do something different, anyone—*anyone*—you tell them this. Write it down." I waited for her to get out her device. "Tell them that Colonel Butler says that if anyone interferes with the computer techs in any way, he will consider it interfering with an official investigation and take appropriate action."

She looked up. "Yes, sir. Got it."

"Use those exact words." It wouldn't stop someone truly determined, but it would make a career-oriented officer like Stirling think twice. The only advantage I had was that he didn't know the extent of what I could do. To be fair, I didn't know either. I hoped we wouldn't have to find out.

"Yes, sir." She waited to be dismissed. "Sir . . ."

"Go ahead."

"Sir, if you don't mind . . . what are you going to do next? I'd like to get ahead."

Good question. No way could I sit and wait on a couple of techs to do their computer magic. I'd go insane.

Inspiration hit me. "I think I'll take another crack at the hospital."

The surprised look that crossed Alenda's face gave me some minor satisfaction. "Really, sir? I thought you said she told you to stay out."

"She did. That's why I'm going to need you to arrange transportation. See, my foot really hurts. I'm not sure I can walk that far." Elliot told me to stay out, but they wouldn't reject a patient. I had the beginning of an idea. Maybe not a great one, going by my history, but it was that or deal with Colonel Karikov and the Special Ops guys.

CHAPTER ELEVEN

THE CAUSTIC SMELL of the hospital permeated the patient wing even more than the administrative. My eyes watered and the inside of my nose burned. How could doctors stand that for long periods? It probably grew on them until they didn't notice it. Probably the same way soldiers got used to combat rations.

I didn't have an appointment, but as I suspected, nobody wanted to turn away a colonel with pain in his foot. And it really did hurt. It hurt every day, but normally didn't bother me enough to stop me from living. Like the smell in the hospital, I'd gotten used to it. It hung around in the background, always there, not really hampering me anymore unless it rose above the normal level. Which it hadn't.

But they didn't know that.

I took off the top of my uniform so that a tall female medical technician could do her job. Was she a nurse? I never could tell the difference. She took my heart rate, temperature, and blood pressure. They always did that, even for pain in the ankle. I never understood that, either.

She frowned at the monitor. "Your blood pressure is high."

"That will happen when you're old, angry, and drink too much."

She glared at me with bright blue eyes a little too large for her narrow face. "High blood pressure is serious, sir. You could have a stroke."

"I know. Sorry. I use humor as a defense mechanism."

"I must have missed the humor." I think the corner of her mouth twitched in a smile. It probably didn't.

A short doctor with too much hair for someone in the military came in, saving me from the awkward silence with the tech-nurse person. I pegged him as a doctor because he entered like he owned the place. The nurse-tech stepped out of his way, then followed him with her eyes, as if waiting for an order. Definitely the guy in charge.

He glanced down at his chart, and spoke without looking at me. "Colonel, what can we do today to help you out?"

"Foot hurts." I started to unlace my boot. I knew the drill.

"I haven't got your records pulled over from SPACECOM yet. Is this an old injury, or something recent?"

"Old. Definitely old." I got my boot off and pulled the sock after. "Robot foot." Medical folks hated when

I called it that, which led me to do it more often. I'd lost a foot about ten years ago on a different planet. I didn't tell the story often, because it's not a good story to tell. Most people didn't even know I had it.

"Where's it hurt?" asked the doctor.

"Everywhere," I said. Complete truth. No matter how good the technology, they couldn't fix your brain. You wouldn't think a fake foot could hurt, but no amount of rehab could stop it from telling your body that something didn't match. They called it ancillary rejection. Big words that meant that your body constantly tried to fix itself, despite having a perfectly operational robot foot. Or cybernetic appendage, if you wanted the medical term.

"Take him for a scan, then to ortho-robotics," said Long-Haired Doctor.

"Yes, Doctor." The pinch-faced tech gave me a set of crutches, and I hobbled down the passageway after her.

"They don't have a portable scanner?" I asked as we passed scurrying orderlies and doctors, a nondescript wave of different-colored garb.

"No, sir," she said.

"Huh. I'd have thought a hospital this busy would have one. How long have you been here?"

The passage opened into a waiting area with padded benches bolted to the walls, occupied by a couple of patients who watched a video screen that hung from the center of the room. We stopped outside of a closed portal with a lighted "Wait" above it. Experience told me that meant the scanner was on the other side, but probably occupied. "Eight months, sir."

"Did you rotate in with a unit, or as an individual?" I wanted to keep her talking. It didn't matter about what.

"We don't do unit rotations," she said. "How about you, sir? How long have you been here?"

Thank you for asking. "I just got here." I spoke loudly, so that people nearby could hear me. Maybe a dozen stood in earshot, including four clerks behind a tall counter on the far side of the room. People passed through, as well, giving me a good audience. I proceeded with my little monologue.

"I'm doing an investigation. Looking into some anomalies in patient records. That sort of thing." I resisted the urge to look around. People would be watching. During a deployment, soldiers looked for anything different to pass the time.

"You're investigating the hospital?" she asked, eyes somehow even wider.

"No, nothing like that. Nobody here is in trouble. I'm just looking for things out of the ordinary."

"Huh. I haven't seen anything," she said. I couldn't tell if she was defensive or sad that she didn't get to participate. It didn't matter. I'd set the bait out. Now I just had to suffer through a checkup of my foot and see if anybody took it.

The door opened to the scanner room and I went through the standard routine. When we finished, the tech led me back to a different treatment room while someone looked at the results. It surprised me a little when Colonel Elliot walked in, her gray hair tucked up mostly under a surgical cap. I guess it shouldn't have—I remembered now that she said her specialty was orthopedic robotics.

"Butler. I wish I could say it was good to see you again."

I smiled and pointed at my foot. "Bad foot."

She nodded. "I see that. I looked at your scan and nothing seems out of the ordinary. There might be a slight infection, so we'll treat that just in case. Odds are good that it's an ancillary rejection. I'll give you a steroid along with the treatment for infection." Elliot glanced over to her assistant. "Kappernon, draw me five cc's of ephmernol."

"Yes, ma'am." The tech moved to a counter and got a large needle. Great. A pissed-off doctor with a needle. This wouldn't end well.

Elliot, for her part, behaved completely professionally. She manipulated my foot around until she found the spots she wanted and marked them with a tool designed for the purpose. She would punch the medicine right into the fake nerves and deaden the pain. I'd seen it done dozens of times.

"This should hold you for six weeks," she said. "I trust we won't see you back again."

"No, the ephmernol usually holds me," I said.

"Good." She took the needle from the tech and tapped it to get the air bubbles out, then lined it up with her mark slightly above my ankle. She pressed half the liquid in on that side and it burned as it entered. She moved to the other side and repeated it on her second mark.

"Thanks." The pain started to dim almost immediately. Its absence would bother me for at least a week—I'd gotten so used to the ache that I missed it when it disappeared.

They left me alone to put my boot back on, and I checked at the desk to make sure they didn't need anything from me before I left. When they said they didn't, I made my way out of the hospital, wobbling a little since I didn't have to compensate for the pain anymore. "Colonel?" I turned but didn't stop walking. A normal stride would catch me anyway, with my awkward gait.

"What's up?" I asked. A short, dark-haired sergeant hurried to catch up. A fine sheen of sweat dusted her light brown skin, like she'd been running. She fell in beside me and matched my pace.

"Someone told me you were here doing an investigation, sir."

"That's right." I forced myself to keep my excitement off my face and kept walking as we neared the exit.

"I have something I want to tell you."

I stopped. "Okay. What's on your mind?"

"Keep walking, sir. Outside." She held the door and I went out first.

"Nobody here wants to talk," I said once we were out of the hospital. "What makes you different?"

She took a moment to answer. "I'm short, sir. Less than a week left before I rotate out. Something's not right, and . . . it's stuck in my head. I feel like if I leave and don't say something, I'll regret it."

I nodded slowly. "Fair enough. What do you know?"

She glanced back over her shoulder at the hatch to the hospital, then shook her head. "Not here. Can you meet me?"

"Yes. Anywhere." I looked behind me. Mac waited a couple dozen meters down the passage, leaning against the wall.

"Not tonight, sir. I have duty. Tomorrow," she said.

I nodded again. I'd have agreed to anything at that point. "Okay. Where?"

"Do you know where the K Bar is?"

"I'll find it." I kept my lips in a flat line, trying not to give anything away even though I felt like I might burst. I didn't like the idea of meeting a female non-com at a bar, but I didn't want to show any hesitation that might spook her.

"Meet me there at twenty-one hundred, sir."

"Will do. See you then." I glanced at her name tag. Santillo. We turned and walked in opposite directions without saying anything else.

"What was that, sir?" Mac pushed himself up off of the wall as I approached.

"I'm not sure. It might have been a break. Might be nothing. Have to wait and see. Have you heard of the K Bar?"

"No, sir."

"I need you to find it tonight. Do a recon, come back and tell me about it. I've got to meet her there tomorrow."

"Roger that, sir. Can do." He smirked slightly.

"What?" I asked, smiling.

He chuckled. "Sorry, sir. Just picturing you with a date."

"Yeah." I rolled my eyes. "I've got a date. Hopefully she puts out some answers."

Mac and I didn't bother with transportation on the way back. I could walk, and it would help me get used to the lack of pain.

CHAPTER TWELVE

MAC FOUND THE K BAR the next day and reported back, almost unable to contain his laughter. He said I wouldn't like it. I didn't doubt him, so I did the natural thing senior officers do when something is going to suck. I made Hardy come with me. He seemed excited to be involved, which ruined some of the fun.

The K Bar resided on K deck. Soldiers don't have much imagination when it comes to nicknames. It sat firmly in the MEDCOM area of the base, and played host mostly to off-duty medical soldiers with the occasional table of contractors. That's what Mac told me. His description didn't prepare me for the reality waiting beyond the wide entryway.

Flashing red and yellow lights accompanied music two decades newer than anything I listened to, driven by a thumping beat that vibrated in my chest. Soldiers occupied 80 percent of the small tables, crowded around with more chairs than someone designed for the space. The half-full dance floor writhed with people, some in uniform, some not. I glanced at Hardy. I had to yell to make myself heard over the noise. "You probably like this, don't you?"

He shrugged. "It's okay, sir."

I leaned in so I didn't have to shout. "I'm going to go to the bar. You go to the other side of the room. I don't want to scare her off."

"Yes, sir," said Hardy. "What do you want me to do over there?"

"Keep your eyes open. See what you see. And try to look less aide-like," I said.

He scratched the top of his head and scrunched his face. "Sir . . . uh . . . what do you mean?"

"Just try to look like you fit in."

"Right. Yes, sir."

I shooed him away with a hand motion and little hope he'd succeed, then pushed past two male soldiers in uniform to get to the bar, where I grabbed an open seat. I had thirty minutes before the meeting. After a day waiting for tech info that didn't come, I hadn't been able to stay in my room any longer. At least I'd be able to get a feel for the place before the soldier arrived. Sergeant Santillo. The woman who hopefully had some information that made it worth coming to a place like the K Bar. Something that would break the investigation open for me.

"You have whiskey?" I asked.

The bartender looked at me over the top of his wire-rimmed glasses. An affectation. Nobody wore glasses. "We have synthanol."

"Great. I'll have beer." I could drink synth in a

pinch, but I wasn't desperate, and I didn't want to be drunk anyway.

The bartender brought me a plastic bottle and his scan pad. I punched in a three-mark tip and placed my thumb against the screen. His eyebrows arched at the amount, which represented a big tip for a soldier bar. I'd get good service the rest of the night.

I turned and leaned my lower back against the bar, took a sip of my not-cold-enough beer, and scanned the room. Groups and couples huddled close so they could talk over the music. In one corner, a guy sat with his hand between his girlfriend's legs, rubbing her thigh. I didn't make eye contact. Technically the rules prohibited stuff like that, but nobody enforced it. We ran an organization full of young people. If they didn't do it here, they'd find a different place.

I zoned in and out for a while, ordered another beer, checked my watch for the fifteenth time: twenty-one fifteen. She was late. I made a lap around the bar to see if maybe she'd come in and I'd missed her, and almost collided with a tipsy tech sergeant who pulled up short when he saw my rank. Probably didn't get a lot of officers at the K Bar. Nobody had taken my seat at the bar by the time I returned, so I resumed my post.

Another thirty minutes and another beer later I'd decided to leave, but hadn't motivated myself to get up yet, when a woman approached me. Not Santillo. This woman had light skin and blonde hair pulled back in a professional-looking bun.

"Colonel Butler?" She got to within a couple steps before she spoke, because of the music. Not as old as me, probably, but she had hints of lines at her eyes that I could see even in the dim bar lighting.

I nodded.

"I heard I might find you here. Karen Plazz, from the *Times*."

The *Times*. Not the *Talca Times*, its official name . . . nobody called it that. Just "the *Times*." Not the biggest media outlet in existence, but arguably the most influential.

Great.

"How'd you know where to find me?" I gestured to the empty seat next to me. She wasn't going to leave, so might as well be polite.

She smiled. "Well I wouldn't be much of a reporter if I revealed my sources, would I?"

I decided I liked her. Didn't trust her. Never would. But that went with the job. "I was actually about to leave."

"So early?"

She asked in a way that left it open for me to explain myself. I didn't. I had no intention of helping her by confirming something she might suspect.

"Yeah. Not as young as I used to be."

She didn't drop her smile. "Not like back on Omicron, huh?"

Omicron Four. I did a tour there twenty-something years ago. She'd done her homework. "No. Not like that."

"Mind if I walk with you?"

I shrugged. "I don't think it's worth your time."

"It might be worth yours. I know why you're here.

Mallot. And I know you're not going to confirm that for me. I don't care. I have information you will want to hear."

I smiled. "So you're going to give *me* information." But even though I smelled BS, it was better than nothing. Hell, she might be telling the truth. I couldn't get a good read. If she did know something though, she wouldn't give it up for free. So I figured it was time to find out the price. I left the last half of my beer on the counter. "Let's go."

The absence of glaring noise away from the bar left a void, and we walked in silence through the well-lighted passage, our footfalls on the deck drowned by the remains of the thumping beat. Footsteps sounded behind us, running. Hardy. I'd left him in the bar. "Sir!"

"Yes, you can stay and drink at the K Bar," I said.

He shook his head back and forth, then glanced at Plazz. I cut my eyes over to her quickly to see if she'd picked up on it, but she had looked down at the floor.

"Excuse us for a moment," I said.

"Sure. I'll be right here." Plazz smiled.

I walked a few steps away, my hand on Hardy's shoulder, pulling him in. "What is it?"

"There was a guy in the bar, sir. He was watching you. He pretended he wasn't, but he kept glancing over."

I clenched my fist, then relaxed it. Santillo not showing up, now this. "Really. What did he look like?"

"Big guy, military haircut, but dressed in civilian clothes," said Hardy. "I could point him out again, but he's gone. He left ten minutes ago."

I nodded and breathed out loudly through my nose. "Probably should have followed him, but good work. Do me a favor. Go see what you can find out about Sergeant Santillo, and why she might have missed our meeting. Start at the hospital. Try to be subtle."

Hardy held his chin high. "Yes, sir."

I rejoined Plazz and she and I started walking. Mac saw us coming and inclined his head slightly, asking me if I found what I came for. I shook my head minutely to tell him no, then gave him a nod to go on ahead and give me some space. He understood, and walked well in front of us. He had a protein shake. No idea where he got that.

"I've always admired how you military folks can communicate like that," said Plazz. She looked at me as she spoke, observing. Looking for my reactions, I think.

It impressed me that she picked up on it, but I didn't let her know that. I wondered what she'd sensed about Hardy, what she might have overheard. "Practice. So you mentioned you know something . . ."

She smiled again. She knew she had me. "I'd love to get a statement from you."

"Sure. Feel free to record it. Ready? Good: Due to the nature of the ongoing investigation, I cannot speak on the matter at this time."

"Oh, come on." She turned one side of her mouth down in a sarcastic frown.

I shrugged. "Yeah, I know. That's what we always say. Doesn't make it less true."

"Not even off the record?"

I laughed. "Come on, I'm not a rookie here."

"Worth a shot."

"What's the story?" I asked. "I don't even see an angle for you at this point."

"I don't know yet." She looked down, then back at me. "My boss wants something, and right now I don't have it. If I had to go with something today, it's you."

"Me?"

"Sure. Decorated veteran sent into the middle of nowhere for an investigation. It's not much, but I can run stuff from your history."

I grimaced. "So a human-interest piece?"

"Sort of," she said. "But one that will run near the splash page. Maybe on it. Mallot is news."

"Mallot isn't news. So you make me the story in hopes that I give you something to make you change your mind. That's dirty."

She shrugged slightly, using only one shoulder. "Only a little dirty. They're going to run something anyway. If I don't send it, they'll find someone who does. Or they'll write it back home."

I sighed. "How much control are you going to have if you do send something? They going to let you run what you want?"

She laughed. "Not a chance."

"That's what I'm afraid of," I said. Sometimes you could trust reporters. Especially the ones that came out to the field. But you could never trust editors. They'd publish whatever drew eyeballs, even if it meant hanging their own reporters out an airlock.

She nodded. "Look. I'll tell you what I know, which

isn't much. But you think about talking to me. Not now, but when you can. When you have something."

"I'll promise you this: If I talk to anyone, it will be you." I didn't know what other outlets had folks here. I didn't care. I didn't have any intention of talking to anyone, and I could live with the half-truth.

She looked at me for a moment, maybe trying to judge my sincerity. I should probably have been insulted, but we both had jobs to do. "Deal." She stuck out her hand and I shook it.

"Like I said, it's not much." She stopped walking, so I stopped too. "Stirling and Elliot had a shouting match over the phone. A long one, and angry. Two, maybe three days after Mallot disappeared."

I paused. I didn't know what it meant, but it did add another wrinkle. "Who told you?"

She shook her head. "Can't tell you."

"What did they say?"

"I don't know," she said. "All I got was that they were yelling. My source only heard one end."

"He was sure it was Stirling and Elliot?"

"He . . . or she . . . was dead sure. Said they argued for five minutes, loudly, but couldn't give me more than that."

"You believe him? Or her?"

"Enough where I'd print it if I had a story."

I nodded. That said a lot. The *Times* had standards, and if she'd print it, she believed it. "Interesting."

"I thought you'd think so."

"I really don't have anything I can give you." I would have given her a nugget if I had one. Her information was worth it. Another tiny crack I could shine a light into.

She looked at me for a moment. "I believe you. But I don't think that will last forever."

I shrugged. "I hope not."

She tapped her device, and mine vibrated in response. "Call me."

I nodded.

We went separate directions, and I replayed the conversation in my head. It almost made me forget about Santillo and what it meant that she hadn't shown up. I didn't know if she'd gotten cold feet or if someone had gotten to her and convinced her not to talk. Hopefully Hardy would find something.

I reached my room and found Lex waiting outside. "You could have gone in," I said. Mac stepped through the door while I stopped to talk.

Alenda's short hair stuck to her head like she'd been working out. She looked down the hallway and found it empty. "The computer techs are done, sir. Would you like to see them tonight or tomorrow?"

"Tonight." *Like I'd sleep knowing they had something to say.*

"Yes, sir. I can have them here in fifteen minutes."

CHAPTER THIRTEEN

PARKER AND GANOS walked in and I ushered them to the couch, trying not to seem too eager. I didn't want to let them know how desperately I needed their information, because it would only put pressure on them. I needed them calm and detached. Ganos sat with her shoulders tensed, her foot tapping. Alenda leaned against the wall to my right, watching the two techs.

"So tell me what you know," I said.

"Sir . . . we found the break." Ganos leaned back, a shy smile on her narrow face.

"And?"

"It was a pro job, sir," said Parker, gesturing with his big hands. "Really high-level stuff."

"We could barely trace it," added Ganos. "If we hadn't known to look, we'd have never found it."

I smiled at them. "But you did."

"Yes, sir," they said, simultaneously.

"And you know who did it . . ."

Their faces dropped.

They didn't know.

"We know who *didn't* do it," offered Parker.

I kept my face as even as I could to hide my disappointment. "That's something. Just tell me what you know."

"It came from outside our headquarters, sir," said Ganos.

"So SPACECOM."

"No, sir. Definitely not SPACECOM. It came from this base."

"You're sure?" I asked.

"Yes, sir," they both said.

I looked at each of them in turn. "So here at Cappa, but not from inside the brigade."

"Unless someone from the brigade left our facilities and accessed from somewhere else, sir," said Ganos.

"Like a public terminal?" I stood up and took a couple of paces, too agitated to sit.

"No, sir," said Parker. "No way. Whoever did this used a military machine to get in. One of ours."

"Definitely no way," Ganos agreed.

"Sir . . ." Ganos looked at Parker, who nodded. "We think that one of the other commands on base broke in and erased the records."

"So either MEDCOM or Spec Ops."

"Yes, sir," said Parker, and Ganos nodded as well.

I scratched my chin. "I'm going to regret this, but how do you know?"

They looked at each other, then Ganos spoke. "Sir, whoever broke into the net was on the WAN, but not on the LAN."

"Those are networks," I said.

"Yes, sir. Local area network and wide area network," said Parker.

"And that means . . ."

"The WAN encompasses the whole base, sir. But each command has its own LAN," said Ganos.

I nodded. I mostly understood. "Any hint as to which command it came from?"

This time Parker took the lead. "Nothing in the computers to give us a hint there, sir. But it's high-end work."

"So you think Spec Ops," I said.

"It's inside their capability, sir," said Parker. "Not that they'd use it on us, but . . . well, they could."

"Okay. Thank you . . . both of you. I can't tell you how important this has been to my work. If anyone asks you what you found, I want you to tell them that you didn't find anything."

They looked at each other. They did that a lot, like they had some secret communication system.

"You already told?" I stopped pacing.

"Not exactly, sir. We didn't tell anyone what we found. But we were pretty excited. I think people kind of know that we found something," said Ganos.

I thought for a few seconds, then nodded. "Yeah. Okay. Well, then people are definitely going to ask. You tell them that I ordered you not to speak of it to anyone. Not even your boss."

Parker hesitated before he spoke. "Yes, sir."

I raised my eyebrows. "Is that going to be a problem? If it's going to be a problem, tell me now."

"It might, sir," said Ganos. "Lieutenant Colonel Beckenridge . . . that's our boss . . . he's a little bit . . ."

"Controlling," said Parker.

"Yes, sir," said Ganos. "Controlling. Like he wants to know all the information that comes out of our shop."

"Okay. I'll handle Beckenridge. The order stands, though. Don't say anything to anybody."

"Yes, sir," they said together.

I let them get out the door and for it to zip shut behind them before I spoke to Alenda. "Are they right about their boss? Will Beckenridge be a problem?"

Lex drew her lips into a flat line, like she was thinking about her words. "I think that's fair; yes, sir. He's a bit of a micromanager."

"I'll need to see him then. Unless you think he'll take it from you."

"I can make him understand, sir," she said.

"Okay. But don't be too soft. Make sure he knows that I will not hesitate to call every communications colonel I know and put the death word out on him."

Lex smiled. "Yes, sir. That will work."

"Good. And I'm going to need to see Colonel Karikov." I'd avoided Karikov up to this point, mostly because I knew he'd be difficult. He had a history. A decorated one, for sure, but also a reputation as a guy who did things his own way. And he'd be mildly interested in my mission at best. With Sergeant Santillo's failure to show pointing toward the hospital, I wasn't convinced that Special Ops had done the hack, but Parker was right about it being inside their capabilities.

"I anticipated that, sir. I contacted Spec Ops. Colonel Karikov is planetside."

I nodded. "Of course he is. When is he coming back?"

"I asked that, too, sir. According to his people, never. He stays down there full-time."

I snorted. "Great." With anyone else I wouldn't believe it, but that fit what I'd read about Karikov. He might have been the one guy in this part of the galaxy with more written about him than me. He'd spent a lot of time on Cappa. It got hard to track where one tour ended and the next started. You could never trust Spec Ops record keeping, anyway.

"Would you like to talk to someone else in the command?" asked Lex.

I considered it. "No. I don't think that would have much utility. I'm going to need to go down to the planet." I took a little satisfaction in the look of surprise that drew from Alenda.

She sat without speaking for a moment before she said, "Sir . . . I'll need to run that by Colonel Stirling. To get approval for the spacecraft."

"Run it by whoever you need to. What else am I supposed to do? You heard Parker and Ganos. Someone cracked the system and deleted data. No way did anyone in Spec Ops take on an operation like that without Karikov knowing about it. Karikov is on the planet. That means the investigation is on the planet."

"Yes, sir." Lex hesitated again.

I let her stew on it for a minute. "What's on your mind?"

She thought about it. "I'm good, sir."

"Come on, Lex. Clearly you're not. Spit it out. I can handle honesty."

She nodded several times before she spoke. "I don't think it's a good idea, sir. Going planetside."

I considered it for a moment, met her eyes. She kept her shoulders square, chin level, unflinching. I'd made my decision, but she needed to speak. "Okay. Why not?"

She thought about it a moment longer, considering her words. "It's an unnecessary risk, sir. You're not going to find Mallot. It's long odds at best. If he was down there, someone would know it. Someone would have reported it. You going to the surface isn't going to change that, regardless of what else you find."

I thought about it for a moment. She had a point. Mallot was gone, and even if I found out why, that wouldn't change. But I couldn't let it go. Maybe it would have been different if I thought I had any chance of getting help from MEDCOM, but I expected that to continue to be a closed airlock.

"It's not that much of a risk," I said. "If it's that dangerous, Stirling will say no."

"You and I both know that's not true," said Lex, not pausing to consider her words.

I smiled in spite of myself. She knew that Stirling was looking out for his own career as well as I did. He *couldn't* say no without looking like he was blocking the investigation. And though he didn't seem the type, it probably crossed his mind that me being killed would clear up a lot of his problems. "Look. If I never stepped on Cappa again, that would make me very happy. I'm sure Karikov knows that, too. But Karikov also knows I'm coming."

I read the confusion on Lex's face, but she'd have to figure it out for herself. Karikov wanted me to come see him. I could feel it. I wasn't smart enough to decline the invitation.

"I'll set it up, sir," she said, after a moment of silence. "It might take a day or two to arrange."

"I'm not in a hurry. Two days is fine. Since I'm going down, I want to visit Mallot's company, too. I can question the soldiers there before I move out to see Karikov. In the meantime, I want to see everything and anything anybody here has on the area. Intel, satellite shots, current friendly and enemy positions and strengths. Whatever you can get your hands on. I even want to see logistics schedules, too." No way would I go to the surface blind.

"Yes, sir. I'll make it happen." She sounded a little surer now. Perhaps I sounded more reasonable. Perhaps she had just accepted it.

"Thanks, Lex."

"Just doing my part, sir. Other people will do the bulk of the work."

I shook my head. "No, not that. Thanks for having the guts to say what's on your mind. I value that." I really did. I still didn't trust her completely, but I definitely respected her more.

STIRLING CALLED ME the next morning and made sure I really wanted to go. He even offered to deny the mission so that I could save face, if I wanted. Smart of him. Always give the other guy a way out. Of course, that would have meant I had brains enough to take it. In truth, I think he wanted me to go, and for a reason that hadn't dawned on me earlier. His network got hacked, and that had to piss him off at least a little.

Alenda loaded my system with everything I needed about the planet, and I'd just sat down with her to look at it when Hardy showed up.

"What did you find out about Santillo?" I gestured to the sofa, in case he wanted to sit.

He hesitated. "Stasis, sir."

"Excuse me?" I glanced at Alenda, and she gave me an almost imperceptible nod, confirming his answer. Of course she'd checked, too.

Hardy sat, the fake-leather sofa squeaking in protest. "Yes, sir. She was scheduled to leave in three days. They moved up her stasis call."

I stared at him. "Huh." It could have been coincidence. On the big troop transports, they put everyone into cryo before launch because they didn't have the staff to handle it in flight. Three days, though. "Did you get a reaction from anyone?"

He shook his head. "I didn't seem to, sir. One guy asked me why I wanted to know, but I made something up. I thought someone followed me out of the hospital, but I took a random turn and he didn't match it."

I put my fist in my palm and mashed them together. Shit. I needed Santillo's information on the hospital. She'd been my only lead. I considered having her pulled out of stasis, but that would take a ton of effort, and it would sound an alarm to anyone who didn't know that I wanted to talk to her. At least it solidified my reasons for going to see Karikov. I had no other decent options.

"Good work, Hardy. Lex, do me a favor. While Hardy and I are gone, poke around and see if you can figure out who gave the order to move up Santillo's stasis call."

"Yes, sir," she answered.

"Where are we going, sir?" Hardy asked.

"Prep your kit. We're going planetside."

CHAPTER FOURTEEN

MAC, HARDY, AND I loaded onto a shuttle with nine other soldiers for our trip to Cappa. The ship had six seats along each wall, and Stirling insisted on filling it, even though we'd land at one of his bases, surrounded by his people. My stomach twisted a little, making me glad I'd skipped breakfast. I hadn't dropped down to a hostile planet in a few years, but the same feeling assaulted me every time. Having a full ship didn't make me feel any safer.

Mac handed me a rifle and a pile of magazines. "Got you a Bitch, sir."

"Nice. What are my loads?"

"Three magazines explosive, four guided. Already coded to your helmet."

"Thanks." I slapped a magazine of guided into the well but didn't charge it. Once I did, though, I'd be able to control the flight of the bullet with my thoughts. Bend it a little. It made it hard to miss. Now if I could get someone to take the shine off my body armor . . .

We planned to drop in to Mallot's old company at Base 17A, spend a day or so there asking questions and getting my bearings, then we'd move by ground to Karikov's headquarters. Pretty easy, as far as combat missions go.

I studied Hardy, trying to see into his mental state. You always had to watch a guy making his first trip into a combat zone. He looked fine, but you could never be sure. We strapped in for the thirty-minute trip to the surface.

"You good?" I asked him.

Hardy nodded. "Yes, sir. A little nervous. A little excited."

"That's normal. Don't worry about it, we're dropping into a pretty friendly area. Not a lot of locals around, and those that *are* there mostly support us."

"That's good, sir. Is that normal?"

I shrugged. "It's been a while since I've been here, but I don't think it's changed that much. Most of the planet supports us being there. Only a small percentage fight against us."

That split of the Cappans—the 90 percent who supported us and the 10 percent who didn't—that's what made Cappa so different. We'd discovered planets with intelligent life before, but never at this level. Cappans were humanoid. Nobody would mistake them for human, with their big, round, bulging eyes; elongated faces; and blue-and-yellow skin. But they were bipedal. They *walked*. If it had only been that, maybe we'd have fought it like any other war. But the sociologists who came in droves to study them found more. They could communicate. Many species communicated with each other, but the Cappans . . . they could talk to *us*. They learned. It took a while to figure it out, the chirping and clicking, but within a couple of years the linguists put it together, and we had rudimentary translation.

That discovery stopped the war. For a time. We brought in diplomats. Settlers. Made an effort at peaceful coexistence. Like most things, humans eventually fucked it up. The money got in the way, and we expanded too quickly trying to get at the silver, which pissed off the Cappans. They'd been happy enough to trade for our technology at first, but as the mining companies continued to push, the Cappans started to resist. Protests turned violent, then turned to flat-out hostility.

That's when we brought in soldiers. Even then, it was like no other war in several hundred years. It had a moral element, and a level of complexity beyond any other fight I'd seen. Because the Cappans chose sides, and we couldn't tell them apart. Eighteen years of fighting hadn't altered the situation much, and left us bogged down fighting an insurgency that we couldn't win, and that politicians and industry wouldn't let us quit.

The bump and acceleration of takeoff settled into the smooth quiet of a trip through space. I closed my eyes and pretended to nap. My body wanted rest but my brain whirled, wide awake. The questions I wanted to ask when we landed ran through my mind in their own little dress rehearsal. After a couple minutes I gave up the pretense of sleep and followed our progress via a wall screen that fed a picture from outside the ship. Cappa filled the display, a mottled brown ball with some splotches of pale green and a few specks of blue. Cappa had a large ocean out of sight on the far side of the planet, but in this hemisphere a lot of the water resided underground, leaving mostly hilly, rocky desert.

I'd hoped to never see that view again.

WE DISMOUNTED AT Base 17A, one of a couple dozen small outposts on the only human-occupied continent on Cappa. The dry heat punched me in the face as I exited the craft, followed quickly by the smell. Cappa in the summer smelled like stale laundry with a hint of sulfur. The base sat in the middle of a flat expanse of hard-packed, gritty dirt interspersed with egg-sized brown rocks. A group of rocky brown hills, speckled with sharp angles and a few tiny spots of vegetation, dominated the horizon in two directions. I knew from study they were minor peaks, maybe fifteen hundred meters tall, but rising abruptly from the flat ground about ten kilometers away, they appeared much bigger. What made them truly significant was they were loaded with silver, meaning mining, which made Base 17A necessary.

The company commander, Captain Zattel, met us at the bottom of the ramp. He didn't have his gear on, which indicated a low threat. His wavy black hair, a bit longer than regulations allowed, rippled from the disturbance of the engines. The hair pissed me off a little since he was a commander, but I decided to give him the benefit of the doubt.

"Welcome to Base Seventeen Alpha, sir," he shouted over the noise.

I nodded and started walking to clear the takeoff zone. Only two of Stirling's men got off with us, and the ship took off as soon as we stepped out of the blast zone. The silence in its wake was almost palpable. When Zattel spoke again, it came across almost like a shout, though he spoke at a normal volume. "Glad to have you, sir."

"Glad to be here." He lied, I lied. The sweat had already started running down my face, and my shirt stuck to my back under my armor.

"I've got the men lined up that you wanted to speak to. You can use my office for your interviews."

"That will work," I said. "When do you want me to start?"

Kawhoompfh. A rocket hit maybe a thousand meters away, close enough where I felt the compression, and I flinched, involuntarily.

Captain Zattel looked to his left and I followed his eyes to where Lieutenant Hardy lay hugging the ground.

"Get up, Hardy," I said. "That wasn't close enough to worry about."

Hardy glanced about, then skittered to his feet. "Sorry, sir."

I waved my hand at him dismissively, ignoring his red face. "No shame. Everyone does that the first time. By the time you hear it it's too late to duck anyway." I turned to Zattel. "That happen often?"

"Not really, sir. Couple times a week, maybe. They aren't accurate. No guidance systems."

"Small blessings. What was that, one hundred twenty-five millimeter?" I knew it was. Munitions made unique sounds. After a while, you learned to recognize them. But I wanted Zattel to know that I knew. He'd give me less trouble if he thought he couldn't bullshit me about things.

"Yes, sir. Probably. We'll get the analysis to be sure, but almost all of them are one twenty-fives."

I nodded. "Just harassing, then."

"Yes, sir." Zattel started walking again and I followed. "Back to your question. We can start the interviews as soon as you're ready."

I wiped sweat from my eyes. I'd forgotten how miserable Cappa could get. "Now's good."

"Yes, sir. I'll get you set in the office and have First Sergeant line them up."

SIX HOURS LATER I emerged from the office and flung my notebook down on a table a little too hard. Part of me wanted to pick it up and fling it again. I'd interviewed twenty-one soldiers and they all told some form of the same story. Nobody had seen anything. Too much commotion. Attention on the fight around them, securing the landing zone. At least six of them were lying. Maybe more, but six for sure. They weren't even good liars. Someone gave them the story, but hadn't rehearsed them well enough to stand up to pressure. They stumbled over words, and more than one locked up and stopped talking altogether.

I tried every interview tactic in the book—and some not in the book—to break through to the truth.

I tried good cop, bad cop, and every cop in between. I tried ordering, intimidating, pleading, tricking. I swore at more than a couple soldiers. I challenged one big corporal's manhood. None of it worked.

"Did you get what you needed, sir?" Zattel approached as I evacuated his office. Bad timing.

Screw you, Zattel. Longhaired asshole. "About as you'd expect," I said.

He stopped short. "I'm sorry sir, I don't understand."

"I think you understand perfectly. Someone told your people to keep their mouths shut. Was that you?" I studied his face, the dirt crusted in the sweat under his eyes and on his cheeks.

His face tightened, eyes narrowed slightly. "No, sir."

I continued to stare, and he met my gaze calmly, his shoulders square and his head level. Shit. I believed him. "Do you know who it was?"

He hesitated.

"I get it. You don't want to roll over on your people. I wouldn't either. But we both know what's going on here."

He stood silently, his eyes cast down, his weight shifting from one foot to the other. I could have pressured him into talking right then, but as much as I wanted answers, I really didn't want him to break faith with his soldiers. The unit might never recover from that kind of betrayal.

"I tell you what, Zattel. I'm going to let it go for now," I said, after letting him stew for a moment. I'd find some way to make his life miserable later.

"Yes, sir." He met my gaze, and a hint of tension

came out of his face. I didn't know if he understood my logic in backing off, but I also didn't feel the need to explain myself.

"I want to move out tomorrow morning to Colonel Karikov's location."

"Yes, sir. Third platoon will take you. Do you want your lieutenant along, or do you want him to wait here?"

"Yes, he's coming with me," I said. Third platoon. Mallot's platoon. Rather, it had been, at one point. They had a new platoon leader now. I hadn't met him, but I'd read the name. Lieutenant Politte.

"Roger that, sir. We'll make sure there's space. We'll get you the departure information tonight."

THE PLATOON STOOD huddled up on the shady side of their four vehicles when I walked up the next morning, the men and women looking top-heavy in their armored vests. Hardy and Mac trailed behind me. I had my rifle clipped to my gear with a single strap that allowed me to shoot without unhooking, and I carried my helmet in my other hand. Mac had put the platoon radio frequency in one ear, company headquarters in the other. I'd be riding in the back of one of the vehicles, and not in charge, but I liked to keep abreast of the situation around me. I tried to stay pretty relaxed back at home base, and even spaceside, but if you relaxed in a hostile fire area, bad things happened.

I reached the back of the cluster of soldiers and joined them, all watching the fresh-faced lieutenant at the front with the holo map. So young. He had his dark hair in a short buzz cut that looked like someone told him to get his hair cut before reporting to the front, but didn't explain how. He started talking as soon as I arrived.

"We went over the route last night. A hundred and fifty klicks." The route lit up on the holo. "It's a cleared route, so no contact expected, but be alert. They've hit cleared routes before, as recently as two months ago. If they hit us, it would likely be at one of these two spots. Choke points." He lit a spot about halfway along the route where the road cut between two hills, and then another at what looked like a small forest about three-quarters of the way there, the only vegetation on the otherwise bleak route.

"My vehicle has lead," he continued. "Sergeant Stanzi second, Sergeant First Class Belham, third, Jones, trail. Platoon freq is per the SOP. Someone gets hit, we secure the vehicle, attack through the enemy, consolidate and call for MEDEVAC as needed. Nothing we haven't done before. Remember, if you see Cappans, ninety-five percent of them don't mean us any harm. Verify the threat before you engage. Questions?" He looked around and predictably got only head nods. Veterans.

"We move out in five," he finished. The young man approached me.

"Sir, I'm Lieutenant Politte." He stood taller than I thought at first. Maybe five centimeters taller than me. That didn't change the fact that with his baby face and red cheeks, he looked fifteen.

"Good to meet you, Politte," I said. "I appreciate the ride today."

"Hooah, sir. I've got you and Staff Sergeant McCann in vehicle three with my platoon sergeant. Did you want your aide with you?"

"Colonels don't have aides. But Hardy can ride with you, if that's okay. Hardy!"

"Yes, sir. I've got a seat," answered Politte.

Hardy trotted up. "Yes, sir."

"Ride with Politte. Give you a chance to see what a platoon leader does."

"Yes, sir," Hardy replied.

"Is that your platoon sergeant?" I nodded toward a short, dark-skinned man with a thick mustache.

"Yes, sir," said Politte. "Sergeant First Class Belham."

"I'll introduce myself." I didn't know Belham. I'd hoped to get lucky and find someone familiar, but it had been a long shot. I didn't recognize anyone in the platoon, except those who I'd questioned yesterday.

"Sir." Belham turned toward me as I approached.

"Sergeant Belham. Good to meet you." I offered my hand, and he took it with a firm grip after shifting his helmet to the other side.

"You been in a Goat before, sir?" The MT-488 hover vehicle, affectionately known as the Goat because it went anywhere and did everything. Not a great fighting vehicle, but well armored and safe. Perfect for a casualty-conscious force.

"Yeah, a few times," I said. Hundreds, in truth. But I didn't want to look like I had something to prove.

"Roger, sir. That's good. So you and your man know the drill if we get hit. You'll be in back. We pull the gunner down out of the turret, keep moving through the kill zone if we can, exit and assault through if we can't. Watch for secondaries on exit."

"Yeah, I've got it. You seeing a lot of secondaries these days?" A secondary device was something the enemy placed to hit us after the main attack, often a potato mine. The Cappans liked to put them in culverts and behind cover. When soldiers dismounted a disabled Goat, they'd naturally seek out those supposed safe spots and trigger the explosives. They created a lot of casualties that way.

"No, sir. Not lately. But you never know." Belham put on his helmet, which had a bullet scar along the top. He'd gotten lucky at some point with that one.

"You ready for us to load?" I asked.

"Yes, sir. One on each side. Middle seats."

I put my helmet on, then triggered the visor, dropping the face shield and heads-up display into place. Once I confirmed that everything was functioning and I could see all the data I needed, I retracted it and climbed up the back ramp into the Goat, ducking my head under the back deck and crouching in the tight space. It had three black seats with high backs down each wall, the two forward ones filled with troopers, the other four empty. I took the middle seat on the left wall and Mac sat across from me. Two more soldiers came in behind us and took the rear. Belham would be in the front next to the driver. Add in the gunner and we had a full load of nine.

One of the soldiers hit the ramp lever and it closed

us in. We still got light through the armored windows on either side, so thick that they distorted any view. We weren't meant to see out from the back, but the windows added a sense of location. I synched my helmet to the internal comms right in time to hear Belham speak.

"We in?"

"Check, Sergeant." The soldier directly beside me spoke. A female voice.

"Moving out." The lieutenant's voice came over the speaker with a slightly different hum that said it was radio, not internal. My helmet could handle up to five communications channels at a time. I could hear all of them, and then switch to broadcast on the one I needed. It took practice to tell the different channels apart as they blended in my earpiece, but I'd had plenty of that. For the moment I had one channel open inside our vehicle, one for the platoon, so I'd hear the four vehicles in our convoy, and one for the line back to company headquarters. On that one I'd hear anything Politte sent back to his boss, or any new incoming orders.

The Goat's engine whined, and the queasy movement in my stomach told me we'd lifted off the ground a meter or so. When we started moving forward my restraining belts dug into my shoulders until our speed normalized. I glanced out the window and watched the blurry base disappear, but there wasn't much to see. The browns of this part of Cappa melded into one endless blur. I leaned my head back and closed my eyes.

"Checkpoint one." The lieutenant again. The first time they'd made a radio call and we'd been traveling nearly ten minutes. Good discipline. A quiet radio was a mark of a veteran unit. The enemy couldn't crack the transmissions, but they could track the energy that pushed the signal. Best to keep conversation to a minimum, even on a cleared route.

We passed two more checkpoints without incident. We'd pass seven before we hit our destination, based on the holo map Politte showed before we left. My head started to bob a bit. I'd been amped up when we started out, but quickly fell back into the routine, and the gentle motion and white noise of the Goat lulled me to sleep.

I'd just drifted off when an explosion jarred me instantly alert . . . a slight concussion shaking the vehicle. Nothing had hit us, but something came close. My heart slammed against my chest the way it does when you're jolted awake. For the length of a breath thc radio remained silent, and it pounded rapidly, echoing in my ears.

Then the net exploded with voices.

"What the fuck!" Belham, on internal. "Lieutenant's hit. Contact, right front. Return fire." The big gun above me rattled into action, adding a new vibration to the Goat, almost shaking it.

"Driver bear right, give them the front armor!" Belham again.

"Goat Two, get past the lead vehicle and secure the front." This time Belham broadcasted over the platoon frequency. With the lieutenant hit, he'd quickly taken over the battle, another sign of a veteran unit. The different communications in my helmet jumbled with each other, but I pieced it together.

The vehicle jerked to the right, jamming me back into my seat and into the soldier to my right at the same time. I tried to breathe in deeply through my nose, calm myself, keep the adrenaline from taking over. I couldn't do anything from the back of the vehicle, but I needed a clear head for when the moment came.

"Roger, Three. I can't see where the fire's coming from." A response from the distant end of the radio.

"Don't worry about the fire. Get up there!" Belham spoke firmly and with authority, but kept his voice under control.

"Roger. Moving."

Bullets slapped against our armor on the side away from me, and my heart started pounding again. Being strapped into the back of a vehicle with a battle going on, unable to see, is a helpless feeling. I wanted to be where I could visualize the fight, where I could act. Instead, I tried not to get slammed into anything too painful as the Goat dipped and turned again.

"Dammit, sergeant, they're in two places!" The gunner, I think. Impossible to say for sure once people get chattering on radio and internal at the same time, unless you know the voice.

"Keep fire on the rocket position. Don't worry about the small arms," said Belham. "Goat Four, suppress right. We need to get up to the LT."

"Roger." A pulse weapon whined behind us. The platoon probably had heavy conventional weapons and pulse guns on alternating vehicles. I should have checked before we left. The heavy vehicle-mounted pulse would do a good job suppressing enemy dismounted troops. It drained a lot of power, but the Goat had that to spare.

"Blue Leader, status." Belham, calling to the lieutenant.

"Leader's down. Multiple wounded," came the response.

"Can you move?" asked Belham.

"Negative, Three. We're cold." I didn't know the voice, but from context it had to be someone in the lead vehicle. The one that got hit. Multiple casualties and an inoperable vehicle on a cleared route. Not good. I slammed my fist into my hand in front of my face. I wasn't pissed that we got hit, but rather that I'd thought we wouldn't. I'd been away from combat, and it had dulled my thinking. I grabbed my belts and almost took them off when the vehicle lurched forward again, and I thought better of it.

"Dammit," said Belham on internal. "Move us up. Prepare to dismount. Pull the casualties out and load as many as we can fit."

"Blue Four, this is Blue Three," Belham transmitted. "Continue to suppress, but follow me up to Leader. Prepare to take on casualties."

"Roger Three. On your lead."

We sped forward, then jerked to a stop. "Ramp!" The man next to me slapped the button for the door and it whooshed down. I hit the release on my belts and followed my lead man out, three of us to each side in a standard dismount. My team had the side away from the immediate fire. That made us the rescue team, the other three the suppression. Thank the Mother of Planets for standardization. Everyone did things the same way, which made it easy for newcomers to the unit like me and Mac.

One of the soldiers next to me gave a hand signal to the other, preparing to move. I followed them forward to the smoking Goat in front of us, now pitched on its side at an ominous angle. If the soldiers were surprised that I followed, neither of them stopped to say so. We hit the ground at the front of the vehicle, kicking up dust and taking prone positions in the scraggly brown grass. Bullets cracked through the air nearby, but not so close that we needed to worry. The acrid tang of the burning vehicle bit at my nose, so I lowered my visor and triggered the air filter in my helmet with a flick of my eyes. A low whir began behind my ears and the clean air pushed out the caustic fumes.

"Load everyone. We need to get the package back to base, we'll MEDEVAC from there." Belham over the radio. It took me a moment to realize he meant me when he said "package."

What.

The.

Fuck.

He intended to pull out and put guys at risk on my account? No fucking way. If we loaded the casualties and bailed out, it meant more time before they got treatment. More chance they wouldn't make it.

I got up from the prone position and hurried around the front of our vehicle. Bullets flew down from the rocky hill that dominated the area and ripped into the side of the Goat, flashing against the armor. I dove for the dirt. My elbow banged on a small rock, shooting a burst of pain down to my fingers.

I spotted the source of the fire quickly, catching a glimpse of a mottled blue face poking out from behind a spiky rock that jutted out of the steep, brown hill. The enemy had picked their ambush site well. Two Cappans continued to fire from a hundred and fifty meters away, maybe forty meters higher than us. I brought my rifle up to return fire but by the time I got it there they had disappeared.

I struggled back to my feet after a few seconds, feeling stupid. The bullets had never been meant for me. Too high. They might have been trying to hit the gunner, who continued to rip off heavy rounds at a high rate from his position up in the turret. My senses were off, my reactions too slow.

I ran four quick steps and caught Belham as he dismounted from the front of the vehicle.

"What the hell are you doing?" I grabbed his kit and got in his face, yelling so he could hear me over the guns and radios.

Belham opened a private channel to me. "Sir! What are you doing? Get down!" The gunner fired a long burst mostly drowning him out, but I got the gist of it. I dropped to one knee and he followed me down.

"Why are we withdrawing? We need to secure the area and call for MEDEVAC."

"Sir, we need to get you—"

"Fuck that!" I cut him off. "We fight through, destroy the enemy, and get our people out. You hear me?"

Belham hesitated for maybe a heartbeat. "Yes, sir!"

His voice came over the platoon net. "Blue Four, Blue Two, assault through the enemy. Blue One, lay down suppressive fire. Everyone get your dismounted troops in the fight. Dismounts follow Goats Four and Two's move." With that, the soldiers who came out of the back of the Goats—the dismounts—sprinted into action.

Belham looked at me.

I waved him away. "Go! You take the dismounts. I'll help with the wounded." Every part of me screamed to join the fight, but that would distract Belham. He needed to lead his troops, not babysit a colonel. He turned and sprinted after the two vehicles, rifle in both hands. I flipped to the company radio net and called to headquarters to give them our coordinates and request air support.

Seven minutes, they replied.

A lifetime.

I wasn't being poetic, either. For some of these soldiers, it could be all they had left in their lives.

I ran back toward the overturned vehicle, ignoring the fire around me this time. Nothing close enough to matter. The initial rocket had shredded the front of the vehicle. Three soldiers struggled to pull the platoon leader out of the mangled, half-open door of the passenger's side. I grabbed on to the jagged metal and pulled, trying to give them another few centimeters. They finally pulled a bloody mess of a body through the gap, their backs exposed to the enemy as they did it.

The four of us carried Politte around to the safe side of the vehicle, putting it between us and the bad guys. The fire had shifted away, focused on the assault force, but we didn't take any chances, in case it started up again.

It didn't matter to Politte. He'd bled out.

Shit.

I knelt down and wiped my bloody hands and forearms on the dirt and thin grass, smearing it and coating myself in reddish-brown mud rather than getting clean.

Hardy lay in a line with the other wounded. They'd evacuated the injured before the dead. Cold, but proper procedure. He bled some from his shoulder, more from his hip, where a piece of bone jutted out, startling white against the crimson wound. A medic hunched over him.

Hardy had his eyes closed, but he seemed to sense me as I walked up, turned his head slightly in my direction. "I'm sorry, sir."

"It's not your fault . . ." I wanted to say more—a lot more—explain the randomness of battle, but I had to turn away before I choked up. I couldn't let a wounded man see that.

"I put him under," said the medic, a few seconds

later. Mini-stasis, we called it. It would slow Hardy's body and his wounds, knock him out so the medic could work.

I nodded without looking back, and walked away. I didn't trust myself to speak.

CHAPTER FIFTEEN

I STOOD NEXT TO Belham, unable to hear anything across my headset for a moment as the engines of the MEDEVAC ship screamed on takeoff. We stood out of the blast area, but barely, and the heat singed my face enough to make me turn away. Five of our team left with the ship. Two dead, including Lieutenant Politte, and three wounded, including Hardy, who along with his shattered hip had lost a lot of blood. I still couldn't believe his dumb ass apologized to me, like it was his fault somehow.

The evac bird disappeared through a small bank of clouds, leaving an empty silence in its wake. When I spoke, I found myself almost yelling at first, even though I no longer needed to. "Continue to the objective or back to base?" I asked Belham.

He took his helmet off and held it in the crook of his arm. "Back to base."

Not the answer I expected. If I thought he would quit on the mission, I might not have given him an option. But I couldn't go back on it after asking. "You sure?"

"Yessir." Belham drew out his "s" and turned it almost into a z-sound, running the words together so they sounded like one. "There's something wrong here. This attack . . . it smells funny. This was a cleared route."

"Cleared routes get hit sometimes," I said.

He paused. "That's not it, though, sir." Something flashed across his face. Confusion? "The Cappans . . . they don't attack like this. A sustained ambush where we can bring our firepower to bear? This never happens. We killed nineteen of them. No saying how many we injured that got away." Not that the injuries really mattered: Cappans had superb healing capabilities and could block out almost all pain. If you didn't kill them, they almost always got away. Or kept fighting.

I thought about it. I'd never seen it before either. Not since the early days, when they learned their lesson about head-on confrontations. After that, they tended to stick to hit-and-run tactics. But I hadn't been here recently, so Belham had newer information. "That does seem unusual. They haven't been attacking like this?"

He met my eyes. "Never, sir."

I chewed on my bottom lip. "What do you think it means?"

"I don't know, sir. But I don't want to push on until I have a chance to think it through. Talk to Intel."

I considered it, then nodded. "Okay. Back to base."

"Besides, sir, there are some guys back there I think you're going to want to talk to."

"I talked to everybody yesterday," I said.

Belham gave me a flat smile. "Not everyone, sir. You only talked to the guys on your list."

"And some of them lied to me." I took a shot in the dark hoping to get lucky. Maybe he wanted to tell me something. Firefights had strange effects on people, changed the way they thought about things, sometimes.

He shrugged. "Maybe. But none of them knew anything anyway. None of the people you talked to saw anything."

"But somebody else did?"

Belham raised his eyebrows. "There are two soldiers you need to talk to, sir."

"Why didn't you . . ." I'd raised my voice, so I cut myself off, and when I spoke again, I controlled my tone. My words still contained a bit more venom than I intended. "Why didn't you tell me this before?"

Belham turned and started walking away from the nearest pair of soldiers, gesturing for me to follow. "No offense intended here, sir. But you showed up from headquarters in your shiny new body armor. We didn't know why you were here, but come on. Colonels from outside don't show up to help."

I paused, then I chuckled. "Yeah. I get it. I'm from your higher headquarters and I'm here to help. So what changed?"

Belham stopped and gestured at some of the men to load up. "You're one of us, sir."

I nodded. "Thanks."

"Thank *you*, sir. I didn't think about air support.

And if we had bugged out instead of fighting through and didn't get the MEDEVAC, I'm not sure Jacobsen would have survived the ride."

I nodded again. "Okay. So back to base, I talk to your people, and then what?"

"Then I try to figure out how the bastards knew we were coming," said Belham.

TRUE TO HIS WORD, Belham ushered two soldiers to meet me a few hours after we got back. We'd all had time to do our after-action reviews and clean up, but not much more than that. Belham didn't want me to talk to them in the headquarters, so he set me up behind one of the vehicles in the motor pool to give us some privacy. The sun hung barely over the horizon, casting long shadows and painting the world with a reddish tint. With the cooler evening air and a slight breeze blowing—and the fact that no one was shooting at me—I'd finally stopped sweating.

He brought me a small wooden stool that someone had taped a foam pad to for me to sit on—perks of rank, I suppose. The soldiers—Essenbach and Xiang—stood, their backs to the vehicle shading them from the remaining sunlight. Both of them fidgeted, like they'd rather be somewhere else. They were the same height, and while it was hard to tell while seated, I figured I'd look them in the eye pretty evenly if I stood. Essenbach wore her service cap over her blonde hair, while Xiang had taken his off. His short black hair rippled slightly in the breeze.

"You want them together or separate?" asked Belham.

"We can start together," I answered. "I can take them separately later to get official statements."

"Roger that, sir. You two answer whatever the colonel asks, you hear me?"

"Yes, Sergeant!" The two soldiers answered in unison.

"Relax," I told them, once Belham left us. They didn't change posture at all. Privates tended to have a tough time slouching in the presence of colonels, even when given the opportunity. "You can lean against the vehicle, if you want."

Neither of them moved.

"Okay then," I said. "Your platoon sergeant says you know something about Lieutenant Mallot."

They glanced at each other, as if silently discussing who would speak. Xiang won. Or lost. I'm not sure which. "Yes, sir. Where should we start?"

"Why don't you start from the beginning? Tell me what happened on the patrol."

Xiang nodded. "Yes, sir. It was at a different base camp. We were augmenting the special forces, providing perimeter guard, convoy security, those types of things."

"Right." I'd read that much in the report, but I didn't let them know that. Better to have them tell me the whole thing in their own words.

"We were out on a patrol, on foot, escorting a few of the operators out to a Cappan camp to do some training. We had some of the friendly Caps with us, walking up front. We got hit hard. Command-detonated mines—you know, remote controlled—and a couple of heavy weapons opened up. They really pinned us down good. LT went down in the initial mine strike, which hit the middle of our column. Blew part of his leg clean off. I remember seeing his boot laying there. The firefight lasted pretty long, until we got air support in, then the enemy bugged out."

Everything he said matched the earlier reports. "What happened next?" I asked.

"One of the special ops guys, a captain—"

"Captain Sessma," interjected Essenbach.

"Right, Sessma," said Xiang. "He started yelling at one of the friendly Cappans on the patrol."

"What did he say?" I asked.

"I couldn't tell, sir. He had his translator on and I didn't have mine."

"But he was yelling?"

"Yes, sir," said Xiang. "For sure. Yelling and walking forward, and the Cappan was talking too, but backing away. I think the captain was blaming him for us getting hit. We took seven casualties and the captain was pissed. But three of the seven were Cappan, so I don't know why he was yelling at them. They'd lost some of theirs, too."

"I see," I said. His story varied slightly from what I'd heard previously, but not significantly. "Then what happened?"

Xiang turned to Essenbach, who nodded. "Then sir, we pulled security so they could bring in a MEDEVAC. Essenbach and I, we had inner perimeter."

"So you were close to the bird when it came in?"

"Yes, sir," they said together.

"Okay, good." I tapped a note into my device. "Now this is important. Did you see them put Lieutenant Mallot on board?"

"Yes, sir," said Xiang.

"You're sure?" I highlighted my note.

"Yes, sir," said Xiang, and Essenbach nodded. "But that's not all."

I tried to contain my elation. This was the first definitive evidence that someone saw Mallot loaded. "Okay. What else?"

"Sir—" Xiang paused. "They loaded all the casualties on the ship."

"Okay," I said. He spoke like it was important, but it seemed simple enough.

Xiang stared directly at me. "Sir, you don't understand. They loaded *all* the casualties. The Cappans too."

A chill ran through me. "On our ship? They put the fucking Cappans on *our* ship?"

"Yes, sir," they said together.

"Where did the ship go?" I knew the answer instinctively, but I had to ask. Taking a living species off their home planet violated at least half a dozen laws. A few pandemics and millions of dead hundreds of years ago made sure those laws stayed on the books and were strictly enforced.

Xiang shrugged. "I don't know, sir. Up."

"So off the planet?" I asked.

Xiang looked at Essenbach again, then back to me. "We can't say for sure, sir. But it looked like any other med bird taking off."

"Holy shit." I stood up and started pacing. "Who else did you tell this to?"

"Nobody, sir," said Xiang.

"Nobody?" I stopped and turned to Xiang. "Why not?"

Xiang flinched, and I realized I'd raised my voice.

"Sorry." I forced myself to sit back down. "Why didn't you tell anyone?"

"Sergeant Belham told us not to," said Essenbach in a high, squeaky voice.

"That's right, sir," said Xiang. "The day after the attack. That's when Sergeant First Class Belham told us to keep our mouths shut."

"I see." I rocked back on my stool so it sat on two legs.

I paused for a moment, fighting the urge to explode, then calming myself before speaking. "Sergeant Belham did the right thing." I wasn't sure it was true, but the privates needed to believe it, regardless.

I CAUGHT UP with Belham coming out of the headquarters after I finished talking to his soldiers. It was one of those fortuitous timing things, where he was coming to look for me at the same time I sought him out. I didn't give him a chance to speak, and I walked up and got right in his face. "Why did you hide these two from the investigation?"

The short sergeant's face dropped like I punched him in the gut, but he recovered quickly. He took a half step back with one foot to put himself at an angle and create space between us. "I take it that they told you something useful then, sir?"

"You know damn well they did." I consciously dropped the volume of my voice so it wouldn't carry to the entire base.

"That's good," he said.

"Yeah, it's good. But if they'd told someone before now, maybe I wouldn't even be here." It came out almost as a hiss. "You intentionally covered up information in an investigation."

Belham paused, pursed his lips. "Yes, sir. I did," he said after a moment.

"That's it?" I gestured at him with my hands, the way I do when I get frustrated. "No explanation?"

"Do you want an explanation, sir?"

"Of course I want a fucking explanation!"

He nodded. "Walk with me, sir." He started walking without waiting to see if I followed. I almost didn't, but something in the way he said it grabbed me. He had too much confidence, and it made me curious.

"I reported the situation by the book, sir," he said, after we'd walked two dozen meters.

"I don't think—"

"Hear me out, sir," he said, cutting off my protest. "Let me say what I've got to say, then you go ahead and pass your judgment and do what you've got to do."

I stopped walking. "Okay. But you tell me everything."

"Yessir. Everything. When we got back off of mission the day LT Mallot got hit, I had Sergeant Caena report what he saw. What his whole team saw. Caena was Essenbach and Xiang's team leader. They all saw the same thing, so he went to HQ and debriefed. Standard procedure."

"Caena told you, too?"

"Yessir, he told me before he told HQ. I'm the one who sent him there. I figured the captain would flip out, but nothing happened. It was late, and we had work to do on our equipment, plus an inventory of Mallot's kit, so I didn't follow up until the next morning."

"You had to know it was a big deal," I said.

"Yessir, I knew what it meant. But when you're down here in the shit, sometimes the big picture doesn't matter as much as the little ones. I did what I had to do, I put my soldiers down to sleep, and I planned to check on it the next morning."

"Planned to . . ."

"Yessir. But then things got crazy that night. Multiple rocket attacks. We were up and down, and didn't get much rest. Long story short, it was almost noon before I made it to Company HQ."

"Wait, before you go further. Who did you specifically speak to at Company?"

"The captain, sir."

"Captain Zattel?"

Belham nodded. "Yes, sir. I spoke to him directly."

"Okay." I blew out air through my nose. "Be very precise. What did you tell him?"

"I told him . . . no, wait, I asked him. I asked him if Caena filed a report. And he told me that he had."

"Then what?" I asked.

"Then the captain said that Caena had reported

nonsense, and he was evacuating him for a psych consult."

I stood silently for at least a half minute, processing. Zattel knew. Or he legitimately thought Caena was crazy, but I didn't believe that for a second. "So what did you do?"

"What do you think I did, sir? I told the captain that my man saw what he saw."

"What did Zattel say to that?"

"He asked me, very deliberately, if I saw anything myself. Which I hadn't. Then he repeated himself. He said Caena. Didn't. See. Anything. That's how he said it. Then he raised his voice, and asked me if I had a problem."

"And what did you say?"

"I said, 'No, sir, I don't have a problem.' You can check it out with anyone who was in the command post that day if you want. Everyone heard that last part . . . the captain yelling."

I nodded. "No, I believe you. So that's why you had Essenbach and Xiang keep their mouths shut."

He nodded. "Yessir."

"Shit." I kicked up dust with the ball of my foot.

"Yessir."

"And when the investigation came around . . ."

"I never gave the major doing the investigation the names. I told him that Caena thought he saw something unusual, but Caena was gone. Told him nobody else saw anything. Didn't want anyone else disappearing off to psych."

"Wait, you told the investigating officer about Caena?" I'd been looking at the dirt, but I looked back up.

"Yes, I definitely did."

"That wasn't in the report." Was it? I know I hadn't seen it, because I'd have remembered. No way did I miss that.

"That I can't help you with, sir. I know I told him."

"As part of your statement?" I asked.

Belham thought for a moment. "No, sir, I don't think so. I think this was before. As the senior guy present the day Mallot got hit, the major talked to me first. Mostly I gave him the names of the people he should talk to."

I punched my palm. "Okay . . . okay."

"What do we do now, sir?"

"Hold on, I need to think." Belham had told the investigator about Caena, and Zattel knew about Caena for sure. *Who else knew, and when?* "I need to look at the report again, but I left it spaceside. I don't want to confront Zattel, because I'd give too much away."

"Yessir. I'd much prefer you didn't talk to the captain."

"That's why you had me talk to your men outside the headquarters."

"Yessir."

"And I still need to get out and talk to Karikov."

"Sir . . . about that . . ."

"Oh just spit it out." I almost chuckled in spite of myself. What else could happen?

"When you were talking to the men, I went and

checked the satellite feeds for the area where we got ambushed. You're not going to believe this."

"No coverage?" I believed it immediately.

"They hit us in a fifty-five minute window between passes," he said.

"What about the geo-synch?" We had two types of satellites: The high-tech ones that gave the most data, that passed over every hour or so, and the lower-resolution geo-synchronous birds that traded off some capability to be able to maintain a persistent stare.

"Geo-synch feed was down. Went down almost an hour before we got hit, and didn't come back on until well after."

I stared at him. "Fuck."

"Yessir."

"That's a lot of coincidences."

"Yessir. Remember after the ambush where I told you something smelled funny? The stink is damn near overpowering now."

"Yeah." I let my arms fall to my sides. We'd been ambushed in a perfect window of time that existed almost never, by a force using tactics they never used, in a location where nobody should have been. I knew what the data told me, but I still didn't want to believe it. And I definitely didn't want to say it out loud. But it all pointed to one thing:

Someone had set us up.

They'd used indigenous forces, so that pointed the arrow at Karikov because his Special Operators worked closely with them. But someone else could have done it, maybe, knowing that I'd think that way.

Perhaps I was overthinking it. Karikov provided the simplest answer.

"Sir?" Belham spoke, and I realized that I'd been standing there for a while without speaking.

"Sorry. We can't go back out until I get some more answers. I need to go spaceside." I made the decision, and instantly knew it was the right one. I couldn't put more soldiers at risk taking me out to see Karikov until I knew who wanted to stop me. And until I knew how far they were willing to go to do it.

"Yessir, I understand." He paused. "Sir, whatever happens, you need to protect my people."

"I'll do what I can," I said.

Belham stepped in front of me as I went to go, his dark eyes staring up at mine. "No, sir. With all due respect, fuck that. Don't give me that officer answer that lets you off the hook when they get screwed, and you say, 'Eh, I did what I could.' I need more than that."

"Belham. *I'll do what I fucking can.*"

He smiled. "Yessir. That's better."

CHAPTER SIXTEEN

I REVIEWED MY NOTES on the shuttle up to Cappa Base. I had a lot of problems, and not a lot of solutions. The disappearance of Sergeant Caena via psych indicated that he'd probably gone through the hospital, where I wouldn't get a warm welcome. First, someone took alien life off of its planet in contravention of law. Second, the crew that did it was dead, and third, I couldn't tell anyone about my two witnesses without putting them in jeopardy. Add to that the possibility that Karikov had organized an ambush of our own forces to prevent us from getting to him, and the lovely fact that I had absolutely no way to prove or disprove it . . . yeah, I was stuck.

My gut said to pursue the Special Ops angle first. I could put some technical folks to work to see what happened to the satellites, and maybe find a lead there. But to do that would alert Stirling, and I didn't know yet if he had something to do with Caena's disappearance—I couldn't rule out the chance that Karikov and Stirling had worked together. Definitely not on everything. No way would Stirling be a party to his own men getting attacked the previous day. Stirling was an asshole, but he'd never go that far. I'd have liked to say the same thing about Karikov, but there were enough signs to give me doubts. Either way, I didn't know the full relationship between the two, and until I did, I didn't want to give away anything to Stirling that I didn't have to.

The shuttle landed in the hangar with a rough thump, a little harder than normal, and it jarred me back into the present. I stood before the door finished opening and hopped down the ramp and through the tunnel into the decontamination chamber, Mac following quickly behind me. The less said about decon, the better. Suffice it to say that you get sprayed and radiated and scanned in uncomfortable ways to make sure you're not carrying any nasty surprises from the surface. It had a weird smell that nobody ever explained to me, like a cross between ammonia and burning toast.

It wasn't the worst thing I'd experienced, but it was in the top ten.

Major Alenda waited immediately outside the chamber, which proved useless since we were still in the hangar and couldn't hear each other until we put some distance between us and the cacophony of engines and machinery.

She spoke once the noise subsided. "How was the trip planetside, sir?"

I gave her a nasty glance. "We got ambushed and Hardy got blown up. How do you think it was? And don't even tell me that you told me so. Not after Hardy got hit."

"Wouldn't think of it, sir."

I nodded curtly. "How is he?"

"He's stable sir. His hip was messed up pretty bad, and they've got him under sedation for at least the next seventy-two hours to speed the repairs. Doctor says he'll probably be laid up for ten days, and another week after that before he's fully fit for duty again."

"Seventeen days for a shattered hip? That's a pretty good facility," I said. "You wouldn't get much better than that back in the civilized part of the galaxy."

"That's a fact, sir. We get some pretty high-end docs out here."

"I guess so." I pushed the button and the door leading out of the hangar whooshed open. "Thanks for checking on him, Lex." I felt like crap that he got hit on his first mission, like somehow I'd been responsible.

Alenda waited for me to enter first, then took a few quick steps to catch back up. "Did you get what you needed for the investigation, sir?"

"Captain Zattel had everything set up when I got there, just like you said he would," I said. Alenda was fishing for something, but that didn't mean I had to make it easy for her. If she wanted to know something, I wanted her to ask it. Something nagged at me about the question. I couldn't explain it, but I started to assume someone else wanted the answers. Someone above her. It might have been my imagination. My brain does funny things when my own people try to kill me in an ambush. We walked in silence until we almost reached the door to my quarters.

"Sir . . ." she said, finally.

"Yes?" I stopped and turned to face her.

"We got reports about the attack, and then the request for the shuttle." She paused. "And nothing else."

I smiled. "I know. That's all I sent."

"Yes, sir. We got a report from Captain Zattel, but all he said was that you conducted interviews, not what they were about."

"Yep." I nodded. "I ordered everyone I interviewed not to talk about it. Glad to see they listened."

"Yes, sir." Alenda looked down at the floor and clasped her hands in front of herself. "It's just . . . my boss doesn't do well with not knowing what's going on in his command."

"I understand. If I were in Colonel Stirling's position, I'd feel the exact same way." I softened my voice a little. "I understand the position that puts you in."

Alenda let out her breath. "That's great, sir. So you'll talk to him?"

I thought for a moment. "Sure, I'll talk to him. Let me get a shower and I'll head right over. You'd think after decon you'd feel clean. I never do. They should work on that."

Alenda gave a half smile. "Thanks, sir."

"Don't mention it." I had no intention of briefing Stirling, but I didn't want Alenda to know that. Now that I knew Stirling was interested, I decided to let him wait. It was kind of a shitty thing to do to Lex, but I didn't exactly have a duffel bag full of other ideas.

"Hey, did you find anything out about Sergeant Santillo's early cryo call?"

Lex shook her head. "It seems on the up and up, sir. They moved cryo earlier for thirty soldiers with one order. I dug deeper, but the only answer I could get was that one of the cryo techs got injured so they had to spread the work out with fewer hands."

"Thanks." I hadn't expected to get any help there. I suppose it was a plausible explanation, though it still felt like too much of a coincidence. I turned and went into my room.

I tossed my stuff on the sofa. They didn't want me at the hospital, and with Hardy unconscious, I couldn't use him as an excuse to visit. I didn't want to talk to Stirling, and Karikov didn't want to talk to me. I had to talk to *someone*. After a minute, I picked up the comm and pulled up the contact info that Karen Plazz gave me. If there was one person I knew nobody was working with, it was the media. She answered on the second buzz and we agreed to meet for chow in forty-five minutes. I stripped out of my stuff and jumped in the shower. It wouldn't do to go meet a reporter smelling like combat and decon.

I BEAT PLAZZ to the mess hall and waited for her before I got in line. She came in with her blonde hair pulled back in her serious-looking bun, wearing a white long-sleeve shirt and tan pants that were a little too tight for space duty. At least five soldiers checked out her ass as she walked past. I doubt that was an accident on her part.

"Good to see you again, Colonel." She took my hand in both of hers when we shook, which annoyed me for some reason. It felt too intimate or something. I don't like touchy people.

"You too," I said.

"I hear you were down planetside. Also heard there was a bit of a fight." She said it casually, though her tight lips and firm gaze came across as anything but casual.

"Yeah, we got in a bit of a dustup. Let's get a plate. I'll tell you about it, but I'm starving."

"Sure," she said.

We split up and met back at an empty table that seated eight. I counted on my rank to scare away anyone else who might think about sitting down. It tended to work that way.

"What do you know about Colonel Karikov?" I asked before she had a chance to start in with her own questions.

She looked at me. "You know, that's not usually how reporters work. Usually I ask you questions, and you tell me things."

I shrugged. "We're off the record, right?"

She smiled at my joke. "Sure. Off the record."

I swallowed a bite of bread. I really was hungry. "So what's it hurt if we give and take a little?"

She stuck her fork into her salad, but didn't take a bite. "Nothing. I suppose we can share information. I assume you have something for me." She seemed suspicious. I didn't blame her.

"Yeah, I do. I'm not sure it's a story, but I was in the action."

She appeared to consider it. "Okay. You've got a deal.

Karikov. I don't know a lot. Special Operators don't exactly open up to reporters, you know."

"I know."

"But he's got history," she continued. "All the bad spots. Rensa 4, Polla 5. Multiple tours."

"No kidding?" I talked through a mouthful of pasta. Probably poor form. "Those *were* some rough spots."

"You'd know." She still hadn't eaten anything, but I didn't let that bother me.

I chuckled, then hid it behind a drink from my water. "I guess you've done your homework."

She met my eyes. "Come on, Carl. Did you ever doubt that?"

"No, I did not. I actually counted on it. What else do you know about Karikov?"

"I know he's been here two and a half years."

I whistled. "That's not normal."

She drew her lips into a thin line. "No. It's not. And he's spent almost the whole time planetside. I can't find anyone who has even seen him up here in more than two years. Okay—my turn to ask a question. Why would they leave someone out here that long?"

I took a bite of some sort of meat to give myself time to think before I answered. It didn't help. "I really don't know." It didn't help her, but it was the truth. I'd never heard of a tour that long. Sometimes guys did an extension, but never more than two years.

"Not sure that's a story," she said. "But it's interesting."

"It is."

"Other than that, it's mostly standard," she said. "His

men are fanatically loyal, but that's nothing new in his line of work. They don't talk, also not unusual. So really, it's about what you'd expect."

"Except that he lives on a hostile planet, and never takes a break."

"Exactly." She gestured with her fork. "I wonder what the shrinks would say about that."

"You haven't asked one?" I wondered about psychs too, but not for the same reason.

"Didn't really see an angle I could use," she said. "So what do you have for me?"

I set my fork down. "We got ambushed. They hit the lead vehicle, then continued to fire on us as we tried to recover the wounded. It took us a good bit of fire and maneuver to break out from it, and we really didn't gain much advantage at all until we got air support. Around twenty enemy killed in action. I'm sure you've got the casualty information from our side."

She rolled her eyes. "That's all you've got? That's pretty weak for a story. I knew most of that already."

I shrugged. "I can't talk about the investigation, if that's what you wanted."

"Why are you fucking with me, Carl?"

I know this is going to sound sexist, but it always has a bigger impact on me when a woman swears than when a man does. I think maybe it's because I don't expect it as much. That didn't include soldiers, though. Male and female soldiers were equal opportunity cussers. But when the reporter did it . . . that woke me up a little. "I didn't think I was," I said. "This attack . . . it wasn't normal."

"Really . . . go on." I had her attention again, her big eyes staring at me.

"It was a new tactic. Nothing we've seen on Cappa in ages. Usually they hit and run before we can bring in firepower. This time, they stayed and fought."

"Interesting." She had stopped pretending to eat, and started tapping into her device.

"Don't quote me on this," I said.

"Okay. I'll call you 'a source.'"

I nodded. "That works."

"What do you think it means?" she asked. "The new tactic by the enemy."

I shrugged. "They hit us at a good spot, with good timing, and with some serious firepower." I wanted to tell her about the satellite coverage gaps, but no way could I get away with giving out that kind of classified stuff. They'd track it back to me for sure.

Karen sat silently for a moment, fixing me with her stare. If she wanted to unnerve me, she was going to be disappointed. I was long past the point of being rattled by a pretty face and big blue eyes. "Why are you telling me this?"

"I owed you something for talking to me about Karikov," I said.

"No." She shook her head. "You *want* this story out there. Why?"

Shit. Had I been that obvious or was she that good? I did want the story in the press. I wanted Karikov to know that I knew something was off. He probably already figured, but I wanted to make sure he had no doubts. I needed to push him to do something. Anything.

"Come on, Carl. You're trying to use me."

"No." I looked down at my hands, then back up. "Maybe. I don't know."

She chuckled. "Okay, which is it?"

"I don't know." I sat quietly for a moment. "I really don't. This investigation is going nowhere, I've got nothing but dead ends, and I really don't know what to do next."

"So no leads on the whereabouts of Lieutenant Mallot."

This lady was good. "No. None."

"Can I use that?" she asked. "Come on, Carl. You're going to want a favor at some point. Hell, you want one now."

"I'm giving you a real story on this attack," I protested.

"I'll give you that." She paused. "But only because it's convenient. Give me something else."

I thought about it for a moment. "Write this down. Word for word. 'A source close to the investigation says that there are no new developments in the disappearance of Lieutenant Mallot.' "

She finished writing in her book. "That's not much."

"That's all you're going to get."

She thought for a second. "Okay. I'll take it. For now."

"For now." I pushed my plate away. "This food sucks."

"That's not news," she said. "One more question?"

"Sure," I said. "Shoot."

"How does a colonel on the back side of his career

who's buried at Student Command end up assigned to investigate such a high-visibility case?"

I started to answer too quickly, then caught myself, smiled, and stood up. "That's a great question. If you figure out the answer, let me know."

CHAPTER SEVENTEEN

I SAT SLUMPED ON the fake-leather sofa in my room several hours later, halfheartedly tabbing through the original investigation for the second time, looking for anything I might have missed in there about Sergeant Caena. I still hadn't found anything when the buzzer from my door sounded.

"Open," I called, and the door voice-activated with a whoosh. I tossed back the end of my whiskey.

"Carl." Stirling walked in, still dressed in his work uniform and giving the impression that he'd just left the office, even though it was late.

"Aaron." I stood and wobbled a little. "You want a drink? I was going to pour myself one. Ferra Three whiskey. Good stuff."

"You look like you've already poured a couple."

I glared at him, but without malice. "Sure." I'd already had three, but who was counting?

He thought about it. "Yeah, I'll have one. Mind if I sit?"

"It's your base. I'm just a guest. Sit wherever you want."

Stirling rolled the chair out from behind the desk and sat it so that it faced the sofa at an angle. "Thanks."

"Ice?" I asked.

"In Ferra Three? Just a little."

"Good man." I poured us both a couple fingers, added two cubes, and handed his over on my way back to the sofa.

"Going over the initial investigation again, I see." He wanted to sound casual, I think, but it wasn't his nature.

I swayed back to the sofa. "Yeah, trying to see if there's something I might have missed now that I've talked to some folks on my own."

He stared into the liquor in his plastic tumbler. "You find anything?"

"Not really, no. Nothing useful." I raised my glass, and he raised his back.

"That's good," he said, after taking a sip. "Major Alenda said you were going to come by and see me."

"I was. Now I don't have to." I wanted to see how long it took Stirling to come find me if I dodged him. About eight hours, as it turned out.

"She said you were coming right away."

"Yeah. Sorry about that. I meant to do it, but I got caught up with that reporter. The blonde one."

"Plazz." He said it flatly, and I took away the impression that he'd dealt with her before and wasn't a fan.

"Yeah. Her."

"What's she want?"

I shrugged and took a sip of my drink. "What do reporters ever want?"

"You didn't give her anything, did you?"

"During an active investigation? Of course not. I gave her a bullshit statement." Mostly true, I thought.

"Okay." Stirling swirled his drink in the cup, still studying it. "You know it's hard for me to help you out if I don't know what's going on."

"Yeah." I let the silence linger for a moment to see if he'd speak more, but he didn't. "I'm not really sure who's helping and who's hurting at this point." I probably shouldn't have said that, but a few drinks in, I favored the direct approach.

"What do you mean by that?" Stirling sat straight up in his chair and lowered his drink.

I shifted to a little less of a slouch. "Nothing." I paused. "No, *not* nothing. What I'm saying is that things in this investigation have seemed to have a high propensity to disappear."

"You're talking about the radar tracks of the MEDEVAC," he said. "You can't think I had anything to do with that."

"I didn't say anyone had something to do with anything. I said things were disappearing." *But it's nice to know that you're defensive about it.* "It's not only the radar feed. There's the female sergeant from the hospital who conveniently disappeared before I could talk to her."

"I heard about that." He relaxed, and took a sip of his drink. No way could I blame him for hospital personnel, so no need to be uptight.

"And you've heard about the ambush yesterday." I watched him closely as I said it.

"Of course."

I took a drink. "Did you see the satellite feeds of the fight?"

"No." He pursed his lips, and wrinkles appeared on his forehead. He knew I wouldn't be asking that question without a reason, but I didn't think he knew the reason.

"Look at them," I said.

"Okay, I will," he agreed. "But why don't you save us some time. Tell me what I'm going to see."

"You're not going to see anything. Because there were no feeds. We got hit in a window without coverage."

He stared blankly. "What about the geo-synch?"

I shook my head. "Down."

"What?"

I chuckled. "Yeah. Exactly."

Stirling breathed out loudly through his nose. "That's a lot of coincidences."

"Yeah. Coincidence."

"Nobody reported that." He paused for several seconds. "Okay. I can see why you're suspicious."

I nodded. "I don't like 'coincidences.' As far as reporting, I'm not sure who knows about the satellites. Zattel down at the company, for sure, but I'm not sure battalion got the word. Although they pushed air to us, so they had to have looked for some sort of feed during the event. Maybe it didn't register."

Stirling tossed back the rest of his drink. "Well, they should have noticed. And they should have reported it. It's on the critical-information list."

"I'll leave that to you, then. Have Alenda let me know what you find," I said.

"Sure. Can I pour another one?" he held up his empty tumbler.

"Of course. I'm good for now." Four was as many as I needed. I still had work to do. Stirling got up and fixed himself a drink, then stopped to look at me. "You think there's something to the satellite feeds being down?"

I considered my words before I spoke. "It seems likely."

He nodded and poured. "Yeah. I don't believe in coincidence either. But that would mean . . . well it could indicate a few things, but none of them are good."

"None of them," I agreed.

He sat back down. "I mean, it's unlikely that the Cappans cracked our feed, but we'll need to check. And if it wasn't them . . ."

I nodded.

"That's preposterous, right?" He didn't specify, but I knew what he meant. He'd come to the same conclusion as me.

Karikov.

But I needed to say it out loud. We'd been dancing around it, and I didn't want to give him a chance to deny it later. So I asked, "What, that our own folks did it?"

He sipped his whiskey. "Right. That's absurd, isn't it?"

I shrugged. "How far a leap is it from deleting radar tracks to shutting down a satellite?"

"It's a long, long way, Carl. One is data. The other

is lives. If somebody did this intentionally, I'll personally hang the bastard."

"I'm good with that."

He set his cup down, making a thunk against the table and causing the amber liquid to leap. "We'll look into it. Hard."

"I'd appreciate hearing the results."

Stirling waved his hand. "Of course. That's what we do. We share information."

It was a nice dig, if not very subtle. "Okay, I hear you. In the spirit of sharing . . ." I paused, picked up the report lying beside me. I waved it in the air. "There's one thing I can't figure out in here."

"What's that?" Stirling leaned back in his chair, savoring his whiskey.

"Why there's no mention of Sergeant Caena."

"Who?" he asked, his lips hidden behind his drink. He was a bad liar.

"Sergeant Caena. From Zattel's company. Transferred out on a psych call."

"Never heard of him." He did a better job keeping his face steady, but I still read him for a lie. I'd have loved to gamble with the man.

"You have to approve any transfers out of theater, even medical if they aren't emergency, right?"

"Yeah. I sign about twenty-five or thirty a month though." I knew it for truth, this time, because it was normal in any unit this size.

"Makes sense," I said. "Turns out, Sergeant Caena might have reported something."

"Oh? What?" There he went again, trying to be casual and failing. It was coming close to pissing me off.

"I don't know. Someone tipped me off that I should talk to him. But my source wouldn't say what." I'm a much better liar than Stirling, even four drinks in.

Stirling thought about it. "I'm sure we can get word to him."

"He's probably on a med ship somewhere in the middle of empty space," I said.

Stirling nodded. "Yeah, you're probably right." He sat silently for a moment. "Who mentioned him?"

"I shouldn't say," I said, intentionally coy.

"Come on, Carl. I thought we were sharing information."

We were. Shit. I wished he hadn't lied to me. I really needed an ally. "All right. Zattel let it slip. What can you tell me about him?"

"Zattel?" The way he said it, I didn't know if he was surprised that Zattel was my source, or buying time to think.

"Yeah. What kind of officer is he?" I decided to change the direction. Throw up some false trails.

"Huh." Stirling tossed back the end of his second whiskey. "Middle of the pack, I guess. Definitely not a top guy, but not bad. Solid. Doesn't take a lot of chances."

"By the book?" I asked.

Stirling thought about it. "I think so. Yeah. I guess you never know."

"Yeah. I'm not sure he even knows he told me. It

wasn't a direct question." In fact, I was quite sure Zattel didn't know he'd told me, since—you know—he hadn't.

"I see," he said. He stared off over my head, as if he was thinking.

I could almost see the gears spinning in his head. Setting Stirling and Zattel at odds with each other was a dick move, but I figured I'd stir things up and see what happened. Neither of them had played straight with me, so they deserved whatever they got. Assholes. If nothing else, the false information about Zattel would throw them off the trail of my real sources for a little while. Cause some confusion. Maybe that would give me time to figure out why Stirling lied about Caena. I was tired of being the only one looking over my shoulder at people he should be able to trust. See how they liked it.

We sat in silence for at least a few moments. I had enough of a buzz to lose sense of time, and to not care about awkward silence.

"Thanks for the drinks," Stirling said, finally.

"Anytime." I didn't get up as he left.

CHAPTER EIGHTEEN

I WOKE UP THE next morning with more of a hangover than normal and a new clarity on how derailed my investigation had become. My best hope rested on the possibility that someone who had lied to me, and very possibly covered up evidence, would come through . . . that made for a steaming pile of crap. I couldn't deny it any longer. I needed help. Unfortunately the nearest person I could completely trust other than Mac sat several months of deep space travel away.

After I showered a little longer than necessary, Parker showed up and hunched over my terminal to do some sort of computer magic. I wanted a few extra levels of encryption on my system.

"You're set up for level-five encryption, now, sir," said the big man.

"So it's secure?"

"Pretty damn secure, sir. We don't usually send anything out beyond level four, and that's only for the serious intel stuff."

"So on the other end, nobody can get it but Serata?"

"That's right, sir. Level five is double bio-encrypted at both ends. Nobody can open it but the recipient."

I knew that, but I wanted to hear him say it. "It can't be hacked?"

"Sir . . . anything can be hacked with enough resources."

"Like the type of resources it would take to erase flight tracks from the computers here?"

Parker smiled. "No, sir. That stuff was level-three encryption, this is level five."

"So more secure."

"Yes, sir. Level three is encrypted at 2048 bit—"

I cut him off. "Normal person words, Parker."

"Level three is protected against outside the network, but once you're in, it's fairly accessible. Level five is protected even from within." He paused, probably dumbing down what he needed to say next. "Basically, only you can access it, sir."

To log into the secure connection, I had to do a thumbprint and a retinal scan. I guess it needed two biometric cues in case someone stole my thumb, although if someone was willing to take my thumb, they probably wouldn't be squeamish about my eye. But that line of thinking seemed somewhat counterproductive. Parker assured me that once I logged out, nobody could read what I wrote, not even him. I couldn't control who saw it on the far end, but Serata would have to log in himself to receive it. I rarely use a keyboard, usually opting for voice recognition, but I didn't want to chance anyone overhearing me, so I sat back down at the terminal.

Sir—Eyes only—reached multiple dead ends in the investigation. Don't trust anyone here to help me out. Hardy got blown up in an ambush. He's fine, but he'll be laid up for a couple of weeks. Shattered hip. Sorry about that. Someone is contaminating the investigation. Maybe more than one entity. Can't be sure. All the radar tracks from the day of Mallot's disappearance have been erased. Signs point to a hack from inside Cappa Base, but outside of Stirling's HQ.

Zero cooperation from the hospital, still. Will re-look that angle later today. Tried to get to Karikov, but got ambushed on the way. Possibility that it was an inside job. I know that sounds ridiculous, but there are too many coincidences.

I don't trust Stirling. I don't think he was involved in the ambush, but he's hiding something. I know he's got a good record, but he's covering up. I don't know what. Just gut instinct at this point. But I'd put a lot of money on it. Not sure I can get this thing closed out with him in charge here. Openly, he's cooperating. But he's keeping tabs on everything (as we all would) and I'm not sure what happens if something points to one of his guys.

Need someone to run a check on a sergeant named Caena. Alfred P. Caena. In theory, he was redeployed for psych. Need to know where he is, and if we can get to him.

He saw something. Cappans being loaded into one of our MEDEVACs, and taken off planet. I know that's outside my investigation, but it's huge. And the MEDEVAC he saw them on was the same one they put Mallot on. So there might be a connection.

I'd tell you to send help, but there's no way it gets here in time to do me any good.

Respectfully, Carl

I read it over one time to make sure I didn't have any glaring mistakes, then hit send and cleared the screen before calling Parker back over to make sure I logged out correctly. "You're sure nobody can get back into this?"

He looked at me with the look that technical types give when you ask a stupid question. "I'm sure, sir."

"It would help me out if you didn't talk about it."

He nodded. "Sure, sir. I'll tell them it was a routine tech issue."

I held out my hand, and he engulfed it in his. "Thanks."

I COULDN'T STAND sitting in my room, looking at the screen and waiting for a message to come in, so I started to wander without really thinking too hard about direction. I ended up over near the hospital. I'm sure someone who evaluated things in people's minds would make something of that, but I took it for random chance and went in.

I hadn't been there for even a minute when a tall doctor walked up to me. He had short-cropped hair, which made him unusual for the hospital. I decided I didn't like him before he even spoke. Instinct.

"Sir, you're not supposed to be here." He confirmed my initial thought. I didn't like him.

"Who are you?" I didn't stop walking, which forced him to scramble to match my pace.

"I'm Lieutenant Colonel Wilson, the deputy commander of the hospital," he said.

My mistake. Not a doctor. If he was a doctor, he'd have used that for a title. Probably an administrator. Maybe a nurse. "That's great. Go get your boss. She can throw me out herself."

"She's off base, which makes me the acting commander."

"Huh. Isn't that nice." *Off base*. What was the hospital commander doing off base? "I'll just wait for her to get back, then."

"I'm afraid that's not possible, sir. She won't be back today." He had a weird voice that pissed me off. He probably didn't really have a weird voice. But he did piss me off.

"Really?" I looked over at him, but I didn't slow down. "I've never heard of a hospital commander leaving base before. Is she just saying that so she doesn't have to talk to me?"

"No, sir." He sounded offended, but it was nothing personal. More like a vague dislike of his entire profession. He might have picked up on that.

"Then where is she?" I asked.

"She's touring the forward medical stations planet-side."

I stopped walking. I'd never seen a hospital officer of any grade go to a forward med station. I didn't know if I should be impressed or suspicious. Given everything else going on, I went with the latter. "She do that often?"

"Once a quarter," said Wilson.

"Good for her. Well you can relax, Wilson. I'm not here to take over the hospital. I just want to see my boy. So if you'll point me toward Lieutenant Hardy, I'll be out of your hair. Maybe you could ring up his doc, too. I'll want to talk to him or her."

He thought for a moment. "Hardy. Hip injury?"

"That's him." I started walking again, mostly because I didn't want Wilson to get the idea I might be leaving.

"I think they still have him under, sir. You won't be able to talk to him."

"Humor me, Wilson. I want to see him. It's either that or you're going to have to try to physically throw me out. I'm an old man, so I'm sure you've got some orderlies who can do it. But do you really want to go down that path?"

Wilson paused, and I had a feeling he was actually considering it. He probably wondered if he could get away with having me roughed up. "Wait here, sir. I'm serious. Right here. I'll get his doctor."

"I won't move. I promise."

CHAPTER NINETEEN

I DIDN'T GET TO see Hardy. Not awake, anyway. They let me look at his unconscious, wired-up body in order to appease me. As if seeing my man laid up like this could do such a thing. His doctor said they wouldn't know anything more for a couple days. That didn't help my mood. I sat around for the better part of the next two days, letting my lack of progress fuel my natural inclination to do nothing. I knew I should move forward, but without somewhere to go I couldn't muster the energy.

The fact that I hadn't heard back from General Serata might have had something to do with my malaise. He'd answered my other communiqués immediately. But I'd sent the most recent more than thirty-six hours ago and hadn't heard a word, despite checking in at the commo shop three times to make sure there were no problems with the networks. I didn't know if he had read it and chosen not to respond, or simply hadn't seen it.

I didn't know which bothered me more.

Plazz's story ran in the *Talcan Times*, far removed

from the splash page. The only reason I even found it is she referenced my name, which triggered an alert I'd set. The whole piece ran barely two paragraphs, and basically said that while they'd sent a decorated veteran out to investigate (me), that we had nothing new to report. She'd stuck to our agreement. Whether that had been out of loyalty or because she had no better options, I couldn't say. I assumed the latter. I had no illusions. She'd run whatever she had if it made a good story. We all had jobs to do.

I'd almost convinced myself to move forward with my own job when the alarm sounded on my terminal for a new message. I hurried over, cursed myself for hurrying, then scanned in and touched the screen to display it.

> *Carl—Not the progress I'd hoped for. I'm sure you'll get there. Sorry for the delay. Some of what you wanted took time. Got you some limited authorities in the hospital. Took a LOT of doing, so don't waste it. Be as discreet and easy to work with as you can. And yes, I know who I'm talking to.*

I chuckled. He really did know. But since he directly said so, I'd tone it down with the hospital. He knew that, too.

> *I've got you a contact with special ops. A major named Chu. She was one of mine back*

in the day. Good woman. Karikov is well connected in his community, though, and will be hard to touch no matter what.

Acknowledged on the potential breach of protocols on alien life. Keep it quiet until you can show definitive proof. If you get evidence, that's critical information, eyes only, to me immediately. If it's true, it's going to cause a wave of crap, so I want you to be sure. What I really want is for you to be wrong about it.

You're going to have to figure out how to work with Stirling. I'm not pulling him out without something really solid. He rotates out in a few months, and doing something sooner than that wouldn't accomplish much. It might make things worse rather than better. If you want, I'll send him a note and tell him to help you out more. I'll do it subtly, but I'll make sure he gets the message. Just let me know.

Checking into Caena. Had the HR folks do a search. He didn't show up in any transfer records. In fact, they couldn't find anything beyond his assignment to Cappa. Something is off there, if he's left his unit. Will work it from this end.

Saw you in the news. Avoid that. Give my best to Hardy. Try not to get blown up.

Serata

I read it through twice, then deleted the message. I had no idea where stuff like this got stored, or who could access it down the road, but it seemed prudent. Even at that point I guess I thought about covering my tracks. Maybe it was just my nature. I opened a new document instead of responding to his.

> *Sir—Acknowledge all. Go ahead and contact Stirling, but don't scare him. Tell him that I'm failing, and that you need him to pick up my slack. Imply lack of confidence that I'll get it done while impressing that it has to get done. Weird on Caena. Will dig into it here, too. Respectfully, Carl.*

THE NEXT MORNING I headed off to the Special Ops wing on foot, going up three decks and down a series of passages heading toward the center of the station. I didn't wait for Mac because I didn't really know where I was going, and security felt like a waste of time. Spec Ops didn't mark any of the hatches or corridors in their area, so I walked around staring at a bunch of similar off-white walls and started opening doors at random. Not all of them functioned for me, but I had enough authorization in the base system that some of them did, and eventually I found a few operators staring at screens and listening to communications. They didn't stop when I walked in, though one of them looked up.

"I'm looking for Major Chu," I announced.

"She's not here," called someone from behind a monitor. He looked up and saw me. "Sir," he added. Still, the skinny, olive-skinned man took his time getting out of his seat. He wore uniform pants and a T-shirt that had neither name nor rank on it, and more than a day's growth of scraggly beard decorated his face.

"Where is she?" I asked without inflection.

"I'm Captain Patel, sir." He waited, as if expecting me to introduce myself as well.

"Nice to meet you, Patel. Where can I find Chu?" I wasn't really in the mood for games, but I knew Patel's type. He wanted me to respond to him, so that he could steer the tenor of the conversation. Not happening. I'm fluent in asshole and all of its dialects.

"She's down, sir. Most of our folks work nights." Night and day were nebulous concepts on a space station, but in this case Patel likely meant how it synched to the planet, which happened to roughly line up with standard time this week. A day on Cappa Three took slightly less than the galactic standard, so over time it would fall back out of synch and repeat on its own cycle.

"I can wait while you get her up," I said.

Patel waited, maybe expecting an explanation, maybe an excuse why I needed to see her now. Since I didn't offer one, he said, "Can I tell her what this is in reference to?"

"Sure. Tell her Colonel Butler wants to talk to her."

Patel apparently realized he wouldn't win the pissing contest he'd started, and after a moment he shuffled out the door. The two other people working in the room kept doing whatever it was they were doing, glancing up at me occasionally while they did it. I smiled at one of the guys, and he immediately looked away.

We continued that game for maybe five minutes before Patel came back in, trailed by someone I assumed was Chu, though dressed in gym clothes and slippers I couldn't be sure.

"I'm Major Chu, sir. Captain Patel said you wanted to see me? Sorry for my appearance." Her short hair had matted on one side.

"No problem. I know you were asleep," I said. "I apologize for waking you up."

"No worries, sir. I'm always on call." She yawned.

"Is there some place we can talk?"

"Yes, sir. We can use my office." She started walking through the room to a hatch on the opposite side, and I followed her.

The door zipped open and lights came on as we entered an office barely big enough to earn the title. It contained a desk, three chairs, and a small bookshelf, all cluttered with disposable tablets, maps, and various other junk. Chu stopped and cleared the stuff off of one of the chairs so I could sit down. She stacked it onto the other chair, increasing the pile there until it looked perilously close to tumbling over. "Sorry about the mess."

"Whatever works for you." I took the seat and waited for Chu to get behind the desk before I continued. "General Serata told me I could count on you."

Chu's face lit up, the corners of her mouth turning

upward in a slight smile. “How is the general?” Her voice held genuine affection.

“He’s well. At least he was when I saw him six months ago. He wanted me to pass on his regards.”

“Thanks, sir. When you talk to him again, I’d appreciate it if you’d thank him for me. He released me early from an assignment so that I could take the qualification test for Special Ops. Right after he told me that he felt it was a waste of a perfectly good infantry officer.” She smiled.

I smiled back. “Yeah, that sounds like him. Where’d you serve with him?”

“Polla Five.”

“Really? I was there. When?” I asked.

She scrunched her face a little. “Like seven years ago? It was near the end of General Serata’s tour there. After the big stuff was done. My company transferred in as replacements.”

“I wonder if you and I overlapped. I deployed with him, but I left early.” I left out the reason why I’d left. Another story I never tell sober.

“I remember your name, sir. I think you’d just left when I arrived, but people talked about you.”

“Don’t believe any of it.” I smiled.

Chu chuckled. “Nah, sir. It was good stuff. Mostly.”

I laughed. “That sounds about right.”

“You mentioned that the general said you could count on me, sir. For what?”

I blew air out through my mouth. “I need to get in touch with Colonel Karikov.”

Chu paused. “The colonel keeps a weird schedule

down on the planet, but I'm sure I can get him on the comm if it's important."

"I need to see him face-to-face," I said.

"Oh." Chu frowned. "That's harder."

I nodded. "If it was easy, I wouldn't need your help."

"Roger that, sir. I can see about putting you on a bird the next time we send one down." She didn't sound hopeful, almost like she wanted to discourage me.

"I'd like to see him up here." I knew the reaction I'd get before I said it, but I had to try.

Chu nodded. "Sir . . . Colonel Karikov . . . he doesn't come spaceside."

"I've heard that. But a councilor's kid disappeared. It's a sensitive situation, and I'm just looking to tie up the loose ends."

"I guess I can ask, sir."

"Yeah. That's all I want you to do. What do you think keeps him down there? Is the situation with the Cappans really that bad? The level of attacks seems pretty steady."

She shook her head. "It's bad, sir. We're keeping it under control, but the insurgents . . . they're brutal. They go after us without mercy, and their own people, too. Women, children . . . it doesn't matter. They have no conscience."

"Huh. I guess he's got his hands full then." I hadn't known the Cappans to be quite so ruthless, but I hadn't spent as much time with them as Chu, and certainly not living as close. "See what you can do. Get word to him personally. Tell him Butler said it was important, and ask if he'll come up. He's due for a break anyway."

“Yes, sir.” Chu paused. “Just so we’re clear . . . I wouldn’t hold out a lot of hope.”

I smiled. “I understand. And I’m not going to put you in a bad spot with your boss. Just make sure he gets the message.”

“Yes, sir. I’ll make the call right away.”

“Thanks,” I said. “I’ll let you get to it so you can get back to the rack.”

“Yes, sir. It was good to meet you and put a face to the stories.”

“Good to meet you, too, Chu. I’m sure I’ll see you again.”

CHAPTER TWENTY

I WENT DIRECTLY FROM Chu's office to the hospital, and after checking in and learning that they still had Hardy sedated to speed his healing, I headed for the command offices to find Colonel Elliot. Or at least to find out if she'd returned from planetside. I got my answer when she intercepted me before I could even enter her wing. Obviously one of her people had warned her upon my arrival.

"Here you go." She waved a reader with a green cover at me. "This is a list of everyone who had duty during the time period that you requested. After twelve hundred on thirteen eleven 3943 and before oh six hundred on fourteen eleven, I think it was."

"Sounds right." I took the reader from her hand. "Thanks."

"The ones with asterisks by them are the ones that are no longer available, mostly due to reassignment."

I tabbed through three sheets of data, consisting of maybe two hundred names. "There are asterisks by almost half of them."

She folded her arms across her chest. "My folks rotate

in and out monthly and do mostly twelve-month tours. It's been what, six months? Half should be about right."

I pursed my lips and bit back a sarcastic comment. I didn't know if she'd completed the list on her own or if she'd gotten pressure from whomever Serata talked to. I also remembered Serata saying not to be a dick. "Great. Can I start tomorrow?"

She kept her face unreadable, her shoulders hunched. "Sure. Oh eight hundred start?"

"That works. How was your trip down to the planet?"

A little of the tension came out of her neck. "It was a good visit. I'm very pleased with the progress we've made with the forward clinics. Any particular order you want to do the interviews?"

"You choose. You know, I've never seen a hospital commander at the front before."

She shrugged. "It's a lesson I learned from an early mentor. You get a lot of value from early treatment planetside. It saves lives."

"Makes sense." I wanted to press her about the Cappans in the med ship, but I couldn't get a read on her. She'd be able to deny it and I wouldn't be sure if she was lying or not. "Do you own the MEDEVAC birds?"

She shook her head and half frowned, pausing to consider her answer. "It's a weird command relationship. I've got operational control, but technically they belong to the air squadron."

"Actually, that makes sense," I said. "You get to schedule the flights and set the hours, but they're responsible for the maintenance."

"That's right," she said. "Why do you ask?"

"Just a question I had when they evacked Lieutenant Hardy."

If the question made her suspicious, it didn't show on her face.

"Thank you, Doctor Elliot. You've been very helpful."

"Don't mention it." She smiled, but it didn't reach her eyes.

I STARTED THE kilometer-and-a-half or so walk back, winding through the corridors and levels of the space station toward my quarters, pretty pleased with how the day had gone so far. I didn't think anything would come from the hospital interviews, but if I pushed on the right person I might get a hint that could lead me to another line of questioning with Elliot.

I'm not sure when I noticed someone following me.

It wasn't a conscious realization at first, but I became aware at some point. Definitely closer to the hospital than my quarters, so it couldn't have been too long. I heard the sound, first. Footsteps behind me, faster than my own, but then they slowed to match my pace. I checked back over my shoulder, trying to look casual. I didn't recognize the man. A big guy, maybe twelve or fifteen centimeters taller than me and broad, dressed in civilian clothes. A contractor, maybe, by what he wore, but he walked like a soldier. That wasn't uncommon. Lots of guys retired and moved into the ranks of civilians who serviced distant bases.

I took a random turn off of the main, high-ceilinged passage down a smaller hallway to clarify for myself that it was more than coincidence. He followed me, fifteen meters behind. I stopped and turned to face him. I wasn't going to outrun him, so that left confrontation. "Can I help you?"

He closed the distance impossibly fast and I barely got my arm up in time to block a blow aimed at my head. My arm flared in pain before going totally numb to the shoulder and falling limp to my side.

Stun stick.

Shit.

A stun stick is an ugly, illegal weapon that works by deadening the neurons around where it hits. I wouldn't be able to use my arm for maybe half an hour. What made it worse is he'd aimed it at my head. A stun stick blow to the head usually wasn't lethal, but shutting down the neurons in your neck and brain . . . not healthy.

I took a step back to gain space as my attacker reset himself, my heart slamming in my chest.

I wished I hadn't left my pistol locked up back in my quarters. Or left without Mac. I looked around for a potential weapon, but the hallway continued unbroken and quiet. Not even a door I might be able to run through.

I exaggerated my injury, hung my head a little. The man moved forward, stalking, and I kept giving ground. I needed to lure him in. I only had one arm and he had a weapon, so a long fight didn't favor me. I'd only get one chance.

"You don't want to do this," I said, still moving backward. I hoped to draw him into conversation and distract him, but he kept moving forward without speaking.

I waited until he stepped forward and had his weight on only one foot, so he wouldn't be able to react. I reversed my direction quickly, stepping forward instead of back. I launched a low side kick at the knee of his planted leg.

I don't know how I missed.

But suddenly his leg wasn't there and I was off balance. My head exploded and the world went dark.

I WOKE ON Polla Five, though the lighting seemed off. Too bright, too white. Polla Five's air gave everything a reddish tint, which was missing. Something dug at the back of my mind, telling me this couldn't be real, but I couldn't shut it down. My foot and lower leg screamed in pain. I'd been hit, and even without looking I knew it was bad.

I slapped at a burning sensation in my arm. When I hit it the pain flared. An IV line. Had the medics reached me? When did that happen? I tried to call out, but it came out of my dry throat more like a croak. Too much dust on Polla.

Sweat dripped from my forehead, down my temples. I needed to roll over onto my front. I couldn't walk. I needed to crawl. Get out of the kill zone. But I had the IV. They must have dragged me clear already. No sense in chancing it.

I couldn't turn over. Something blocked me, and I couldn't get my head turned around to identify it.

"Colonel Butler." A female voice. The calm, authoritative tone of someone in charge. Why was she on my radio? How could I hear my radio without my helmet?

"Colonel Butler." The same voice. I hadn't misheard it.

"This is Butler. I'm hit and I need immediate evacuation. They hit us hard. We need air support."

"Colonel Butler, this is Colonel Mary Elliot. Do you know where you are?"

Elliot. On Polla? That wasn't right.

"Give him five cc's. I don't want to put him to sleep, just calm him down." Elliot speaking again, to someone else this time. Softer. Distant.

"Elliot?" My own voice sounded far away, like speaking under water almost.

"Butler, listen to me. You are in the hospital at Cappa Base. Do you understand?"

Cappa, she said. Not Polla. I opened my eyes, then immediately shut them again against the blinding light. Cappa. Tears formed under my eyelids, leaking out. I could feel my pounding heart slowing. Cappa.

I nodded, though I don't know how much my head actually moved. It hurt, but in the dull way that things hurt when narcotics mask the pain.

"Good," said Elliot. "You're safe here. You have a mask on to help you breathe, and you've got IVs in both arms. Nod again if you understand."

I nodded, stronger this time.

"Good. I've given you a mild sedative. Continue to focus on where you are. Cappa Base. Sergeant Mac is here. You remember him?"

I nodded again.

"Okay. He's going to stay with you and talk to you. You're going to be fine. I will be back in a little while."

I nodded.

"Keep him calm. Do not rile him up. Do you fucking hear me, Sergeant?" I assumed she was talking to Mac.

"Yes, ma'am." Mac's voice sounded defeated, like he'd been through a fight and lost.

"Can you take the mask off?" I croaked. "Thanks," I said, once someone removed it. My voice came back. "I can breathe. The mask always makes me feel like someone is choking me."

"I'll be back in about half an hour," said Elliot.

"Can you turn down that light?" I asked.

Elliot chuckled. "Sure." The light pouring through my eyelids dimmed.

"Thanks, Doc."

I listened to people shuffling out of the room. More than two, but how many I couldn't say.

"You okay, sir?" Mac asked.

"Yeah, I'm good. We alone?"

"Maybe," he said. "There's nobody in the room with us, but I wouldn't rule out someone listening."

"That's okay. What happened?" I forced myself to open my eyes. It took a moment for things to come into focus, and even then, I was looking straight up, so I didn't see much.

"I was going to ask you the same thing, sir." Mac stood close to the bed, and I could see the worry on his face.

"Someone jumped me."

Mac grunted. "That much I know. I showed up just as he hit you."

"You . . . how?" I started to get my voice back.

"I spent all morning trying to track you down," he said. "I was headed to the hospital when I heard something. Imagine my surprise."

"Yeah. Sorry I ditched you."

Mac chuckled. "Bet you won't do it again, sir."

"You're right about that."

"Sir, I shot at the guy."

"Good. He had it coming."

"No, sir, you don't understand. I shot at him and I *missed*."

I paused. "That's okay, we all miss."

"No, sir, we don't. *I* don't. Not from that range. Not with a guided bullet. It's impossible."

"Weapon malfunction?"

"No, sir. I checked. And from that range it shouldn't have even mattered. He moved . . . I don't know."

"No, finish that thought. He moved how?" I got a chill that I didn't think had anything to do with my current condition.

"He moved too fast, sir. He took off, and I shot. I led him . . . fired right where he had to go. Except he didn't. I know that sounds—"

"No, it doesn't. My brain got scrambled a little by that stun stick, but I saw the same thing. The guy was super quick. One moment he was there, the next moment I missed a kick that should have hit."

Mac stopped pacing. "Maybe I'm not losing my mind then."

"I'm not ruling out me losing mine. How long have I been out?"

"Maybe two hours? I didn't really check the time, sir. We got you here, then they mostly shoved me out of the way while they treated you. A lot of docs. Scanners and other stuff too. They were worried for a few minutes."

I blew out a deep breath. "Shit."

"Yes, sir. You feel okay?"

"You mean other than the flashbacks and the splitting headache?" I thought about it, wiggled my fingers and toes. My left foot didn't work right. It had that weird feeling I can't describe that comes with the robotics. Like it might be moving, but you can't quite tell.

I started to sweat again, and the light dimmed. There was something in my arm. IV. Right. Hospital. Cappa Base. "I'm at Cappa."

"Sir . . . yes, sir. You're at Cappa. Where else would you be?"

Cappa. Cappa. I repeated it in my head until I started to calm down again. "Sorry."

"Sir . . . are you okay?"

I nodded. "Yeah, I think so."

"Was that . . ." he stopped.

"A neural rejection flashback? Yes." I lay there in silence for a moment. "It's okay."

"Sorry, sir. I've heard about them, but I've never actually seen one before. I didn't know it was so . . ."

"Yeah. It's real. It's really fucking real." It didn't bother me, Mac's thoughts. A lot of people didn't really believe. Things that are in your head are hard for people to see. No outward signs, most of the time. I'd gotten over worrying about what other people thought.

Mac sat down. "I'm really sorry, sir."

"I'm sorry too, Mac. Sorry I didn't wait for you." He wouldn't say anything, but I knew that for a personal security officer, your primary getting hit had to feel like a kick in the nuts. It didn't matter that I'd deserted him. He'd still blame himself. He was too good to do otherwise. "They find the guy?"

"No, sir. Not yet. They're doing a search. Colonel Stirling's people. But the guy was long gone. Once they run through all the camera feeds they're going to show me some pictures. I can ID him."

That was one benefit of being on a space station. There were only so many places a guy could run to. We sat mostly in silence until Elliot came back in, a flock of hospital staff trailing her in a neat formation. They started buzzing around the room, checking monitors, poking and prodding me.

"Did you have any episodes?" Elliot asked.

"One," I said.

"And?" She raised her eyebrows, looking directly down at me, watching my response.

"And I controlled it."

"Just like that."

"Not my first time," I said.

She stared a moment longer, then nodded. "Good." She stepped back and let her minions do their work.

"Okay, give us the room," she said, apparently satisfied they'd attended to everything.

The staffers swarmed for the door, as organized leaving as coming in. "I said give us the room." Elliot turned to Mac, who hadn't followed the others out.

"Sir?"

"It's okay, Mac." I waited for Elliot to explode, but she stood silently and watched him leave.

"I'll be right outside, sir," he said as he reached the door.

"Thanks, Mac."

"You're going to have to talk to him," Elliot said, once the door sealed behind him.

"Why's that?" I thought I probably knew the answer, but it seemed the proper question to keep the conversation moving.

She put her hands on her hips. "I've cut him a lot of slack. Even let him bring his weapon in the hospital, given that there's still an attacker at large. But he's been threatening my staff, and I can't have that."

I nodded. "I'll talk to him. He's just feeling protective. But you're right, he can't do that."

"Thanks." She paused a moment. "The irony of you being here, needing treatment in my facility is pretty rich, if you think about it."

I started to chuckle, but ended up coughing. "Forgive me if it's lost on me at the moment. So what happened? Medically speaking."

"Best that I can tell, when you got hit in the head with the stun stick, it scrambled your brain a bit. That's my technical, medical opinion." She smiled. "Remember all of the neural training you did when you got your cybernetic appendage?"

"Yes." *How could I forget?* It had been the worst three months of my life. Constant agony, headaches, nausea, flashbacks. They never put that in the advertisements. They always showed the benefits of robotics, but didn't mention that your brain would rebel against it. They never mentioned that without neural training, it would drive you insane . . . but that the neural training comes close to driving you insane too. And I just had a foot. Some people had full limbs. That had to be harder. Much harder. It pushed the very limit of what the human brain could withstand. It actually made it so that you couldn't replace more than one limb. The brain couldn't handle it.

"Colonel Butler?" said Elliot.

"Yes?"

"Are you with me?"

She'd said something, and I'd missed it. "Sorry."

She continued. "As I was saying, when you got stunned, some of that neural training got scrambled, which—"

"Which brought me back to where I was when I lost my foot." Ghosting, they called it. Something in your mind that nobody could figure out. It took you back to when you lost the limb, sometimes. The neural training made it better. Mostly.

"Yes, that's what we think," said Elliot.

"I can't do that training again." I tried to sit up, and Elliot helped me by propping two pillows under my head and upper back.

"I don't think you'll have to. Maybe you do one training day. It should come back much, much quicker. I can't say for sure, though, so don't hold me to it."

"Shit."

"Sorry." She sounded like she meant it.

I sighed. "You know it never really goes away. Even with the neural training. They say it will. The doctors. They say that it gets better. It never does."

"I'm a doctor of robotics and orthopedics." She looked directly at my eyes. "I've had hundreds of patients. I know."

I nodded and closed my eyes. She probably did know. But then she couldn't. Not really.

"We're working on ways to help," she said. I opened my eyes and looked at her, skeptical. "Really," she continued. "It's very promising. It's leading toward breakthroughs for double amputees. Triple, maybe."

"That's great. How come I've never heard of it? I stay pretty well informed on robotics, as you might expect."

She nodded, pacing, full of energy. "It's experimental still. But it's going to work. It *is* working."

"That's great," I said. Anything that made neural training easier.

"I could put your name in. See if you fit the test criteria. It could mean a serious upgrade in quality of life. Patients have shown complete dissipation of pain symptoms and a reduction of mental stress in sixty percent of cases."

I almost couldn't believe what she was saying. "Those are good odds." I didn't mind a gamble. I'd bet half my pay on something if I thought I had a sixty percent chance of winning. But experimental medicine . . . it rubbed me the wrong way. "Is it okay if I think on it?"

She stopped pacing and looked at me, like she hadn't expected that answer for some reason. "Of course. Take your time."

"Something wrong?" I asked.

"No, of course not. . . . well . . . to be honest, you're the first person who didn't immediately say yes."

"Don't take it personally," I said. "I've had a rough day, and I'm not thinking straight."

"No, no, it's nothing like that." She pulled over a rolling chair and sat. "I'm passionate about my work. You probably are too. But whatever the patient wants."

"Right now, the patient wants to get out of here and get back to work." I tried to smile, hoping it didn't look strained and gruesome.

She laughed. "Typical combat officer."

"Seriously, Doc, when do you think I can go?"

"You want my best medical advice, or my minimum standard that will ensure you don't die?"

I laughed for real this time.

"That's what I thought," she said. "You should stay here a week. But I'd like you to at least stay here overnight. You've got some signs of a concussion, and we need to observe you."

I nodded. "Overnight I can do."

"Good. It won't be a good night of sleep. We'll have someone in every hour to check on you. But I'll discharge you personally tomorrow. I want to be very clear that we don't know for sure what kind of lingering effects you're going to have regarding your previous injury. I think you should expect increased symptoms. I can prescribe something that will help, but if it gets too bad, or if you still feel like you need the meds after a few days, you should come back."

I nodded again. "I understand."

"Are you up to seeing visitors? Stirling and his people have wanted to come in but I've put them off. If you need some time, I can forbid them to see you. Medical reasons."

"I could use a couple hours. Maybe the night. Tell them they can come by in the morning?"

"I can do that." She stood to leave. "Don't forget to talk to your man."

"I won't. Hey, Doc?"

She stopped by the door and looked back.

"Thanks."

"Don't mention it," she said. "Just doing my job."

CHAPTER TWENTY-ONE

I HAD ONLY FINISHED half my first cup of coffee when Stirling arrived at my quarters. "You look like shit," he said.

"Thanks. Rough night. Coffee?"

"I'm good." He didn't sit down, which led me to believe it might be a short meeting. One could hope.

"You learn anything about Sergeant Caena?" I asked.

"That's what you want to talk about? Carl, you were in the hospital yesterday."

"I'm fine. I've had a lot of practice."

Stirling grunted what might have been a chuckle in another man. "I'm more concerned with the events leading to you being there than your actual time under care."

"Right." I took a sip of coffee. "I'd probably be worried about that too if someone attacked someone else with an illegal weapon on my base."

"Don't be so damn self-righteous, Carl. You know as well as I do that every base in the history of the galaxy has a black market. You yourself smuggled whiskey in. You think you're the only one?"

He had a valid point. I was being a bit of a dick, but having your head used as a piñata will do that. Not that I needed much of a push to be an asshole. "You find the guy?"

"No. We'll need to get a statement later, if that works for you."

"No? Aren't there cameras? Door logs? It's a closed station. It shouldn't be that hard."

Stirling had the decency to look embarrassed. "We're not really where we need to be with that type of thing. There are dark spots, and this guy used one."

"Whatever," I said. "Just send the investigating officer by. I'm going to take it easy here for a day or so. Doc says I had a minor concussion."

"Sure. What's your gut tell you?"

"It tells me not to mess with big guys carrying stun sticks."

Stirling stared at me, then decided to sit, taking the desk chair and spinning it around. So much for a short meeting.

"Sorry," I said, without meaning it. "It wasn't a random occurrence, if that's what you were asking. Guy was a pro. Dressed like a contractor, but definitely military. Fastest man I've ever seen."

Stirling nodded. "Your sergeant said the same thing."

I took another sip of coffee. "Can't explain it. He just . . . moved."

He blew air out through pursed lips. "Unfortunately it's hard to do a personnel screen for quick."

"Yeah, I hear you." I thought about it for a moment.

"Big guy. Almost two meters, at least a hundred kilos. Maybe a hundred and ten. Light skin, dark hair a little longer than military cut, no facial hair." I thought some more. "That's all I've got."

"If nothing else, the size will rule a lot of people out," he said.

"You really doing a screen?"

Stirling sighed. "Trying. With all the different contractors involved, it's almost impossible to get an accurate picture. I've got less control of this place than one would think."

I grunted. "You'd think it would be easy, but it never is." Despite it being a military base, contractors flew in on their own commercial ships, and getting an accurate manifest was always a struggle. When you asked their leadership for personnel numbers, they always claimed that giving an exact picture would hurt their ability to compete for future contracts, because somebody could try to undercut their next bid.

"We're giving it a go. Making everyone report all their names and show proof of their screening. We needed to do it anyway. Your incident gave me an excuse."

"Glad I could get my skull mashed in for the cause."

"You think this has something to do with your investigation?" asked Stirling.

I shrugged. "Don't know. Who do you think I pissed off?"

"Everyone," said Stirling. "But enough to assault you? That feels more personal. Who has the most to lose from your investigation?"

"Honestly?" I thought about it for a minute. "Probably you. But you aren't big enough."

"Be serious for a minute," he said.

"I am being serious. You asked who had the most to lose. I've got next to no authority over anyone in the hospital and less over anyone in Special Ops. That leaves your command as the ones with the most to lose from anything I find out."

He thought about it. "Guess I didn't think of it like that."

"For the record, I don't think you did it. And I don't really suspect anyone in your command. Line soldiers aren't wired that way. They aren't blindly loyal enough where they'd attack a colonel. Not usually, anyway. Maybe at a lower level, like if it happened down on the planet. A guy protecting his buddy."

"Yeah," he said. "You know I had to send up the incident report. So you can expect that the boss has seen it by now."

"Serata?"

Stirling nodded.

"He send anything back?" I asked.

"Not to me. You might want to check your messages."

"Okay, I will. Thanks."

"Carl . . . I want to put some guys on you."

"What, security? I'm good. I just went out without my man. And my pistol." I tapped my sidearm, which I wore at my hip now.

"Humor me," he said. "If it makes you feel better,

you can say it's a favor to me. If something else happens to you and I didn't put measures in place, I won't need an investigation to get fired."

I tossed back the bottom of my coffee, suppressing a chuckle at his sense of self-preservation. "Fair point. Okay. Two soldiers, they report directly to me. Part of my team."

"Two teams of two, so they can go around the clock," he said. "Twelve on and twelve off."

"Agreed," I said. "Have the senior person come see me first."

"He's waiting outside with your PSO," said Stirling.

I laughed. "That's convenient."

He shrugged. "I knew who I was dealing with. We're both reasonable men."

"I'm not sure about that part, but in this case, I guess we are. Would you have Alenda come by? I want her to pull some satellite shots for me."

"Sure. You looking for something specific?"

"I need to get a better look at what Karikov is doing down there. I've got to go back down and see him at some point, unless he agrees to come here."

"He won't," Stirling said.

"I don't think so either," I said. "So I'm planning ahead."

"You think—"

"I don't think anything," I said, cutting him off. "But if you're looking for guys who inspire fanatical loyalty, where would you start?"

"Probably the same place." Stirling started to the door, then stopped. "Be careful."

I put my plastic tumbler back into the coffee dispenser and hit the button. "I plan on it."

MAC HAD THE security detail stay outside the door. I suggested having them inside, but he insisted, so I let it go. Gutierrez and Guildsten. It paid to know the people protecting your ass by name. I promptly renamed them G One and G Two, with Gutierrez being G One on account of her seniority.

Alenda sat in front of my terminal, feeding data to a giant screen she'd had wheeled in. "Where do you want to start, sir?" It was the first time she'd spoken in several minutes. She'd been quiet, since my attack. Shaken a little, I think.

"I want everything," I said. "Every satellite picture we've got of the area around Karikov's base, in every spectrum we've got. I want infrared, I want chemical emissions, I want power usage. If we've got a sensor that picks it up, I want to see it. And I want to look at how it has changed over time. Let's go back six months to start. We'll know if we need to go back farther once we see what we've got."

It was a lot of data, but I had time. I'd put off interviewing the folks at the hospital for a couple of days.

"I'll start bringing them up, sir. If we've got multiple passes of the same sensor, I can parse it down so we only see one or two per month."

"Okay, but keep the rest handy."

"Yes, sir. Sir?"

"Yeah?"

"What are we looking for?"

"I have no idea."

Alenda looked at me as if to say, *Really?* She was too polite to actually say it though. "I get the feeling that you don't trust me, sir. You're keeping me in the dark."

I thought about my response for a moment. "I really don't know what I'm looking for. I'll know it when I see it." I hoped that was true. I believed it though, and had a history of making it work. I often had no idea what I was doing until the moment when it fell together. I didn't feel the need to mess with a successful formula.

"Sir, I want to be a real part of this investigation."

I sighed. "Sit down, Lex."

She sat on the sofa, but remained stiff.

"You are a critical part of this investigation."

"I fetch things, sir. I'm good at it, I get that. But I'm not really a part. You're keeping most everything from me."

"I understand the situation you're in, with your boss," I said.

"Sir . . ." she paused. "Sir, I . . ."

"Go ahead. Say what you've got to say," I said.

"Sir, I don't give a shit about my situation." She paused. "I'm half in, and that doesn't work. I want to be part of the team. For real. Help figure this out."

I sat silently, looking at her, considering. I decided she meant it. I couldn't say why I got that impression, but I trusted my instincts. "Okay," I said.

"Okay, sir?" Her eyes narrowed.

"Okay, you're in." I would have said it even if I

didn't mean it. I needed her help, and if I pushed her away now I risked losing her. But once it came out of my mouth, it felt right. I meant it. I trusted her.

She sat silently for a moment.

"You good?" I asked.

She nodded. "Yes, sir. I just didn't expect that to work."

I shrugged. "Sometimes things surprise you and you get what you ask for."

"Glad to be on your team, sir."

"Glad to have you," I answered. "With that said, I still don't know what I'm looking for in the data."

A laugh escaped her, then she choked it off, but laughed again at the awkward snort. "We'll figure it out, sir."

Alenda busied herself talking to my computer terminal, calling up the data she needed to populate the big screen. She transferred the first piece, a high-resolution image of a series of buildings. I could barely make out the people in the image, but it did a great job of showing the overall layout of the area six months ago. I stored that in my mind while Alenda filed it for ready access on the computer. We'd be able to touch screen back through them later, as quickly as we wanted. Flip back and forth, looking for changes.

She moved faster than me, so I had a bunch of maps in queue when she finished her task. "You want me to help you go through them, sir?"

"First, I want you to get some information about the hospital folks without going through the hospital."

"Yes, sir." The fact that she didn't ask me how showed her professionalism. I had no idea. She'd figure it out.

"I want to know where Colonel Elliot went on her trip planetside. And while you're at it, I want to know what other doctors went with her. I also want to know if there were other trips, where Elliot didn't go. In that case, I want to know what doctors went, and where."

"Yes, sir. You suspect Colonel Elliot?"

"Lex, at this point, I suspect everybody. So we just chase leads and see what comes from it."

She pursed her lips. "We could look at their flight plans."

I punched my fist into my other hand. "Yes! Good idea. We could even follow the tracks, if we knew when they flew."

"Yes, sir." Alenda's face lit up. "We know about when Colonel Elliot went, so that shouldn't be too hard."

"She doesn't own her own aircraft," I mumbled, more to myself than to Lex.

Alenda stopped. "She doesn't?"

"She doesn't," I said. "The flight squadron owns them. Does their maintenance . . ."

"Keeps their flight logs," said Alenda. "I'm on it."

"Good. I'm going to make more coffee and keep at these maps until they reveal to me the great secret they're hiding."

Alenda stared.

"Hey, it sounded good."

"Yes, sir." Her tone suggested she didn't believe me.

GENERAL SERATA'S MESSAGE came up on my splash screen as soon as I authenticated. The brevity of it surprised me. The content surprised me more. I expected restrictions. At the very least, I expected some detailed instructions, after the attack on me.

> *Carl. Read about the incident. I've increased your authorities over all SPACECOM assets in sector, up to and including command. Haven't made that public, so Stirling won't know until you exercise authority. Tell him to check the orders when you need to use them. That gives you flexibility to do what you need to do. Take care of business.*
>
> *Serata*

Shit. I didn't know exactly how far the powers he granted me extended, but "including command" made me think I could fire Stirling and take over the base if I needed to.

Shit.

Shit shit shit.

I couldn't imagine a situation where you'd take an investigating officer and put him in charge, and I knew that wasn't what Serata meant for me to do.

So why give me the authority? If it had been anybody but Serata, I'd have thought he was setting me up. Give me the ability to fire Stirling knowing I wouldn't use it, then if it turns out that Stirling really should have been fired, I'm responsible for not doing it. But Serata wouldn't do that. Would he?

Shit. He wouldn't.

I couldn't start doubting the things I knew to be true. So if he wouldn't do that, he had another reason. The only other reason would be that he thought I might *need* to use it. And that meant he had to be under more pressure than I knew.

I touched the respond button on the screen.

Sir. Clarification requested. Authorities include relief of current commander?

Butler

I looked at it a long moment before I hit send, and sat there for another after I completed the action and the screen cleared.

Shit.

CHAPTER TWENTY-TWO

I LAY WIDE AWAKE on my sweat-soaked sheets at 0415 the next morning. I'd screwed up my drinking the night prior. The secret to drinking yourself to sleep is to drink just the right amount. You need to have enough to get you to sleep, but not so much that you pass out and then wake up four hours later, unable to get back to sleep. It was an art . . . and usually I was a master.

The pills that Elliot gave me threw me off, I think. After taking one and having one whiskey, I felt a little loopy. Some people would have taken that as a sign to stop drinking. I ignored it and had another, because I couldn't possibly be drunk off one drink. I didn't take the pills during the day because I didn't like how they made my head feel fuzzy. Fuzzy at night was perfectly fine. Apparently I was wrong.

After a few more minutes of pretending I had any chance of slumber, I decided I may as well get up and do some work. I checked the news and found nothing from Plazz, which was good, then popped open my messages to see if I got anything from Sharon. I needed to write her. However, I stopped when I saw the first message in the queue had Serata's name on it.

I touched the screen to open it.

Regarding your request for clarification: Do whatever you need to do.

Serata

That could mean anything. Hell, the message was for me, and even I wasn't sure what it meant. Why was he being so vague? He certainly meant it. He'd never have sent it if he didn't. Not Serata. But by telling me to do what I needed to do, he gave me a lot of leeway. Either he didn't know what to do and assumed I'd have better information, or he knew me well enough that he thought he knew what I *would* do. Maybe both.

I sipped my coffee and brought up the next map of Karikov's compound. It showed heat signatures. Infrared. A set of buildings with similar characteristics clustered together in a compound, but didn't show anything unexpected. There was one large facility, maybe two klicks away from the others, which did seem odd, and I pondered it for a bit. Maybe a lower-level headquarters collocated with the main. I didn't know enough about Karikov's command structure to say for sure.

I called the same location up in high resolution from a daylight pass. The lone building looked different from that perspective, barely military at all. It had a low silhouette with a slightly rounded roof. I hadn't seen anything like it during any of my deployments. That didn't necessarily mean anything. Special Ops did lots of things I hadn't seen before. I was merely pondering before, but now it seriously made me curious.

I pulled it up in the energy spectrum. The building shone three times as bright as any other building, including what I believed to be Karikov's headquarters. A building shouldn't use that much power. I flipped the map back to the high res, but didn't notice anything I didn't see on my first pass.

I went to the same set of maps a month prior. Same thing. Nighttime, no change. Another month prior, still similar. Before I knew it my alarm went off in the other room: 0630. Time to get up. I shut it down, and stopped to make another coffee. On a whim I stopped at the comm and buzzed Alenda.

"Major Alenda." She answered after one buzz.

"Alenda. Butler here. You awake?"

"Yes, sir."

"Good. Get over here. I want your take on something."

"On the way, sir."

I didn't know how long she'd take. She could have still been in bed and she'd have said she was awake once I asked. Any good officer would. She buzzed my door five minutes later.

"Good morning, sir." She wore a pressed uniform, sharp as ever.

"Look at this. What do you make of this low building here?" I showed her the high-res picture, first from overhead, then offset at an oblique angle.

She considered it for a moment. "Never seen it before, sir."

"Me either." I pulled up the electromagnetic emissions.

"Wow." She got closer to the screen to read something. "That's a lot of power."

"Yeah, that's what I thought. What on Cappa would need that much energy?"

She scratched her head. "I don't know, sir. I wonder . . ." she trailed off.

"What?" I moved closer so I could see around her.

"Yesterday I told them to pull all the flight tracks from the last week. That looks like a landing pad there, on the west side of the building. I wonder if any of the tracks will correlate. Maybe we can tell what it is by seeing what lands there."

"You're a genius, Alenda. I don't care what the other officers in your outfit say about you."

Alenda turned to me, narrowing her eyes.

"It's a joke," I said. "You want coffee?"

"Yes, sir. I'll get it. Let me use the terminal for a moment first, and get them to start dropping the radar tracks into a form we can use."

I waved her off. "I'll get it. How do you take it?"

"Black, sir."

I rinsed out another tumbler and fixed Alenda a coffee. I went to sit down after that, but quickly stood again. Lack of sleep, half a hangover, and caffeine made me edgy. Not to mention being given authority over the entire sector, which I'd never seen happen before.

"We've got about two hours to wait," said Alenda, after maybe ten minutes.

I finally sat down. "Waiting. Great."

"You have kids, sir?" asked Alenda, probably trying to take my mind off waiting.

"I do," I said. "Two. Boy and a girl. And a grandson."

"Damn, sir. You don't look old enough for grandkids."

I chuckled. "You lie. But also, thirteen years in cryo will do that to you. He's two. My son's son. He and his parents live near my wife. She's quite happy about that."

"That's awesome, sir. What about your daughter?"

"She was killed in action," I said.

"Oh, shit, sir. I'm sorry."

I took a sip of coffee. "It's okay. It happened a long time ago."

Alenda sat quietly for a moment, drinking from her plastic tumbler. "If you don't mind me asking, sir. Where did it happen?"

I tried to force a smile, but probably failed. I normally kept this sort of thing forced down, didn't think about it. Alenda couldn't have known that. It was a natural question. "I don't mind. It happened on Cappa."

Awkward silence followed. What else would happen after that exchange? I hated that more than anything, at this point. The awkwardness. Some things people just don't talk about.

"Did you get anywhere with the squadron and who

they flew where?" I asked, after a couple moments, to break the tension.

"Yes, sir." Lex looked relieved at the chance to change the subject as well. "They said they'd get me some information today. I'd call them, but it's the squadron, so there's no way there are any leaders up at this hour."

"Good point." Pilots never got up early if they could avoid it. I finished my coffee and thought about another, then thought better of it. "Damn. Guess I'll go to the gym. Why don't you get the tracks, get some breakfast, see what you can get from the flying folk, and meet me back here in three or four hours?"

I felt a bit ridiculous going to the gym with three armed guards, but I forced my way through it. Then, after a shower, I decided to head over to see Chu before Alenda made it back.

When I arrived in the Special Ops area this time, they immediately sent someone to wake the major. She came in dressed in full uniform, like she'd been up already and expecting me.

"What's the word?" I asked.

"Can we talk in my office, sir?"

"Sure." From the tone of her voice, I assumed she had bad news. I expected all along that Karikov would say no, so I'd prepared for it.

"Sir, Colonel Karikov sends his apologies, but he has multiple meetings on the surface daily. It's a delicate time with our allies, and he feels that his leaving to come back up spaceside would adversely impact the mission."

"Those were *his* words?" I didn't buy it. It sounded too much like a statement I'd give a reporter.

"I'm paraphrasing, sir."

"You talked to him personally?"

"No, sir. But I talked to the XO."

"I wanted Karikov to get the request directly, so I could be sure it made it to him."

"Sorry, sir. The XO assured me that he delivered your message."

"You trust him?"

"The XO? Yes, sir. He and Colonel Karikov have served together for years. Multiple assignments. Talking to the XO is as good as talking to the boss."

Again, no surprise. I thought about it, considered faking a blowup and demanding that she get me on directly with Karikov. I wasn't sure that would be productive, though, so I held it in reserve in case I needed it later. "Can I get a phone call?"

"Yes, sir. We can set that up anytime, as long as it doesn't conflict with his obligations to the Cappans. The Cappan elders are very sensitive to slights, and sometimes they take a changed meeting as an offense."

"Sure. I get it. See what you can work out."

"Will do, sir." I didn't really believe her boss would follow through, but it didn't hurt to give her a chance.

Truth was, I didn't have other options at the moment.

BY THE TIME I got back to my room, Alenda was there waiting.

"Tell me something good," I said.

"Working on it, sir. I've got a list of the doctors who either traveled with Colonel Elliot regularly or made trips to the surface on their own. What do you think that's going to tell us?"

"Probably nothing. But if I gather enough data, I'm going to eventually get lucky and it's going to be useful."

"I see, sir." From her tone, I didn't think she actually saw. I have that problem, sometimes. People think I'm joking when I'm actually serious.

"It's one of my skill sets, Lex. I can't really explain it. I fill my brain with stuff, and expect that it will pop back out when it matters."

"Yes, sir. What do you want me to do with the names of the doctors?"

I thought about it. "How many are there?"

"Six. Doctors McDaniel, Jones, Emory, Kepple, and Kwan. And of course Doctor Elliot."

"They've made multiple trips?"

"Yes, sir. All of them. Kwan only started two months back. It's possible that she just rotated in, though."

"Makes sense, Elliot said they all do twelve-month individual tours."

Alenda frowned.

"What?"

"I've been here ten months, sir. A little more than that. Colonel Elliot has been here since before I got here. So if she did a twelve-month tour, she'd be due to rotate out any day."

"Huh. Maybe the commander is the continuity. Maybe she does eighteen months. I'll ask her about it the next time I see her. Print out the names of the docs and let me have a copy. I'll see if any of them are on the list of folks I'm interviewing tomorrow."

"Yes, sir." Lex touched the screen and my device vibrated in response.

"Thanks," I said. "Can we pull up the radar tracks, now?"

"We can, sir, but I don't think we're going to find much. Apparently we don't track the really low-level stuff from up here. The Cappans control that part of the airspace since their own planes only fly inside the atmosphere. So we can see the general area where ships are headed, but not with the accuracy we'd need in order to tell us what pad they landed on."

"So what's it tell us?"

"Sir . . . it tells us that there's an armada of ships going into that area. Mostly Spec Ops, but a lot of contracted stuff too."

"That's not really that surprising." Special Ops guys had a huge budget and expedited contracting standards, so they tended to contract anything they needed.

"No, sir. But this one is." She touched the screen and brought up a single track.

"What am I looking at here?"

"Sorry, sir. This is a track from earlier this week. When we hover over it, we get the flight information."

"And?"

"This is Colonel Elliot's shuttle."

"Flying right into the area of Karikov's headquarters."

"Yes, sir."

"I think maybe I'd have led with that instead of the list of doctors," I said.

"I wanted to nail a big finish, sir."

"You're turning into a smart-ass, Alenda."

"Sorry, sir." She tried to hold it, but a quick smirk escaped.

"Don't be. It's a good look on you. I wouldn't try it out on Stirling, though."

"No, sir. That wouldn't go well."

"Right. So Elliot flew to meet Karikov. This week."

"We can't say that for sure, sir. But she definitely flew close."

I paced a bit. "Does Karikov have a clinic? I mean, if he did, it wouldn't respond to MEDCOM anyway. He'd have his own folks staffing it. Maybe something for the Cappans? An outreach project?"

"Not sure our docs could work on Cappans, sir."

I bit my lip on one side. "Yeah, me neither. I think I might need to visit the hospital again. Hardy should be awake today."

"Roger, sir. I'm going to visit the squadron and see if maybe I can find the pilot who flew Colonel Elliot. He or she could tell me where they went."

"Good thought. Be careful."

"What do you mean, sir? It's the squadron."

"And someone attacked me. We don't know why. Watch yourself. Stick to areas with other people around."

Alenda looked at me, and I didn't see fear. It made me worry more.

CHAPTER TWENTY-THREE

HARDY SAT PROPPED up by a couple of pillows in his elevated bed, smiling when I walked in. Two pretty women in hospital gear stood nearby, which explained his expression.

"Sir," he said.

"Don't get up," I joked.

He looked at me, puzzled. Young people don't get my humor anymore. It's time to retire.

"Sir, this is Lieutenant Morietta, the physical therapist who's going to be working with me. We were going over some of the training I'll be doing."

He was lying. If she'd explained the pain he'd experience over the next week, he wouldn't be smiling. But I didn't call him out on it. Let the young man have his chance to screw things up on his own. "Good to meet you, Morietta. Take good care of my boy here."

"Will do, sir," said the taller of the two women. "We'll let you two have the room."

I waited for them to leave, noticing Hardy follow them out with his eyes. "You know she's going to torture you, right?"

"I think I'm okay with that, sir."

I laughed. "Good to see they didn't blow up your spirit. How are you feeling?"

"I'm okay, sir. They kept me under until most of the fast-healing finished. It just aches, now. Stiff. I feel like if I could walk it out, I'd be good."

"Yeah. Don't do that. Wait for the PT. Do what she says."

"Yes, sir."

I fixed his eyes with mine. "I'm serious, Hardy. You're going to want to push it, and you're going to want to show off for her. Don't do it. I say this even though I firmly understand that it's pointless, since you're young and stupid. And when I was in your place, I did exactly the same thing."

"Yes, sir."

"The reason I'm telling you is so that when you ignore me, and push it, and you really, really hurt, I can call you a dumbass and not feel bad about it."

He laughed. "Understood, sir. I'm sorry about all this."

I waved dismissively. "You got unlucky, Hardy. It happens. If it happens too many times, people will stop wanting to ride with you. We had one guy who got hit four times. Nobody would take him out again. But it's too early for that yet. It's one time. It's war. Bad shit happens. Besides, it's more my fault than yours. I should have known it was coming."

"How could you know that, sir?"

"I don't know." I sighed. "But I should have. I missed something, somewhere. Probably a lot of things."

"So the investigation isn't going well?"

"I'm not sure. I think I've found some threads to pull, I'm just not sure what's attached to the ends of them yet. But a lot of them seem to be connected to the hospital."

"What do you mean, sir?" asked Hardy.

"Some of the doctors have taken trips planetside. I have no idea why, but it feels funny. Never mind that, though. You worry about getting better. I don't want to have to answer to General Serata as to why I broke his aide."

"I'm not his aide anymore, sir. I'll get a new job when I get back."

"Yep. And if you don't do what I say and take your recovery seriously, that job will be as a night clerk in Student Command Headquarters."

Hardy smiled. "That's harsh, sir."

"It is. I'd never do that to you. You're a damn war hero."

His face went a little dark. "I got blown up, sir. I never even saw the enemy."

"Speaking for war heroes everywhere, you're not going to want to lead with that."

"I don't want to lie about it, sir."

"You don't have to lie." I pulled a chair away from the wall and sat down. "Listen to me. This is important. When you go home . . . even before you go home, but to a lesser extent . . . people are going to want to talk to you about your experience. All the time. It's going to happen so much that you're going to get sick of it, and it's going to frustrate you, because it's all anybody is going to want to talk about. It's not their fault. They've read about it, seen it in the holos, read it on the news feeds, but obviously they've never actually experienced it. It's new and different to them, and you're right there.

"Don't take me the wrong way," I continued. "I'm not bitter about it. It's much better that they care than if they didn't. It's still going to happen though, so you may as well prepare yourself."

Hardy nodded. "Yes, sir."

"Plus, it might get you laid, so you know, the good with the bad. Either way, you want to have a go-to response. Something respectful, but dismissive, for those times you don't want to talk. Something that tells people that it's not a subject for discussion. Remember, it's *your* experience. You don't owe it to anybody. If you want to talk about it, talk about it. But don't feel obligated. The people who really care about you will get it."

Hardy looked confused. I hadn't meant to get into the subject so deeply. It just came up, because it struck close to home for me. But I'm glad it did come up. He'd understand when it happened, and think back to this conversation.

"Don't worry about it too much," I said. "Trust me. You want a line that answers 'how did it happen?' Something like, 'I was just doing my job.' It's not a lie. You were doing your job."

He nodded again, recognition on his face this time. "I get it, sir."

"You will. For now, get yourself well. Be glad they aren't giving you a robot hip."

"No, sir. No robotics. Just a polymer plate and two rods and a bunch of other hardware."

"I'll let you get some rest. You're going to need it for that physical therapy."

"Thanks, sir. For everything."

"Don't mention it. I got you blown up. I owe you."

KAREN PLAZZ AMBUSHED me outside the hospital. Not that an unarmed fifty-kilo woman can truly ambush a man with three armed guards. She stood there, leaning against the wall, and glared at me like I'd done something wrong.

"Hello." I smiled, trying to defuse whatever it was.

"You've been avoiding my calls," she said.

"I haven't been avoiding them. I haven't received them." I stopped, and G One and G Two stopped with me until Mac gestured for them to give me some space.

"What do you mean?" she asked.

"Exactly what I said. What calls?"

"I called the extension he gave me. Did you check your messages?"

I nodded. "Every day."

"That bastard gave me a fake number."

"Who?" I asked.

"What?" She gave me a fake innocent look that made me almost laugh.

"Who was the bastard who gave you the fake number?"

"You know I can't tell you that."

"Well, you know, you really have to be careful when you take information from strangers," I said.

"You're not funny, you know." She kind of half scowled. "You think you are, but you aren't. It doesn't matter. Clearly he was protecting you."

I made my eyes big in fake surprise. "Protecting me from what? Am I in danger?"

"I heard that maybe you are. That's why I called."

"Huh. Who knew?"

"So what can you tell me about the attack?" asked Plazz.

I shrugged. "Certainly nothing you don't know."

"But you're in danger."

I looked around suspiciously. "Am I?"

"You have three armed soldiers walking with you."

I glanced over at my guards. "Yeah, but I don't think they're that dangerous."

"You're avoiding the question."

"I really am."

"Come on, Carl. I thought we were working together here."

"I'd love to help you, Karen, but I've got to keep a low profile."

"Can I print that?"

I sighed. "I wish you wouldn't."

"Come on, give me one thing. I won't use your name."

"I really can't."

"Nothing? I'll put away my recorder." She made

a dramatic gesture of turning off her device. I'm not sure it was actually on.

"I don't know. Give me a day. If I can come up with something that people won't trace back to me, I'll give you a line."

She narrowed her eyes. "You're not very helpful, you know."

"I don't think you're the first person to say that."

She glared again, but then she started laughing. "Asshole."

"You're definitely not the first one to say that."

Another laugh. "You seem to have fully recovered from your attack."

"I can neither confirm nor deny that."

"Tomorrow," she said.

I smiled. "I'll do what I can."

CHAPTER TWENTY-FOUR

I CHECKED ON HARDY the next morning but they had already shuffled him off to therapy, and I don't like to hear people screaming, so I set up in an office in the hospital and prepared for my hours of interviews.

"What are you doing?" I asked Mac, as he set a chair for himself in the corner of the room.

"Someone has to stay in the room with you, sir."

"No. No way, Mac. What do you think, someone is going to try to kill me here in the hospital?"

Mac's look said he didn't rule it out.

"Look, you wait outside. If someone does kill me, you have my permission to shoot him when he comes out."

He thought about it.

"Just go," I said. "And don't intimidate people on the way in, either. I need them to open up."

"Roger, sir." He said it in that way non-coms talk when they're going to ignore you.

"I'm going to ask people when they come in, you know. They're going to tell me if you gave them shit."

"Roger, sir." He didn't care. He and the two Gs

were starting to take their job too seriously, but I didn't really want to tell the people guarding me to relax, either.

Fifteen interviews later, I regretted my decision to not let Mac rough some people up a little bit. Fifteen sets of questions, fifteen sets of the same answers. No deviation. I'm not a natural conspiracy theorist, but someone had rehearsed them. I tried asking the questions in different ways, making them open-ended, but I got the same pat responses. It frustrated me at first, then I got angry. But we were in the room without any witnesses, so nobody could prove that. I apologized. Sort of.

"I need a break," I said as I walked out the door. I'd gotten a little ahead of schedule when I gave up hope on the last few interviews. "I'm going to the latrine. I don't need a guard."

Mac nodded to G Two, who got up and followed me. Junior man gets to guard the toilet, I guess.

"You really don't have to come in," I told him, when we neared the door.

"Yes, sir," he said, before ignoring me and following me anyway. That was the thing with soldiers. You could give them orders, but in the end they'd always listen to their sergeants. Survival mechanism.

"Let's go see Hardy." I had another fifteen minutes to spare before I needed to start interviewing again. G Two fell in beside me and slightly behind. He didn't talk much.

"How did the questioning go, sir?" Hardy asked when I got to his room.

"Complete waste of time. How was physical therapy?"

"It was tough, sir."

I didn't believe him. He didn't look like a man who'd suffered.

"I did find out something about the doctors who went planetside," he said.

I stopped wishing pain on him. Okay, I never really wished pain on him. Not too much. "What did you find out? How?"

"Elizabeth told me—"

"Who's Elizabeth?" I interrupted.

"Sorry, sir. Lieutenant Morietta. The PT."

Of course. "Right, sorry. Continue."

"Yes, sir. It's the subject of a lot of discussion here with the staff. The doctors who go down on the trips, some of them don't really have jobs up here, I guess."

I nodded, not wanting to interrupt.

"Doctor Emory kind of creeps everyone out. He's a geneticist, and he works in a secured—"

"He's a what?"

"A geneticist, sir."

"What the hell do they need a geneticist, for?"

"Not *a* geneticist. Two of them. And nobody knows, sir. I guess it's supposed to be secret, but some of the staff know. Other doctors talk. There are some weird theories."

I quirked my eyebrows. "Such as?"

"Well some of them aren't weird. Research is the most rational."

"Yeah, great. What's the most irrational?"

Hardy narrowed his eyes for a moment. "I guess that they are genetically creating a super soldier who's better adapted to planetary warfare?"

"Sounds like something you'd see in a holo. And not a good one."

"Yes, sir. Nobody really buys that one. But the stories are out there. I can get more."

"I think I can too." I couldn't believe I'd missed that line of questioning.

I GOT SET back up in the office for the next interview and checked my list. Captain Tracotti. Good. I was glad it was an officer, because I wouldn't feel as bad about beating him up.

"Have a seat, Tracotti. Is it Doctor?"

"Yes, sir." I could have imagined it, but he might have looked down his nose at me a little. I just assume it with doctors, I think. I kind of wanted to punch him in the face, just on principle. He'd have less nose to look down.

"What's your specialty?" I asked instead of hitting him.

"Ortho, sir. Wrists and hands are my subspecialty. I was told there's a sworn statement I need to fill out?"

"There might be. I want to ask you a couple of questions, see what kind of answers you have, and if there's anything I need for the investigation, we'll make it official and put it on paper."

"Sounds good, sir."

"Do you know a doctor named McDaniel?" I asked.

Tracotti started to answer, then stopped and sat silent for a second, narrowing his eyes. He pushed his too-long hair back out of his face. "Excuse me, sir?"

"It's an easy question. Do you know McDaniel?" I tried to make my voice extra condescending.

"Yes, sir. I don't see what—"

"What's his specialty?"

"Ortho and robotics, sir."

"Oh, like Doctor Elliot."

He scrunched up his face. "Yes, sir. Actually, Doctor McDaniel runs the service and Doctor Elliot, she jumps in when she has time she can spare away from her administrative duties."

"That makes sense." I smiled, trying to put him at ease. More trying to send conflicting messages. "You know Doctor Jones? Or Emory?" I asked.

"Yes, sir."

"What do they do?"

"Genetics, I think, sir. I don't see them around the hospital much, just back at quarters or in the mess." He fidgeted in his seat, kept looking down at his hands, folded on the table.

"But they work genetics."

"Yes, sir. I think so. We don't share any patients. We haven't yet, at least."

"Would you ever share a patient with a geneticist?"

"I haven't yet, sir, but I've only been practicing a few years."

"Thanks. Did you see anything unusual on the night of thirteen eleven 3943?"

"No, sir. It was a normal night."

"Great." Same answer as everyone else. "Do you know Doctor Kwan?"

"Yes, sir. She works with me in Ortho. She's mostly lower body."

I made a fake note on my device. "What about Doctor Kepple?"

"I've heard the name, sir. Sorry, I don't know him personally."

"Thanks, Doctor. You've been very helpful."

He glanced around, as if looking for something. "I don't need to do a statement?"

I gave him a cold smile. "No, it's pretty clear that nobody saw anything. It's a formality at this point."

"Yes, sir."

I brought in four more people. I didn't question the enlisted folks much. Just made conversation. But I asked a nurse and a doctor the same questions as Tracotti, and got similar answers. I learned that Kepple was a psych.

I stepped outside. "Interviews are over. You can send the rest of the people away."

"All of them, sir?" asked Mac.

"Yeah. I'm done. I've got what I need. You stay here. G Two, you come with me."

"Sir, where are you going?" asked Mac.

I grinned. "One more piece of business."

I WALKED THROUGH Elliot's outer office and past her assistant without stopping. "G, if that guy moves, I want you to shoot him."

"Yes, sir." G set himself into a ready position by the door.

The lieutenant at the desk stammered, but couldn't form words.

"G, I'm joking. Just don't let him bother us. Don't let anybody bother us."

"Roger, sir."

The lieutenant's eyes had gone large, but he kept his seat. I'd either intimidated him or confused him. I could live with either case.

"How come you have geneticists on your staff?" I pulled the door closed behind me.

"Good afternoon to you, too." Elliot put half of a sandwich down on a plastic tray on her desk. Something healthy-looking on wheat bread. She picked up her water and took a sip. Buying time, thinking through my question.

"You didn't answer," I said.

She glared at me, and the look made me glad she didn't have a weapon. "I don't have to answer, especially when you barge in without as much as knocking."

"You do have to answer. SPACECOM worked it out with MEDCOM."

She stared for a moment. "That's not the order I got. The order I got said that I should cooperate with you where possible, and where it didn't excessively hinder the mission. If you want to make an appointment, I'm sure we can work something out."

"So you can prepare your answers like the rest of your command?"

"I don't know what you're talking about." She gave me a flat smile.

"Of course not." I had to walk a line here. I couldn't

directly accuse her, because if I ended up using her statement she could say I badgered her into it. "What do you know about bringing Cappans up off the planet on one of your MEDEVACs?"

She looked like she was about to say something, but she stopped. She picked up her water and had a sip. "Who told you?"

"Does it matter?"

She inhaled deeply. "Probably not."

"You want to tell me about it?"

She sat for a moment and composed herself. "It was a mistake. The med crew loaded them. Once we figured out what they'd done, we followed the correct protocols to contain it."

"Where are the Cappans now?"

"Incinerated. Per the protocol. Everyone and everything that touched them went into quarantine, just as if they'd had contact planetside."

"And you didn't report it," I said.

"I started an investigation. Then three days later the MEDEVAC involved got shot down, killing everyone on board. I could have continued the investigation, but I didn't want to sully the reputation of a pilot who otherwise served honorably."

I thought about her answer for a moment. Something in the way she said it rang false. Like she'd rehearsed it. She could have. She had to have known that someone would question it one day. Secrets always get out on a military base. I didn't know how to press her though, without coming off like a total asshole. The pilot was dead, that much I knew.

I nodded after a moment. "That makes sense. No need to drag him into it."

"But you'll still put it in your report," she said.

"I might. Depends on what else I learn and how it applies. I can hardly avoid the fact that there were Cappans on the same MEDEVAC that the missing lieutenant flew on."

She paused for a moment, then nodded. "The lieutenant never arrived here."

"How is that possible? They were on the same ship."

"Were they? One of my people told you that?" She considered it. "I think not." She sipped her water again, this time watching me over the rim of her cup.

I sat down, opened my device, and pretended to read something. I didn't like how she'd reversed the direction of the questioning. I didn't want to give her the impression that I got the information planetside.

"How was your meeting with Karikov?" I asked.

She stopped moving, her glass halfway to the table, then she set it down gently, almost arranging it on the surface of her desk. "He's well."

She'd decided not to lie about meeting him. I didn't know what that meant. Maybe she couldn't think of anything quick enough. "What was the visit about?"

She looked at me without emotion. "He's a patient. The nature of our discussion is private."

"So you were there to see him medically."

"Yes, and to check on his clinic."

"Special Ops clinics don't fall under MEDCOM."

She pulled her lips into a flat line. "They don't. But we have an agreement, Karikov and I, where I give him courtesy inspections and help fill any supply shortages they might have. It's in writing, if you want to see it."

I fixed her eyes. "Interesting. Is that common?"

"I don't concern myself with what's common. I do what I think is right for the mission. This is right." She stared back at me, unblinking, as if daring me to challenge her.

I glanced back down at my notes, stalling. I considered asking what the geneticists did planetside, but decided against it. She'd recovered her balance too quickly with my other lines of questioning. She'd have a prepared answer for that, as well. I needed to keep something in reserve. Dig some more. "I'd like to get you on the record with a sworn statement."

"Given your questions here, I don't think that's going to happen."

"No? MEDCOM said to cooperate."

"And now I find it outside my ability to accommodate."

I nodded. "So I guess I send them a formal request, complete with the reasons why I feel that you need to be part of the investigation. With all the details."

She glared for a moment, then relaxed. "I'm not going to answer questions about the Cappans. Not in a statement. I didn't report it, and that's a clear violation. If you want to charge me, charge me, and I'll speak with my attorney before talking to you."

"I see." I sat silently for a moment, tapping my finger on the screen of my device. "What if I agree not to ask about the Cappans?"

She narrowed her eyes, furrows deepening on either side of the top of her nose. "What would you ask, then? I don't see what I can provide that you don't already have."

"Background. The subject of your visits to the planet. Why you think they're important."

She studied me. "I don't see where you're going with this."

I gave her my most innocent look. "You could just trust me."

She half laughed, half snorted, which made me smirk too. "I think there are a lot of things more likely than either one of us trusting the other," she said.

I shrugged. "What do you have to lose? If you don't like the result, you don't sign the statement."

"And if I don't like the questions, I report you for threatening the life of my assistant."

I smiled. "I hardly think that happened. Clearly a misunderstanding."

"Indeed," she said. "What's your interest in Karikov?"

"I don't know," I said. "The fact that when I tried to visit him someone blew up my convoy?"

She frowned. "Surely you don't think he did it."

"Like I said, I don't know. I've never met the man. That's why I asked."

She thought about it. "He wouldn't do that."

"See, that's something I didn't know." It was thin, but I didn't have much to work with. "What makes you say that?"

She thought some more. "Karikov cares about soldiers. He wants what's best for them. Having them attacked . . . no. I don't see it. Is that all?"

"One last thing. How long is your tour? Standard is twelve months, right?"

She nodded. "That's right. I extended for six months. I've been here thirteen so far."

I stood. "Thanks. I appreciate your time."

"And I appreciate your people behaving in my hospital. I let them carry weapons, but not so they can threaten my staff."

"I'll talk to them about that," I said. "Let's go, G." G Two followed me out the hatch of the outer office and into the corridor.

I thought through what I learned in the exchange. Elliot didn't think Karikov would have us ambushed. I wasn't sure about that, but I did believe that *she* believed it, and she'd met the man in person, which gave her a perspective I didn't have. But I still didn't trust her to tell me the truth, which colored my thinking about everything she told me, casting the matter right back into doubt. Too, she knew about the Cappans and hadn't reported it, which was something. But not much. She had a plausible reason for her actions.

I needed to find a new way to approach the problem.

"WHAT IF WE just dropped in on Karikov?"

"I thought Chu got you a call scheduled, sir," said Alenda. She sat on the sofa, reading something on a tablet. I think she'd gotten a haircut, shorter and spiky, though I couldn't say for sure it hadn't been that way the previous day.

"She did. She messaged me an hour ago to set it up for tomorrow night. But what if I didn't wait? We could get in ships and fly in. Get off at his base."

She lowered her tablet to her lap. "To what end, sir?"

"I need to talk to him."

"You've booked a call."

"Right. But you can't read somebody over the comm . . . I'd get a lot more talking to him face-to-face. Besides, I don't think he's really going to take the call. I think he's just putting me off another day."

"I'll take that bet, sir," she said.

"You're on," I answered. "Anyway, I'm thinking it might be a good plan."

"We don't have any authority there," said Alenda.

"I know we don't. But it doesn't matter. It would let me put this thing to rest." It started out as a lark, but the idea started to grow on me.

"You still need to find the lieutenant, sir." She looked at me, her head tilted sideways.

"Right." I stood up and started pacing. "But Karikov knows where he is."

"Forgive me, sir, but let me . . . How do you know he knows?"

"People keep asking me questions like that," I said.

"Like what, sir?"

"Ones I can't answer. I don't know how I know, I just know."

"That's thin, sir. Begging your pardon."

"You can stop begging my pardon. Just say what's

on your mind. And you're right. It's thin. Really fucking thin. But I *know* Karikov knows." I didn't really know, but I felt like I did. If I was Karikov and it happened in my unit, I'd know.

Alenda sat without speaking, which was probably smart, because if she dumped on my intuition again I might have thrown something at her.

"We could go at first light and be back in time for lunch," I said.

"Yes, sir. Sir . . . I don't think I'll be able to set that up without you talking to Colonel Stirling. If I ask, the answer is going to be no."

I stopped and looked at her, then nodded. "Yeah, you're probably right. I'll go talk to him."

She grabbed up her tablet and stood to go. "If you're going planetside, I want to go with you, sir."

I turned and looked at her. "Why?"

"If that's where the answers are, I want to be there. Plus you don't have Hardy available."

"The reason I don't have Hardy available is that I got him blown up. I'm not making that mistake again."

"You're taking Mac."

"That's his job." I knew it was bullshit when I said it.

"It's all of our jobs, sir."

I started to snap off another answer, but held myself. "I'll think on it."

She stood silently for a moment, breathing through her nose, locking her eyes with mine. I think we both knew I was lying. "When do you want to go, sir?"

"Tomorrow morning." Just like that I decided. I was going.

STIRLING WAS IN his office when I arrived. "Carl. What can I do for you?"

"I need a couple ships," I said.

"Sure. What for?"

"I want to drop in on Karikov."

He stopped dead still, looking almost comical in his reaction, like if he had been drinking something he'd have spit it out. "I'm not sure that's a great idea," he said, after a moment.

Understatement.

"Why not?"

He looked down for a moment, then back at me. "I think you have to consider the possibility that he had something to do with the attack on our convoy. Not that he ordered it, but that he knew about it."

"Why do you say that?" I sat on the edge of his table, keeping my feet on the floor. I agreed with him, but I wanted to hear his reasoning.

"The satellite stuff. Something happened there."

"What happened?" I asked.

He took a deep breath, then let it out. "I still don't know for sure. But it wasn't a routine outage."

"Interesting. How sure are you?"

"Sure enough," he said.

"Shit."

He nodded. "Exactly. So you see why I'm hesitant."

"I still need to go. We'll simply have to take precautions."

"Like what? You're going to drop in with a couple of troop ships. You don't have much protection there."

"What are they going to do, shoot us down?" After

the words left my mouth, I considered the possibility for the first time.

"The Cappans own the airspace now. We clear all flights through their control once we drop in below eight thousand meters."

I met his eyes. "And you think they'll do something?"

He shrugged. "They shouldn't. But then, they shouldn't have attacked your convoy, either. The thing is, I don't know what's going to happen. And I don't like reacting."

I nodded absently, thinking. He was right. Reacting means your enemy is dictating what you do, and that's never good. "We could put some gunships alongside for escort."

He thought about it a moment. "We could. And I want full teams on each landing ship. You and your PSO with ten of my people in one bird, another dozen in the other. That way you've got some firepower once you're on the ground."

I paused, soaking in that the tenor of the conversation had changed from *if* we'd go to *how* we'd go. "Sure," I said. I went along with his thought even though I didn't think twenty-two soldiers would matter much if there was a problem.

"Dawn tomorrow?" he asked.

"That works." I pushed myself up off of the edge of the table.

"Okay. I'll have it set up." He put his hand out, and I shook it.

"Alenda wants to come," I said.

"Your call." He kept his face neutral, giving no indication of his thoughts on the matter.

"I'm not taking her." That would piss her off, but I could live with that. I couldn't live with dead. Like I said before, I knew it for total bullshit, but I had to do it. If not for her good, then for mine.

CHAPTER TWENTY-FIVE

I WOKE UP WITH my heart hammering in my chest, drenched in sweat. I could hear heavy gunfire still ringing in my ears. My foot throbbed from where I'd been hit. Something was off, though. I couldn't see any of the rest of the team in the dark. I sat up and whipped my head around, but there was a wall behind me. How did that get there? They were all dead, and it was my fault. I couldn't be sure because I couldn't see them, but I knew. They were fucking dead.

There shouldn't have been a wall on Polla like that.

Polla . . .

No, not Polla. Cappa.

"I'm on Cappa Base. I'm on Cappa Base."

I told myself that over and over, but it took a moment for my nervous system to register it and for my heart rate to slow to something approaching normal. I felt a bit of a hangover headache coming, so I got up and drank some water, and splashed some on my face to wash off the sweat. I checked the time: 0211. I'd slept maybe ninety minutes.

I got back into bed and lay down, my hands shaking from the adrenaline dump. I concentrated on taking deep breaths, tried to clear my mind of everything else except the sound of my breathing. I did the exercises the doctor gave me, relaxing different parts of my body every time I exhaled, as if blowing the stress out. After a time—I'm not sure how long—I fell back asleep.

When I woke to my alarm at 0545, I didn't feel rested.

I showered and got coffee and decided against eating anything. I didn't like to drop into the atmosphere on a full stomach. I didn't puke, like some people, but it screwed with my digestion enough to make me uncomfortable all day. Better to be hungry.

Mac came by to pick me up at 0630 and we made our way to the hangar for mission brief. He walked beside me, letting the two soldiers provide security for the trip. We were both kitted out in our body armor and heavily armed, so we made for a tough target. Mac chugged on another one of his nasty concoctions as we walked.

"You know those things are going to kill you," I said.

"So is dropping into a Spec Ops base in the middle of nowhere without coordination, sir." He had a point. We walked the rest of the way in amicable silence.

We had a basic mission plan. A simple transport down to a friendly landing pad. We still spent twenty-five minutes going over contingencies. What to do if we landed somewhere hostile, what to do if we lost a ship. All the things you don't want to think about before you encase yourself in metal and drop out of space. I closed my eyes for a moment while the lieutenant briefed.

I wondered if anyone told her how lieutenants who traveled with me had fared lately. One dead, one in the hospital. Not a great record. But then, I'd never been particularly good luck for those around me. We'd won some fights, sure. But I'd lost people. So many that I couldn't name them without the list I kept laminated on a card in my pocket. I needed to add the five soldiers from my last trip to Cappa. They hadn't been under my command, but I was still responsible, at least in my mind. Of course, my mind wasn't a very good judge of anything at the moment, but they were on my bill all the same.

I tried to focus on the words of the briefing, but they slid off of my brain. After a while, we loaded into the two transports. I didn't worry about it much. I'd done this so many times that the briefing didn't matter anyway. I slapped a magazine into my Bitch, checking the load first to make sure I had guided rounds, then I synched my helmet's receiver to the ship's internal frequency.

"This is Butler, can you hear me?"

"Loud and clear, sir. I'm your pilot, Captain Jurzic." A deep male voice that almost vibrated in the speaker of my helmet. "We'll be ready to go momentarily. Looking at just under a thirty-minute trip. Destination is almost directly below us. Skies look good around the landing area, so we should have a clean ride."

"Great," I said. "Keep me informed."

"Yes, sir. We'll let you know when we're ready to launch. Waiting on the gunship escort to finish prep."

I leaned my head back into the headrest and closed my eyes. The next time the pilot spoke it jarred me, as if I'd drifted off for a moment without realizing it.

"We're ready to go, sir. Are you clear back there?"

I gave the lieutenant sitting across from me a look to ask if she was ready.

She looked down the ship, checking the soldiers seated on either side, then flashed me the thumbs-up.

"We're ready," I said. I closed my eyes again and let the G-force from the launch wash over me. The belts bit into my shoulders and pushed me against Mac. Since I was in the front seat, there was nobody to my right to lean into me. Yet another privilege of rank.

After a moment the ride smoothed out and settled down into that space-travel feeling where you're not gaining or losing speed, so it feels like standing still. Only a slight vibration of the ship indicated movement at all as we switched from the initial booster engine to the smoother fusion one. I dozed in and out until we hit the atmosphere and things got bumpy.

"We're clear of the worst of it, sir," said the pilot. "Approximately ten to destination."

"Roger."

"Sir . . ." The pilot came back on the internal channel a minute later and his voice had that universal quality that something was fucked up. "Sir . . . we have a problem."

"Go ahead," I said.

"We're being directed to an alternate landing zone

by the Cappan air control. About two and a half klicks northeast."

"Screw that," I said. "Ignore them. Land at our initial destination."

"That's just it, sir. We can't. They've shut down the instruments on the pad there. We'd be going in blind."

"So go in blind. You've done an assault landing before." It seemed a simple solution, and it perturbed me that they even brought it up.

The channel remained quiet for a moment.

"Tell me you've done an assault landing before," I said.

"Yes, sir," came the response. "On the simulator."

I muted my microphone and bit back a scream of frustration. Another thing I failed to check. If I kept screwing up, someone else was going to get killed over one of my mistakes. Maybe me. I should have aborted the mission right then, no doubt. Easy call.

But I didn't.

I could make up a bunch of reasons why, but being honest, I don't know. I think I just wanted the thing to be over, one way or another. A stupid reason to make a decision.

I flipped the channel back open. "Can you pull up a map of the new landing area?"

"Yes, sir. It looks like a warehouse complex. Multiple large pads. Probably where they bring in supplies." The co-pilot, this time. Female voice.

"Hold on, I'm coming up to see it." I unbuckled myself and stood, then lurched forward into the dark-skinned lieutenant sitting across from me. Baxter. She caught me so I didn't face-plant. She didn't say anything, and my respect for her went up a notch. I half walked, half crawled to the door to the cockpit.

"Show me," I said.

"Sir, you shouldn't be unbuckled. It's dangerous," said the co-pilot.

"As opposed to landing in an unsecure area on a hostile planet? Because that's completely safe. Show me the map."

"On the screen, sir," she said.

The screen between them showed the original landing pad, highlighted in red, while the new pad flashed blue. "Can you zoom in?" I asked.

The co-pilot pushed a couple buttons and the resolution increased around the new site. The pads looked like commercial landings, fit for ships well bigger than our landing craft. A series of rectangular buildings lined either side of the pads in orderly rows. Supply depot, just like the co-pilot said.

"Can you pull up a live feed?"

"No, sir, just the map," she said. "There's no coverage there right now."

Of course. "Okay. Treat it like it's hostile. Have the gunships fly a recon pass before we get there, then come in as hot as you can without putting us at risk."

"Yes, sir," they answered simultaneously.

"Pass the map of the new area back to the lieutenant," I said, then shuffle-walked back to the passenger compartment and knelt down in front of the platoon leader.

I opened a private channel to Baxter and pointed

to her handheld. "New landing zone!" I didn't want to broadcast where everyone could hear until I let her know. Let her tell her own people. They'd respond better that way.

Baxter looked at the device strapped to her wrist and pulled up the map, then nodded.

"Situation unknown. Hit it like it's hostile. We'll march to our objective," I said.

"Roger, sir!"

I sat down and buckled myself in while the lieutenant started barking orders into her mouthpiece. Down the ship, soldiers started checking their weapons, tightening their kit. They didn't require much direction. These were pros who knew what to do.

Mac looked at me and I gave him a confident nod. He'd have been listening in on the platoon's channel and heard the word from the lieutenant. He offered me one of his grenades, but I waved him off. Nobody needed a colonel throwing grenades.

"Fighters made their pass, sir," called the co-pilot. "No movement reported."

"Roger." I allowed myself a moment of hope. Maybe the diverted landing was legit. With twenty-two soldiers plus me and Mac, a short move through a reasonably friendly area was an inconvenience, not a major threat.

"Plenty of room on the pad. We'll land in a forward stagger, the other ship to our left rear," said the pilot. "We'll pop both doors for exit on either side."

I looked across at the lieutenant to see if she heard, and she nodded. "Roger," I said. The staggered landing allowed our exiting troops clear fields of fire with minimum masking from the other ship. We'd still be easy targets in an ambush, but at least we'd get to shoot back without hitting our own people.

The last minute before landing stretched with anticipation. We came in fast and hit the ground with a thud that jolted me in my seat. I popped my belts off but stayed seated to let the soldiers hit the ground before me. They'd have the battle drill down and I didn't want to get in the way. Two or three troops went out each door before I heard shouting over the idling engines. Excited shouting.

Bad shouting.

I jumped up and forced my way into the line of exiting soldiers, pushing someone out of the way. The heat and light hit me as I stepped out, almost physically stopping me. As my vision adjusted I saw what had to be a couple dozen Cappans with their elongated yellowish faces and large, round eyes, thin rifles leveled at the human troops who escorted me. Soldiers hit the ground and took up prone firing positions, their rifles pointed back at the unexpected welcome party. It was a miracle nobody had fired a shot yet.

I could hear the lieutenant yelling from the opposite side of the ship, but I couldn't understand her. "Translate," I said into my helmet, and after a brief hesitation the sounds resolved into recognizable words.

"Lower your weapons." The Cappan's voice came across in the metallic sound of the translator.

"You lower your weapons!" Lieutenant Baxter's voice, loud, but under control.

"Where did they come from?" I asked, using the ship's frequency.

"They were hiding inside the buildings, sir. There are at least eighty," said the co-pilot. "Maybe more inside."

"Scan the buildings," I told her. "How did the fighters miss that? Bring the fighters in low and fast, but tell them not to engage without my express order. I don't care what happens here . . . not without my order."

"Yes, sir," she responded. "Not without your order."

I walked around the front of the spacecraft and past the lieutenant. Mac scrambled behind me and I could hear him shouting, but I ignored him. "I'm Colonel Butler. Are you our escort?" I didn't know which of the Cappans had command, but I made a guess based on their positioning and directed my comments at one near the front.

"Lower your weapons," the Cappan answered.

"We'll lower our weapons, you lower yours." I turned and faced back toward the ship just as Mac got there and flung his head around, probably looking for an angle he could take to block fire from hitting me. It was useless. They had us surrounded, and more shooters on the roof.

"Lower your weapons," I said to the lieutenant.

"But sir . . ."

"Lower. Your. Fucking. Weapons." I broadcast over her frequency so that every soldier heard me. They didn't react quickly, but tension released, fingers came off triggers. Gradually they lowered their barrels, though they stayed in prone positions and could aim again quickly.

I turned back around to find that some of the Cappans had lowered theirs. The scream of two fighters grew into a deafening roar as they passed overhead, low enough to kick up a cloud from the dirt road between the landing pad and the warehouses. A few more Cappans lowered their weapons. If somebody shot here, a lot of folks were going to die on both sides, and everybody knew it.

I walked further forward, my rifle hanging from a strap, my sidearm still holstered. "Stay back, Mac," I said, as he made to follow. I didn't look to see if he complied, keeping my eyes on the Cappan leader. He was a good fifteen centimeters shorter than me, which was about average for his race. He wore a brown tunic and lighter brown leggings, nearly identical to all his companions.

"We got diverted from our original landing location. We'd appreciate your help getting to Colonel Karikov's headquarters."

It took the Cappan a moment to answer. I didn't see a transmitter or a receiver, but I assumed he was talking to his leader. Cappans never put the real leader out in front, and whatever they'd expected when we got off the ships, I didn't imagine it was someone asking for an escort. I treated them like they were friendly. No reason not to. If they weren't, this had only one ending anyway.

"Come, follow," said the Cappan after what seemed like five minutes, but was probably closer to one. Sweat dripped down my back under my armor, and not just from the Cappan heat.

We walked along a dirt road wide enough for two large ground vehicles to pass, every step kicking up dust that the light breeze didn't have the energy to clear. A full five dozen Cappans escorted us, keeping to the outside, weaving their way around the low scrub brush and a few scraggly trees, making it abundantly clear that we weren't free to deviate from the chosen route. I didn't care, as long as it got me to Karikov without anybody getting shot. I'd put us in the situation. Nothing to do but to play it out. The fighters continued to orbit above us, high enough that I couldn't see them, but I heard them talking on the ship's frequency. They'd get back quickly if I needed them.

The shuttles checked in with me before they took off, roaring overhead and back into space. They were too vulnerable on the ground without support, and I didn't want to split our force to defend them. I hoped we wouldn't need them in a hurry.

I walked close to the lieutenant in the center of the formation. "When we get there, no matter what happens and what you see, keep your people alert. Don't relax, even if you see humans. Don't trust anybody."

Lieutenant Baxter looked at me and her eyes grew wide inside her dark face. She started to speak, then stopped and nodded.

"Listen, Baxter. Everything is fine. I just don't like

when things deviate from plan, so I'm not taking any chances. Got me?"

"Yes, sir." Her voice sounded slightly stronger. It made me sorry for lying to her. Nothing was fine about this. I should have aborted the mission.

I walked on.

CHAPTER TWENTY-SIX

WE APPROACHED WHAT looked to be Karikov's camp along the same packed dirt road. They'd cleared away the trees around it, leaving only a bit of scrub. Nothing that could provide cover for someone approaching. Four poles marked the entrance to the camp, two on either side of the road creating a sort of entryway in the dust leading up to the gate. Something hung from each pole, heavy and not moving in the light wind. I didn't recognize them until we drew closer.

Cappan corpses.

Mother of Planets . . .

Three of the four blue and yellow splotched bodies had darkened to a brownish bruise color, as if they'd hung there a while. Two of them had had their eyes gouged out, leaving sockets caked with old blood. The freshest corpse had blood vessels bulging out in its sclera, as if maybe someone had choked it to death.

I stopped for a moment, as did several of my human escorts. If the Cappans walking with us noticed, they gave no indication, and only slowed when they realized we'd stopped following.

"Come, this is the camp," said the Cappan I'd first spoken to upon arrival. He was the only one who'd communicated with me during the entire operation.

"What are those?" I asked, gesturing toward the bodies with my head, so I didn't have to point with my hand and be obvious.

The Cappan glanced up at his dead brothers. "Enemies." He started walking again, not waiting to see if I followed. After a few more seconds I gestured to Baxter, and walked into camp through the gate that one of our escorts opened. I scanned up and down the fence line, looking for human guards. From the look Mac gave me, he'd noticed the absence too.

Most of the Cappans remained outside; maybe a dozen led us into the compound where the road widened into a dirt courtyard with six or seven buildings on either side, mostly prefab military polymer, but with some added construction out of a gray, local wood. Our boots crunched on thin gravel, providing the only sound beyond the low hum of generators that ran outside each building. The military facilities had small armo-glass windows, but the tinting reflected light and blocked any view inside. I'd have felt much better if I saw a human anywhere.

We approached the largest of the buildings, a boxy two-story thing maybe forty meters along the front. Karikov's headquarters, probably. We stopped and the first Cappan walked up to the door and punched a code into the old-fashioned keypad. The door slid upward. *The Cappans had unescorted access to the headquarters.* I hadn't seen that before. Either the humans completely trusted Cappan security or there were no humans. Regardless of trust, I'd still prefer my compound guarded. The door shut behind the Cappan, leaving us standing out in the sun. Even early in the day it caused sweat to bead on my forehead.

Baxter circulated among her milling soldiers, talking to each one quietly. More than one glanced around afterward, checking the surroundings. Over the next couple minutes they casually drifted apart some, spreading out. If the Cappan escorts noticed, they didn't react. Neither side raised a weapon, but nobody exactly let one fall, either.

Maybe five minutes later the Cappan came back out with a human captain. He had no headgear and an ill-fitting uniform, and sported a two-day growth of beard. He waved a lazy salute at me as he approached.

"Sir, glad you made it." He held out his hand, which I considered ignoring, but shook.

"What's with us not landing here?" I asked.

"Transmitter's out, sir. Fried. Lightning. Two big storms this week. Contract techs are due in today to work on it."

Bullshit. "But you knew I was coming."

"Yes, sir. Sure did."

"And you didn't think to let us know the transmitter was out."

He looked puzzled. "We published it in the air order, sir. We thought you knew."

I wiped a drop of sweat out of my eyes. "So what was that with the welcome party?"

"The Cappans, sir?"

"Yeah. The Cappans." I tried to keep the edge out of my voice, but I'm pretty sure I failed.

The Captain—Benton, according to his name tag—gave me the same puzzled look. "They secure that area, sir. We've only got twenty people here. We don't go out except on mission. The Cappans do everything."

I bit back a nasty reply. I had to remember that Special Ops did things their own way. Blowing up on a captain wouldn't help, anyway. "Where's Colonel Karikov?"

"This way, sir."

I expected to go into the headquarters building but instead we walked to the next structure down, a small, wooden building with a low polymer-panel roof set well off the road near the back corner of the headquarters. The door had a hand pad, but Benton ignored it, knocking instead. We stood for half a minute or so before something inside scraped toward the door. After a few more seconds a lock turned with a click and the manual door swung open.

I waited for the captain to go in before me, but when it became clear he intended to stay outside, I stepped through into the darkness. The room smelled of sweat, urine, and dust. It went dark when the door closed behind me. Shapes took a moment to resolve as my eyes adjusted, but even in the shadowy darkness I could make out Karikov walking with an exaggerated limp, like one of his legs didn't work. It dragged on the dirt floor, caught on a small carpet for a moment, bending up the edge of it.

"Colonel Karikov?"

He sat on something that might have been a cot, but I couldn't tell without lights. The only illumination came from small cracks between the weathered boards. "Yeah. You Butler?"

"Yes." The shadows grew more distinct as my eyes dialed in, showing me shapes, if not colors.

"Didn't think you'd make it." His voice had a rasp, like he'd been drinking dust.

"I tried to get here a week ago. My convoy got hit by Cappans." I kept my voice neutral. I thought I'd feel anger when I met Karikov face to face, but I found my curiosity held it in check.

"Haashaaw!" He made some half-laugh, half-cough noise. "Figures."

I waited for him to explain, but he sat quietly in the dark.

"You know why they did it?" I asked.

"Haashaaw! It's what they do. Fuckers."

I didn't understand him. He sounded like he meant something specific, but it could have been anything. "I saw the bodies. On the poles by the gate. What's that about?"

"It's a warning."

"It's barbaric," I said. "You work with Cappans, but you display their dead like that?"

He coughed. "Those are bad guys."

"They look the same, though. How can you tell?"

"They know. The Cappans. They know."

"It's not right, putting them on display."

"No, it's not," he agreed, his voice trailing off a little. "There's a chair if you want."

"Then why do you do it?" I found the crude wooden chair in the dark and sat.

"It's not us. It's them."

"Who?" I asked.

"The Cappans. They put them up there."

"They strung up their own people?" I asked.

"Haashaaw! Shit. You don't know the half of it. They do worse than that."

"The Cappans."

"Listen, Butler." He paused. "The Cappans are a brutal, ruthless people. You don't know. I live here. I've seen what they're capable of doing. And they're a hell of a lot smarter than anyone gives them credit for, too."

"So tell me." If there was a chance the Cappans conducted the attack on my convoy without his knowing, I wanted to hear it.

Karikov didn't answer for a moment. "The Cappans would kill every one of us if they had their way. Every human they could touch."

"You're still alive."

"Pfft. Because they need me. And they know if they took us out, we'd come in stronger. Scorch the earth and then dig through their bodies to get the silver." His head slumped, and I wondered if maybe he'd somehow fallen asleep.

"What happened to your leg?" I took a different line of questioning to get him speaking again.

"Huunh. Old injury. Robot leg stopped working."

"Elliot came here." I didn't ask, because I didn't want to give him a chance to deny it.

"Fuck Elliot!" He nearly stood up, and his sudden shout jarred me.

I sat for a moment, waiting for his rage to subside. "I'm not a fan of hers either. But she's a good doctor."

"Kwwwaaaha!" He wailed, then broke down into a fit of coughing.

I waited, this time, letting the silence drag out more than a minute until he spoke again.

"You don't know, Butler," he whispered. "What I had to go through, what she wanted me to go through again. You don't understand."

"I do understand," I said. "I don't have it as bad as you with a full leg, but I lost a foot. Above the ankle. I know what the therapy is like."

He sat silently once again and I thought he may have fallen asleep until I heard him, either giggling or sobbing, his body shaking slightly. "You don't understand."

"Then help me fucking understand!" I didn't know what to do. I felt like I was so close to answers, but I didn't know the questions. I shouldn't have lost my temper like that, but Karikov threw me. I dug my fingers into my thighs to regain focus and bring myself back under control.

His sobbing grew louder, clearer, wracking his body, his head in his hands. After a moment he reached out with a shadowy, trembling arm and hit a switch. Four globes lit up from the wooden ceiling, bathing the room in a harsh light.

The furniture consisted of the small cot, the chair, a wooden stool that he'd converted into a nightstand, and a wobbly-looking square table. Bits of trash lay strewn about the dirt floor, but not enough to clutter the small room. But the man himself drew my attention more than the room.

Karikov's hair flew from his head in a wild mess, his beard unkempt, shot through with gray. His eyes sucked back into the worn leather of his face with black circles under them so pronounced it looked like someone had punched him in the nose. His skin had an unnatural yellowish tint, hanging off of a frame that might not have seen nutrition in days.

His eyes grabbed me. His pupils didn't contract in the light, nearly filling his irises. His pupils . . . they weren't round. They were oval . . . like a Cappan's. "What happened to you?" I whispered.

"Haashaaw! Haashaaw!" He threw his head back like someone laughing maniacally, but the sound he made didn't match. I began to wonder if he might be mad. Two and a half years planetside . . . but if he was insane, surely someone would have reported it. He didn't leave, but others rotated in and out. Didn't they? They had to know. His head stopped and he seemed to focus on something off to the side.

"Karikov?"

He brought his head slowly around until he faced me again. "Elliot."

"Elliot what? What's Elliot got to do with this? Your eyes . . ."

"Elliot happened." His voice faded into a whisper

and he stared off again. I followed his eyes, but if something else was in the room, it was only visible to him.

"Karikov. This is important. What did Elliot do?"

He looked back at me. "This."

After a few moments of silence, hoping he'd say something else, I stood.

"They won't let you go," he said, his voice clearer.

"Who won't?"

"The Cappans. Them. If they intended to let you leave, they'd have never let you talk to me. Her people."

"Her people? Elliot's?"

"Not hers. But she made them. She mixed them. Mixed *us*."

His eyes. His skin. Cappan. Elliot mixed them? Then it clicked: *The geneticists*. But no, she couldn't have. Nobody would allow it. "There's no way."

He grunted, sounding much saner than his previous outbursts. "There's a way. They spliced our DNA. The healing powers of the Cappans were supposed to help with our robotics. Let our bodies and minds handle the strain. It worked, too. At first. Double amputees walking again. They didn't know the price."

"She told me." I sat, stunned. She'd offered me a solution to my neural rejection. "She told me she could help me."

"That's why they let you through," he said. "I didn't understand. That's why. They want you to take my place."

"Take your place? How could I do that? Why?"

"Because I'm dying. My body is shutting down. My

mind. I was one of the first converts, when the concept was new."

"So when Elliot came to see you . . ."

"She wanted to update me. Start over. She knows I'm dying. Knows . . . thought . . . I was desperate. I told her to fuck off."

"She talked to me after that. After her visit," I said.

Karikov nodded. "They want you. They're not going to let you leave. You or your people."

"But they let us in."

"Exactly," he said.

"How will they stop us?"

"Convert you. Or kill you."

"They can't. We'll call in reinforcements. Stirling will—"

He cut me off. "Stirling. Ha! Stirling . . ."

"There's no way . . ."

Karikov stared at me. "Stirling knows we're losing this war. Lost it. It's only a matter of time. We never had a chance. We had technology that was beyond them. We thought we were so much smarter. Maybe we were, once. But they learned. And our guys . . . the guys she changed . . . they're helping them. *My* guys."

"If Stirling knows, then others have to know."

"Not as many as you think. Stirling knows the war is lost. He knows who will get blamed for it too. Unless he holds on long enough."

I shook my head. "This is ridiculous! Radios—"

"Jammed. Or controlled by them."

"There's no way. Supplies come in and out. Ships."

"Contractors. Paid in silver."

"No. I don't buy it. We'd crush them."

Karikov drew his lip into a thin line. "Do you know how many of them there are? Millions. How many men can Stirling put down here? Four thousand? Three?"

"Our technology—"

"Has been stolen. They've got it. Copied it."

Copied? How much could they do? How did we not know? "We'd have seen them—"

"In the mines. So many mines. A whole underground world. The conventional forces stay too far away."

"Impossible!" But was it? The Cappans ran the mines. Stirling knew? "We'll bring the fleet. More men."

He looked at the floor, then back up at me. "Will we? Why?"

"You know why. The silver."

He shook his head slowly. "The silver's already flowing. Five times more than the authorities know about. If the Cappans can deliver that . . . what's easier, an enemy or a trade partner?"

I thought about it. Would we fight? *Should* we? "Maybe. That's a big risk they'd be taking."

"It won't matter," he said. "They'll break down. Kill each other. The leaders. Elliot's folks. They're not stable. They'll be like me. It may take longer, but it's inevitable. The two systems can't coexist."

"So we pull back. Wait it out." I put my fist into my palm and squeezed it.

Karikov shrugged. "Maybe. But they learn fast. They'll be off the planet soon, then we're all fucked."

My breath caught and a chill ripped through me

despite the uncomfortable heat. "Off the planet. You're sure? Why didn't you report it?"

His hollowed eyes widened, then he shrugged. "What's 'sure' mean?"

"This is important." I took a step toward him. "How close are they?"

His alien eyes met mine, but without recognition. He rocked back and forth, slowly. I sat there a long time before I got up. I hit the switch and killed the lights before I left.

CAPTAIN BENTON WAITED outside at a respectful distance. "Sir, there's a call for you in the Ops center."

I squinted against the bright sun. "Really?" Maybe Stirling's people wanted to know what happened. The shuttle pilots should have called that in, though. And why wouldn't they have talked to Baxter? "Who is it?"

"They wouldn't say, sir." Benton led the way back to the larger building and punched in the door code. We walked down a narrow hall, boots echoing off the hard floor. We entered a large room with three giant screens on the wall, all manner of data scrolling across them. Two rows of low desks faced the display, but only one seat had an occupant. A muscular woman wearing uniform pants and a tank top handed me a handset.

"Butler here."

"Sir, this is Captain Mallot."

I almost dropped the handset. *Mallot. Holy shit.* "Captain?"

"Yes, sir. I got promoted."

"You're alive," I said, stalling for time until my brain started working. *Mallot.*

"Sir, we need to talk."

"I agree," I said. "I've been looking for you."

"I know, sir. I'll explain everything face-to-face."

Something in his tone made the hairs on my arms stand up. "Sure. Come on in and let's talk. Where are you?"

"I'm not far, sir. Just outside the base. But I'm not coming in."

"Why not?"

"Sir, why don't you come out? Alone."

I glanced around the room to see if anyone was watching, but neither of the two paid me any attention. "What's going on, Mallot?"

"You have to see it for yourself, sir. You're not in any danger if you come alone."

"What if I don't?"

"Sir, that . . . that would be unfortunate."

If I hadn't made up my mind before, that did it. It sounded too much like a threat for me to tolerate it. "Guess we're going to have to disagree."

"Yes, sir. Sorry, sir." The line went dead.

Twenty seconds later an explosion shook the building, knocking dust from the ceiling, and I flinched, then went down to one knee.

A rocket.

The dull rattle of gunfire came from a distance, then from closer. Return fire. The crack of Bitches and the whine of a pulse rifle, muted by the thick walls of the headquarters.

I looked to Benton and the comms operator, but they didn't react. I gripped my weapon and ran down the hall. I stopped and collected myself, heart hammering and my breath already short. I hit the button to open the door and dove through.

CHAPTER TWENTY-SEVEN

SOMEONE HAD POPPED a smoke grenade that hazed the battlefield and blurred images. I dropped my visor and switched my eye shield to thermal so I could see heat signatures through the growing visual obstruction.

Bullets whizzed from different directions, and I spotted muzzle flashes on two sides of us. Another explosion ripped through the compound, close, compressing my chest and raining dirt and bits of rock onto my helmet and back. My ears rang, and sound dulled around me as my helmet filtered out noise to protect my hearing. So far the fire stayed far enough away from me to be safe, but I needed to move. I whipped my head around, looking for friendlies. I wouldn't have traded my helmet for anything right then, but it severely limited my peripheral vision.

The area in front of me consisted of open space. Kill zone. I hoped whoever was shooting at us couldn't see through the smoke. I leaped to my feet and sprinted around to the nearest side of the building—the side closest to Karikov's hut. I hit the dirt as soon as I rounded the corner, stones biting into my elbows and forearms. I hugged the polymer prefab wall, and bullets ripped up dust where I'd been a second before. The building provided cover from only one direction, but that beat being caught in a crossfire.

My headset remained strangely silent. My heads-up display showed no malfunctions, so it had to be jamming.

I couldn't tell how many fighters the enemy had inside the compound, but the volume of fire said "a lot." Three human bodies lay dead, or close to it, in the center of the open ground. *How many more had been hit?*

I tried my comm, but got only static. Jamming for sure. I tried an external frequency to get air support. No joy there, either. Karikov hadn't lied.

I sighted through the scope of my rifle, magnifying my view to five times. A Cappan poked its head out from behind a stack of metal containers a hundred meters away and I squeezed off a shot without thinking. He ducked. I tried to guide the bullet to follow him, but I doubt it bent fast enough to find the mark.

Hugging the wall and staying in a crouch, I circled toward the back of the building away from the fire. The enemy ignored me. Or at least they didn't shoot me, which was all that really mattered. The bullets snapping around didn't come close.

Behind the building I found half a dozen of my security detail, two pulling cover and the other four with their heads together, talking. One of them snapped a rifle up, leveling it at me as I approached.

I put one hand up. "Whoa! Where's Baxter?"

"Don't know, sir! You okay?" The man moved toward me so we could hear each other.

"Yeah. How many?" I asked.

"A lot. Fifty. Maybe more. Hit us by surprise, but the LT had us waiting." He flinched at an explosion a hundred meters away.

"We need to find the rest of our people."

"Yes, sir. We're going to assault around the side. You join the support by fire team."

I nodded vigorously. "Roger!"

"We're going to try to get to the building closest to the gate. That's the last place we saw the lieutenant."

"I'll move on your go." As the support by fire element, we'd lay down covering fire for the initial movement team. Once they got in place, they'd fire so we could move.

We took off down the sheltered back side of the building and broke around the opposite side from where I started. The low building by the gate lay fifty meters ahead across an open area. Four of us hit the ground and started firing across the compound toward the heaviest enemy fire. I couldn't pick out targets, but it didn't matter. We just needed to put their heads down so our people could make a run. After the enemy bullets slowed, three soldiers took off running and we poured on more fire. I caught sight of a Cappan peeking around the corner of a building and put one into its head and another into its shoulder.

I dropped my empty magazine and loaded a second, this time with explosive tips. Now I didn't aim at all. I ripped into any spot that even looked like it might hold a shooter.

I spared a glance at our moving team. One of them went down, blood exploding from his neck where a bullet slipped between his helmet and armor. One of his buddies stopped to get him.

"Leave him! Keep running!" I yelled.

The soldier didn't hear me, or he didn't listen. Dragging his comrade, he made an easy target. His body jerked as bullets slammed into his armor. Body armor would keep you alive through one shot. Maybe two. But the force of the projectiles had to go somewhere, and a body could only take so much of it. After a spasmodic dance, he fell.

"Fuck!" I yelled at nobody in particular. One of the Cappans found my position, and three or four rounds skipped off of the dirt in front of me, somehow missing. I rolled to the right, my heart hammering in my chest, my breathing echoing in my ears.

By the time I reset, the third soldier had made it to the building and hit the dirt as bullets flashed off the side of the structure above him. I stood and fired the last half dozen rounds of my clip at the source of the fire and it stopped. I dropped back down and rolled over twice to change my location, hopefully without being seen.

Two smoke grenades flew from the far building—our destination—and landed in the area we had to traverse, giving us concealment. A few seconds later several Bitches and at least one heavier gun opened fire, a couple on the roof of the building.

"Let's go!" I shouted, but the others had already seen it and started moving. I sprinted the fifty meters without stopping. It probably took me nine or ten seconds, but it felt like two minutes, what with nothing but smoke between me and death.

I skidded to a stop and dropped to a knee. The *fwap* of a pulse weapon nearby drowned out all other sound. I sucked air in through my mouth, trying to calm myself for a moment before skittering around to the front of the building. Someone opened the door and pulled me in, then had it closing before I fully made it through.

"Shit!"

"Sir!" Baxter stood half a meter away, shouting. The clattering of weapons firing rattled off of the walls. The building had ports to shoot from, and a soldier manned each of the two on the front side.

"Status," I said.

"Unknown." Baxter put her face close to mine so we could hear each other. "At least six down."

"Five made it here in my group."

"That gives us twelve," she said. "That leaves six unaccounted for."

"Is Mac here?"

She shook her head.

Shit. He'd have been right outside the headquarters. I should have had him come inside.

The two riflemen stopped firing at the same time, throwing the room into a relative silence so that when Baxter next shouted, it seemed out of place. "This building is armored!"

"Yeah, got it," I said in a normal tone. "What's happening? Why isn't there firing?" The sounds from outside had died out, too.

"They pulled back, sir." One of the riflemen turned from his firing position and spoke over his shoulder.

"Keep an eye out," said Baxter. "I don't like it."

"Me neither," I said. "Let me see." I moved up to one of the firing stations and looked out through the tiny window. The smoke had cleared some, but I couldn't make out much, even checking both visible and thermal. I'd never done well looking through little apertures. I hated armored vehicles for that reason, though if someone had brought me a Goat right then, I'd have taken it gladly.

We stood inside the building. A woman treated a man for a bullet wound to his lower leg. Another soldier worked on a damaged pulse weapon, trying to fit a tiny part back into its firing mechanism.

"What are they up to?" I said to myself.

"I'm not sure, sir. Maybe they pulled back because they had enough." Baxter had come up behind me and heard my question.

"You believe that?" I looked at her.

"Not for a minute."

"They're planning something. Maybe they're waiting for reinforcements."

She nodded once. "Makes sense. They probably expected to take us by surprise. They didn't."

Wham. The building shook, and I stumbled, barely keeping my balance.

"Maybe they're waiting for heavier weapons," I said.

"That was at least a one twenty-five," said one of the riflemen.

It was bigger than a 125 millimeter, but I didn't correct him. He didn't want to know. Four more huge explosions followed in quick succession, none as close as the first. Either they didn't have the range right or they intentionally spread their fire across the compound.

A series of smaller reports came next. Smaller rockets that produced a higher pitched explosion, more of a crack than the thud of the heavier weapons. Someone screamed outside. The barrage hammered us for ten minutes that felt like a lifetime. The rational corner of my mind—the part not flinching at explosions—knew that the rocket fire prevented the enemy from assaulting. They could soften us up, but they'd have to lift the fire to come forward again.

"How many of the Special Ops guys are in the fight?" I asked.

"On which side?" asked Baxter.

I stared. "What do you know?"

"At least two or three of them were shooting at us," she said. "I didn't see any shooting at the Cappans. Not sure how many of them are left alive."

A rocket slammed into the roof and knocked me to my knees. Baxter kept her feet, but barely. "Fuck!" she yelled. "I had soldiers on the roof!"

"We've got to get the hell out of here," I said.

"In case you missed it, sir, it's raining rockets out there!"

"And as soon as it stops, we're going to have a few

hundred Cappans up our ass. I'll take my chances with the rockets. How many people can we gather?"

"No idea, sir. Where are we going?"

"Where would they expect us to go?" I asked.

She pursed her lips and paused. "They probably expect us to sit and fight, keep trying to get through the commo jam and get air support. Reinforcements. If not, they probably expect us to head for the nearest known friendlies. That's a hundred klicks, straight through the enemy."

"So we go the other way. Out the back door," I said.

"There's nothing that way except hills, mines, and Cappans," said Baxter.

"There might be commo, though. If we can get out of the range of the jam . . ."

Baxter's dark eyes met mine. "Yes, sir. That's our best chance. We can maybe get some distance on them before they realize what we're doing. But every time we light up our commo to try, they're going to get a new fix."

"Right," I said. "So we don't transmit for a while. We get as much ground as we can get before things go to shit."

She nodded once to acknowledge. "Right. We move in three. They've stopped jamming internal frequency, so I'll put it out."

"Wait—why'd they stop jamming it? They might be listening in," I said.

She shrugged. "Yes, sir. If they broke the crypto. But I don't have all of our people here, and I'm not leaving the rest of the team without telling them where we're headed. Satellite comms are still down. I think we've just got to hope we got lucky here. If not, we're screwed anyway."

"Roger," I said. She had it right, but I'd have agreed with her either way. No time for second-guessing. We needed a plan and we needed to execute it before the enemy came down on us. Another rocket cracked nearby, followed by a secondary explosion. A fuel tank, maybe. One of the generators.

"White platoon, this is White Leader. We're moving out to the southwest. We'll blow a hole in the wall. Consolidate as much ammo and water as you can carry. Jackson, you take two soldiers and provide cover for ninety seconds."

"Ma'am, what about wounded?" A male voice over the radio I didn't recognize.

A pause lingered on the channel. "Take them if you can, leave them if you have to. We've got a long move. It's all we can do."

Nobody responded. "Let's move," she said.

I heard someone moving on the roof. At least somebody survived that blast. I had no idea how. Inside, the half dozen soldiers scrambled to grab ammo magazines and check their kit.

Baxter opened the door and two soldiers led her out. I followed close behind, ducking into a crouch for a moment as a rocket hit back toward the headquarters. The barrage had me spooked. I shouldn't have paused. It hadn't been close enough to hurt me. I jumped back up and kept going.

Someone threw more smoke into the open area in front of our building to mask our movement. We sprinted toward the back of the building and across the open area to the larger headquarters, which now had smoke pouring from the roof in two different places. A demolition charge ripped the air in front of us, a sharper crack than those of the rocket explosions. Some of the smoke and dust cleared, revealing a hole in the outer wall.

A heavy gun opened up somewhere behind us, but the bullets didn't come close. From the sound of it, maybe they were still shooting our vacated building.

I flipped my air purifier on to stop the smoke as I ran through and found cover on the far side. I whipped my head around and took a quick head count. Eleven, including me. At least two wounded. One had a bandage wrapped around her arm, blood showing dark on the outside of it. The other limped from what looked like a calf wound. I ran to him. "Can you run?"

"Yes, sir," he said, grimacing. "For a bit."

I met his eyes, then glanced at his name on my heads-up display. "Okay, Billings. Don't be afraid to lean on someone. We've got a long way to go."

"I'll make it, sir," he said. "I'm sure as shit not staying here."

"I'm with you on that. Let's move now, we'll get a head start."

"Roger that, sir." He and I took off running directly away from the compound. Baxter could catch us soon enough and choose the route. We needed to get to the first hill. Get to the trees, and out of the open.

Toward what, I didn't know.

CHAPTER TWENTY-EIGHT

WE REACHED THE second hill before we came under fire. Forty-five minutes. That was longer than I'd thought we'd get. Scattered stubby trees provided some cover, but not enough. The enemy fired in a wide pattern. They didn't hit us, but it did enough to slow us down.

Billings gasped as he crouched, grabbing at his leg. He'd taken a piece of shrapnel in the calf, which wasn't a horrible wound if you got it treated. But with the jagged metal still embedded, it had to be torture every time he moved. A dark stain covered the entire lower portion of his pant leg.

"I'm done," he said.

"You can make it," I told him.

"How far, sir?"

I didn't respond.

"Lieutenant Baxter," he called.

"What is it, Billings?"

"Take the rest of the group and go. I'll hold them up here for a while." He grimaced as he spoke.

Baxter looked like she might say something, then after a moment she nodded. "You have grenades?"

"Two. I could use one more."

Baxter took one off of her own kit and tossed it to him. "Make it count," she said.

Billings forced a smile. "Always."

"Let's move. Do not return fire." Baxter's voice over the radio. "Keep radio silence except for Billings. Billings, you open a channel as soon as we move."

"Roger," he answered.

Smart. If he keyed his radio from the current position, anybody looking for an electronic signal would home in on him, which would buy us another couple of minutes.

"Moving," called another voice. Jackson, the second in charge of the group.

"Roger," said Baxter. "Move."

The rest of us half sprinted, half jogged, using the hill as cover, trying to put it between us and where we imagined the enemy.

"They're getting closer," said Billings. "I'm going to lay down some fire." We'd been running less than a minute when he opened up with a dozen shots that echoed through the open microphone as well as the air. "Didn't hit anyone," he called. "But they know I'm here."

He squeezed off three more rounds, more controlled this time. "Got one that time. There's a human with them. No, two. Shit. They're not wearing our gear, though. I don't think they were Special Ops guys. They're too coordinated with the Cappans. Definitely human, though."

Nobody responded, but I could tell from the glances among the running soldiers that they all had the same thought. This was fucked up.

"I'm going to put one of the humans down. Grenade, first, to force them to cover up." A few seconds later the bass of the grenade exploding added to the symphony of higher-pitched snapping bullets. "I'm hit!" Silence on the radio for several seconds. "I'm okay. They've zeroed in on me, though."

Whump. Another grenade, farther away from us, or maybe it just sounded that way because we kept running, adding distance. No way to know if it was Billings's or the enemy's. Rifle fire from close to the microphone said that Billings still had some fight left.

"Holy shit!" he called. "I had one of the humans dead on, but he jumped like five meters into the air. Damn that guy is fast!"

My breathing echoed in my helmet between Billings's reports. Even with my mind on survival, his image registered. The guy who attacked me spaceside had been fast. It had to be related.

"There's at least two of them," called Billings. "They're covering each other. Too fast for me to get a bead on them, even with guided bullets. I'm switching to explosive. Going to try to get lucky."

Silence for a couple seconds. "Here I go," he said. "Keep running. If this doesn't work, you won't have long. There's something weird here."

Four shots rang over the net, then silence. With the radio quiet, the shots sounded in the distance. Probably half a klick. If we were lucky, we'd get farther before they realized that Billings was alone. We needed some luck.

Nothing else came over the net for what felt like a minute. Hard to say exactly, since I still pounded across tough terrain, trying to keep pace with a bunch of young people.

"Over here!" It came across the net, but sounded distant. Someone not near the microphone. "There's only one. Decoy!"

"Is he alive?" A second male voice, human, not translated Cappan.

"No. Bullet through the neck." The first voice.

Billings died with his transmitter still on. "Tracks lead that way. The rest of them can't be far. Shit, he's still broadcasting." The voice grew stronger, more distinct, until it sounded like he spoke directly into the transmitter.

"This is Captain Trey Mallot. I'm one of you. All we want is the colonel. If you give him up, I promise no harm will come to you. If not . . . ?"

I tripped and slammed to the ground, scraping my hands as I caught myself. My mind shut down for a minute, and I couldn't seem to find my way back to my feet. Even though I had talked to him before, somehow this made it more real.

"There are hundreds of Cappans here," Mallot continued. "They know where you are, and I'm afraid I can't protect you. You all know what Cappans do to prisoners."

A soldier grabbed me by the arm and helped me to my feet. She had her visor up, and I searched her face, trying to see if the propaganda had made her think. She breathed through her mouth, tired from the run. I couldn't read her.

Baxter signaled two fingers to everyone.

"What does that mean?" I asked the soldier.

"Alternate frequency. It should already be in your helmet, just flip it, sir."

I toggled it with my eyes, but didn't check in. We were still keeping net silence to hide our location. I reopened the initial channel as well, on monitor only. Baxter switched her people off of it because she didn't want them hearing any more of Mallot's crap, but it didn't bother me beyond that initial shock. Maybe I'd learn something listening to him. More important, anyone we left behind wouldn't know to switch channels. If they came looking for us, it would be on channel one. Mac was back there. Hopefully.

Mallot was working with the Cappans. The whole reason we were here, and he was trying to kill us. Trying to turn my own soldiers against me. Asshole.

A dull, thumping explosion thundered in the distance and Billings's transmitter cut out. His last grenade, probably. He must have booby trapped himself with it. I hoped he got Mallot.

The trees around us now reached more than twice the height of a person, and grew about three or four meters apart. They'd give us some concealment from a distance, but up close they wouldn't do a lot of good.

After a minute for water, we started jogging again, circling the hill about halfway up. The soft ground kept wanting to slide out from under my feet. We needed another hill between us and the enemy. As it got steeper, more than one soldier fell, sliding downward until they found something to grab at.

Mallot and the Cappans. I couldn't concentrate.

An explosion rumbled from the low ground in front of us, maybe a klick and a half away. We stopped in unison. Baxter glanced at me, and I trotted over to her.

"That's bad," she said.

I wiped sweat from my forehead and eyes. "It's good. If their rockets are that far off, they don't know where we are."

"But they're shooting in front of us," she said. "They know where we're going, and they're trying to keep us from traveling that direction."

I didn't want that thought to take root. "What are the odds that they hit you with an unobserved one ten?" One-hundred-ten-millimeter rockets were notoriously inaccurate. "One in a thousand? We can accept those odds at this point."

"Roger, sir. Thanks."

"No problem." I didn't mention how much worse our odds got if they planted someone on top of one of the taller hills to direct the fire.

I think a lot of guys would have simply taken over command. I considered it more than once. Nobody would have balked at the idea, but Baxter's people trusted her, and she was getting the job done. I could always take over later if I had to.

Rockets slammed on all sides with increasing frequency as we continued to trot forward. We avoided the center of the next low ground, as if that was somehow the aim point. In reality, the fire appeared random. Some hit closer, but none near enough to cause damage.

Several shacks sprouted, scattered across the next hill. Rural Cappans. They didn't cluster together the way humans would in a settlement, but close enough to support each other. Farmers, maybe, or perhaps there was a mine nearby. We had definitely entered mine country.

I didn't know how the locals would react, or if their presence would keep the other Cappans from shooting at us. Everything we knew from our intelligence said that the locals didn't support the insurgency, but I didn't trust those reports—hell, Karikov's team had provided a lot of the intelligence.

The trees here in the lowland grew larger, with sharp, rigid leaves the size of a human head. We could avoid the lower branches easily enough during the day, but the shadows grew long. Nightfall would be a mixed blessing. We had better night vision, but the enemy knew the terrain. The cold wouldn't bother us as long as we kept moving, but we were soaked with perspiration. If we stopped too long, we'd freeze.

Baxter steered us away from the huts as long as she could. Even if the locals didn't directly impede us, it only took one calling in our location to give us away to those who followed.

Our run slowed to a jog, then further to a fast walk. When the first bullet skipped off of the ground in our midst it came as a shock, but not a surprise. Before much longer, rounds whipped through the trees all over. They definitely had our position, directing in additional forces. They still fired from long range—maybe five or six hundred meters—but we didn't have long.

Baxter trotted over and walked next to me. "Do you think we've gone far enough to get out from under the jam?"

I had no idea. "We're probably only going to get one shot at it. And if it's a mobile jammer that they brought with them, we've got no chance. Thing is, I don't know enough about their technology."

"I'd really like to have that next high ground. Map says there's a mine there, but if we have to fight—" Her words trailed off.

"It's a good plan. But if there's a mine in that hill, there will be more Cappans."

"Yes, sir," she said. "I think we have to risk that. We *know* the guys behind us want us dead. So we worry about the known."

"Let's do it."

The enemy had other ideas. They always do. Fire ripped into us from the opposite direction, and one female soldier went down with a scream. The rest of us hit the ground. They'd either gotten someone around us or called in another force. Regardless, they had us from two directions. Pinned down.

Baxter shouted orders and gestured with her hands, orienting some of her people in each direction. Soldiers began to scan the sector looking for targets, but didn't fire. Smart. We had to be disciplined. We only had the ammo we'd carried with us.

Someone crawled over to the wounded soldier, then shook his head.

Baxter crawled over to me. "I'm going to try the satcom. We don't have enough firepower to fight through this new blocking position with another force coming up behind us."

"If it doesn't work and we stay here, they're going to dial in on us with heavy weapons," I said. A bullet cracked into the tree a meter above us, raining splinters down on my helmet. "But I think you've got to try."

She nodded. I didn't follow her progress. A figure zipped across my sightline and I fired. I tried to guide the round into him, but I had the wrong ammo loaded. My explosive bullet detonated harmlessly well beyond the target. I'm not sure I'd have gotten him even with the right ammunition. Too fast.

How many superhuman soldiers did they have? I dismissed the thought. It didn't matter. At least thirty enemy fired at us now, so at a minimum they had us by three to one, and they had the ability to reinforce. We didn't. Superhuman or no, we were in trouble.

I glanced to Baxter who had her head down and her ears covered against the noise. We had one shot. If it didn't work, we could measure our remaining time in minutes. As if to punctuate my thought, a rocket exploded about eighty meters short of our position, flinging up dirt and dust. No way to tell where it came from, but when the next one fell on the opposite side of our position, it didn't matter. They had our range.

CHAPTER TWENTY-NINE

"KAPPA BASE, THIS is White Leader, contact my coordinates. Request air support and extraction." Baxter spoke into the transmitter, but I didn't have her feed, so I couldn't tell if anyone answered. Someone opened up on us with a heavy weapon, and large-caliber bullets ripped the ground around our position. I hugged the ground and tried to make myself smaller. Splinters from a nearby tree pelted me, but my armor absorbed it. How the bullets didn't hit me, I'll never know. Lucky, I guess, but I was due some luck.

They had at least three heavy guns by the sounds of it, maybe four, and they used them all to tear at us. Screams cut through the sounds of fire, but between the rockets impacting and the bullets flying everywhere, the dust made it impossible to tell who'd been hit, or how many. I could barely make out the enemy advancing on us in two waves, half at a time. One group fired while the other moved.

They'd drawn within two hundred meters, their shapes showing up in the dying light by heat signature in my night optics. The thermal imagery made it hard to get an exact count, but it had to be more than forty. Cappan or human, I couldn't distinguish at that distance.

"Six minutes until air cover, eleven minutes to extraction!" Baxter transmitted to me across a private channel.

Eleven minutes. That meant that our team had something down near the planet waiting on our call, not all the way back at Cappa Base. Good. Unfortunately we didn't have eleven minutes. We had about two minutes until the enemy assaulted through our position.

A target flashed from behind a tree, forty meters away. I fired off three rounds, guided, but they all slammed into the trunk. The figure closed the ground to the next cover before I could aim again. One of the humans. It had to be. Cappans weren't that fast.

Then again, neither were humans.

The enemy fire slowed. It had to, because they'd risk hitting their own assault force. That came as sort of a mixed blessing for us.

They could have sat back and worn us down with their superior fire and eventually beat us. We'd have run out of ammo. But that would have taken time. Maybe they knew we had air support inbound, and that they only had minutes. So they didn't wait.

A figure flew through the air and landed inside our small perimeter. He had to have leaped more than twenty meters. He pointed his weapon at Baxter, who lay in a prone firing position and hadn't turned to face him yet.

"Mallot!" I yelled, playing a hunch.

He hesitated for a second, his head turning toward me.

It wasn't Mallot.

Baxter slammed her foot up into his groin, and he groaned and sagged, but recovered enough to level his rifle at her face.

His head exploded.

Baxter lay on her back and stared at the body as it fell, her body armor covered in brain matter and blood.

A new source of fire came from a different direction. "Sir, tell everyone to get down. Anyone standing is an enemy." Mac's voice on the radio, calling on the old frequency.

"Everyone stay down! Friendlies coming from sixty degrees." I relayed the message to the platoon on the current channel. I didn't know how many of us could stand, anyway.

For a moment we stemmed the enemy attack. Mac's force coming from a new direction caused them to hesitate, and we took several of them down before they could regroup. I didn't know how many soldiers Mac had with him, but it had to be three or four, given the volume of fire.

Our advantage only lasted a minute. The enemy brought their heavier weapons to bear, and Mac's team had to go to ground.

"Two minutes." Baxter over the radio. "Flip on your markers."

"Mac, air inbound. Markers," I relayed. I didn't

want to take time to bring everyone onto the same channel with the fight going on, but his team needed to mark themselves. By turning on the beacons in their helmets, they'd light up to the inbound aircraft, allowing the pilots to pick out the good guys.

The enemy fire started to dwindle and draw farther away. They must have known about the air support.

I gave a silent thank-you for their mistake. They should have come closer, made a mad rush. Being on top of us would have made it impossible for the bombs to hit them without hitting us, too. I'm glad I didn't have to make that decision. Dropping bombs on your own position was a last resort I didn't want to try. If the enemy wanted to help us out, I'd happily take the assist.

The two ships screamed overhead and I instinctively put my head down. Whatever munition they fired in their first pass, we wouldn't hear it over the sound of the engines until it hit. I didn't know what information Baxter fed them, if any, or what she requested. It didn't matter. The birds would pick out the targets and blow the shit out of them.

The impact came from both directions almost simultaneously, hitting the attackers on both sides. The force wave nearly lifted me from the ground. Sonic cutters mixed with some high explosives, if I had to guess. The world went quiet for a moment in the wake of the aircrafts' hasty departure.

"We're coming in, sir!" Mac saw his opportunity to close our ranks and took it. Great thinking. At least somebody's brain didn't get scrambled by the air support.

"Hold your fire. Friendlies coming in," I relayed to whatever was left of our force.

Mac hit the ground right beside me. "Didn't think we were going to find you. If the whole world hadn't lit up with gunfire, we wouldn't have."

"You picked a good time to show," I said, but my last words were drowned in the whine of the fighters on their second pass. "Alternate frequency," I shouted before they'd quite departed. The second set of bombs shook the ground. My hearing came back just in time to register a large tree falling slowly through the dark a couple hundred meters away.

"Fighters picked a good time to show too," he said.

"Extract in ninety seconds," said Baxter.

I looked at Mac to see if he heard it and had the new frequency. He nodded.

"One more fighter pass," I said. He nodded again, then laid his face to his rifle and looked through his scope, scanning for targets.

The fighters zipped through again, this time firing rockets. They'd be targeting small groups of enemy survivors. The rockets sliced through the air with an evil hiss, followed by flashes from half a dozen locations, the sound and shockwave coming a few seconds later.

"Call in for extract," radioed Baxter. One by one our crew called in. Six, including Baxter and me.

After a moment of silence on the net, Mac spoke.

"Four plus me for five more, ma'am." Eleven. Less than half of what we started the day with. No telling how many of the eleven were wounded. Probably most, though Mac's team seemed to move well, so maybe they'd avoided the worst of it.

The two lift aircraft came in slower than the fighters, but still fast. The trick to spotting them was to look ahead of where you heard the noise. By the time you heard them, they'd already moved from that location.

I tried to find one, only to watch a yellow-and-orange fireball light the sky. A split second later the loud *fwaaaap* of a large pulse weapon cut through the night. More distortion of light and sound. A ship had exploded before we heard the weapon that killed it.

One of the landing craft had disintegrated.

Light streaked across the sky in golden fingers. Missiles. At least six, maybe more. Another flash, then another less than a second behind it. Both fighters hit, one explosion eclipsing the other.

A sinking, queasy feeling grabbed at my gut. They'd just eliminated our rescue with a big pulse weapon and a bunch of surface-to-air missiles. But the enemy didn't have those weapons—they weren't supposed to, anyway. Those missiles hadn't been small shoulder-fired SAMs, either. They had high-end stuff. Dangerous.

I put the implications of what just happened behind me for a minute and scanned the sky. We still had one transport left, and with our reduced numbers, they had space to carry us all out if they could get to us.

Another missile streaked into the sky like a fiery sword.

The second transport flung flares from its hull and dove hard, but the missile had locked in. A golden blossom of death lit the sky and the transport spun toward the ground, spitting flames. A quirk of fate set its descent almost directly toward the source of the missile that killed it.

"Ejects," said Mac, softly so it didn't carry.

I scanned the sky and found the pilots with my night-vision optics. "Got them. Looks like they both popped clear. You think anyone else popped? From the other birds?" The chutes drifted toward Cappa in a controlled fall.

"Don't know, sir," said Mac. "I doubt it. They flashed pretty big."

"Yeah," I said.

Baxter stood and hurried over to me, taking a knee. "Sir, what the fuck do we do?" Her voice rose a few notes.

"Call it in," I said.

"Sir, the jammer. We've got no off-planet commo again."

Shit. "They must have moved in a mobile." Even as I said it, I doubted it. The enemy had pulled back when the fighters attacked. Nothing could have survived that barrage. They had to be jamming the satellites directly. That meant a bigger problem, but one for another day. We had to live through this, first.

My mind scrambled for a solution. "There's no way that Cappa Base doesn't know what's going on now."

I kept my voice level, hoping it would help Baxter do the same. "They'll send help. Wait for the next ships to come into range, then signal them in. You'll know they're close, because they're going to blow the crap out of that anti-aircraft site before they get here, now that they know about it."

"It will take at least twenty-five or thirty minutes until they arrive," she said.

She was right, and we didn't have thirty minutes. With the ships down, the enemy would move back in. "Let's go," I said.

"Where, sir?" she asked.

"Anywhere but here. Let's not give them an easy target."

"We should head for the downed pilots," said Mac.

"Perfect," I answered. "They'll have beacons, not the markers we've got. Transmitters that broadcast without satellites. All the pilots do. And if there's one thing you can guarantee, it's that the squadron isn't going to leave their fellow pilots down here."

"Yes, sir," said Baxter, her voice steady, the moment of indecision gone. She was going to make it in our business, assuming she lived through this fight. That's what the good ones did. If they panicked, they got over it fast.

"Move now, two groups of four, three in the middle," radioed Baxter.

"We've got tail," I told her. Mac grabbed two of the soldiers who came with him to round out our team and linked the others up with another element. We started moving fifteen seconds later, three wedges, our trailing group inverted so the point faced back. If the fighters hadn't destroyed the enemy in front of us, we'd know soon. And if we made it past that, I hoped that the downed pilots didn't shoot at us thinking we were enemy. We didn't have any way to speak to them, and trusting scared pilots on the ground was risky. Another problem for later.

Even with night vision, the branches slapped against my face plate, and low scrub grabbed at my feet and ankles. It kept us to a quick walk, and we still made more noise than I'd have liked. *Thirty minutes.*

Less than five minutes later, four rockets slammed the ground to our front, throwing dirt, rock, and branches, shaking our already wobbly legs. They knew we were moving. They had to. They only missed by a hundred meters. By unspoken accord, we picked up our pace. Someone might fall in a hole or smash a knee on a rock, but it beat being cut in half by hot metal.

Another barrage ripped through the trees, off to the right this time, farther away. An enemy machine gun tore through the night, also off the mark. The bullets hunted through the woods, meandering slowly, looking for a target without knowing where to start.

Recon by fire. They wanted us to shoot back. I flipped open the channel to tell everyone to hold their fire.

Too late.

The man beside me let off a three-round burst. "Cease fire." I tried to keep my voice calm on the net. No use yelling about it now.

"I had his position marked," said the soldier who fired. She sounded confused more than defensive.

"We don't want to give away *our* position," I called over the net. "We need to move. Now."

Two heavy weapons and at least a dozen smaller ones raked the ground around us, ripping chunks out of trees and flinging up dirt, flashing off of rocks. Without firing back, we had nothing to keep the enemy's head down. Even from three hundred meters, if they kept enough bullets flying, they'd get lucky soon enough.

"Keep moving," I radioed. "My team will stop and pour down some fire for thirty seconds, then catch up."

Mac flashed me a thumbs-up to show me that he heard. He grabbed one of the other soldiers and physically put her into position behind a head-sized rock. He put the other behind a tree. That didn't leave much cover for him or me, so we grabbed the ground and got as low as we could.

"Fire when I do," I radioed. "Slow and steady. Thirty seconds, twenty rounds. Explosive if you've still got them. Pick targets if you can, if not, try to silence the bigger guns."

I took a deep breath and silently counted to three for no particular reason. I squeezed my first shot off in the direction of one of the heavy guns, then fired three more in a pattern right around it. The staccato burst of my own team firing close by drowned out the sound of the enemy. Vaguely I sensed bullets getting closer.

Something cracked into my left shoulder, wrenching my weapon from that hand. A burst of molten fire jolted my shoulder joint, then my whole arm went numb.

I didn't think the bullet penetrated my armor, though I had no way to tell in the dark. The force of the bullet did enough, even with the protection I had from my gear. I shook my numb hand, trying to find some feeling.

Belatedly, I rolled over twice to a new position in case someone had homed in on my location. Always have to remember the fundamentals.

A dozen bullets ricocheted off the rock our soldier hid behind, throwing sparks into the air and momentarily screwing with my night optics.

I aimed in the general direction of the fire with my one working arm and squeezed off half a dozen useless shots before rolling again.

"Ten seconds until we move," I said. "Shoot 'em if you got 'em." The pops around me intensified. No fire came from behind the rock, so I crawled on my belly toward the soldier's position, pulling with my good arm.

She lay still, her helmet shattered.

I grabbed her and rolled her toward me, but I knew even before I finished moving her that we'd lost her. Too many cracks in the helmet, too many bullets.

Shit. I didn't even know her name. I grabbed her ammo.

"Let's go," I called. "We're just three. On my move." I leaped to my feet, not waiting to see if Mac or the other soldier followed.

The next fifteen seconds felt like an hour, running

uphill with death chasing us. I sprinted, then tripped after a moment, sprawling. I caught myself with my bad arm, and screamed for half a heartbeat before cutting it off. At least I felt it.

I pushed off with my good arm and scrambled to my feet, scanning as I ran, trying to find where Baxter and the team had gone.

"Left a hundred mils." Baxter on the radio. I still didn't see her, but she could see me. I turned left by a small margin and kept running, sharp Cappan leaves scraping as they bounced off my visor.

"Keep on the same course," said Baxter. "We're in a cave."

I almost tripped again, this time on a fallen log, jumping over it at the last second. *A cave.*

Shit.

I saw the dark spot in the hillside and ran through. Baxter's people opened fire from the mouth of the cave right after we passed, the reassuring pops of their weapons once again drowning out the enemy. For a moment it almost made me forget we were trapped.

I paused for a minute to gasp at some air. My thighs burned, though that paled in comparison to the pain in my shoulder.

I found Baxter. "We've got to get out of here."

"Why, sir? This is good cover."

As if to answer, heavy bullets ripped into the opening. A male soldier screamed and crumpled.

"Never mind. They've got us pinned in. What is this place?"

"It's a mine, sir."

"How deep does it go?"

"I don't know, sir," said Baxter. "A ways. There's equipment at the back of this section."

"How long do you think we've got to hold out?" asked Mac.

"I don't know. Depends how long it takes our ships to find us," I answered.

"Shit, sir, that's at least fifteen minutes," said Mac.

I looked at him, a red blob in my thermals, identified by his name in pale blue text on my heads-up. "See what's here that we can use for a barricade."

"Yes, sir." He disappeared at a run. Bullets continued to screech off the walls and roof.

I checked my ammunition. A magazine and a half. We wouldn't give them a fight for very long. "How much fire you got left?"

Baxter checked her kit. "One, sir. How much you got, Ramirez?"

"Half, ma'am," answered a soldier.

I tossed Ramirez my half magazine and loaded my last one. "Explosive. Make them count."

"Yes, sir."

"Pull your people back from the entrance. We'll try to make a stand farther back," I said.

"Roger that, sir," answered Baxter.

I headed for the back of the cave and found Mac in the dark, throwing around metal boxes. "What is this stuff?"

"Military equipment boxes," he said. "They're empty, but they'll stop bullets."

"That'll have to do," I said. I didn't have time to

worry about why a mine had military equipment boxes in it.

"How are we going to get to the birds when they show, sir?"

"No idea."

The remnants of the team arrived a few seconds later. They limped and staggered, one man holding another up. The fire outside ceased, and every scraping footstep echoed off the walls in the silence.

Soldiers' heads darted back and forth, searching for answers, nobody wanting to speak.

"They're gearing up for an assault," said Mac.

"Fire discipline," said Baxter. "Single shots, pick your targets. We're low on ammo."

A flash lit the mouth of the cave, blinding me, followed by a *whump* that threw me backward two meters and onto my ass. I coughed, my lungs filling with dust and grit until my air filter caught up.

I crawled forward to our makeshift barrier and prepared myself for the attack.

"Colonel Butler." An amplified voice from outside. "Colonel Butler. If Colonel Butler is alive, he's the only one we want. Send him out and the rest of you live."

CHAPTER THIRTY

FOR A MINUTE everyone looked at each other, but nobody spoke. I took my last magazine of ammunition and handed it to Mac.

"What are you doing, sir?" He pulled his hand back and didn't take it.

"I'm going out. Take it."

"Sir, you can't trust them."

"They've got rockets, Mac. If we stay here, they're going to bring this whole place down on us, and everyone dies. If I go out, at least there's a chance." I shook the magazine and he finally grabbed it.

"Baxter," I called.

"Yes, sir."

"Once I'm clear, do whatever you have to in order to get back spaceside. No heroics. Just get out of here if you can."

She hesitated before finally speaking. "Yes, sir."

"This is Colonel Butler. I'm coming out!" I walked toward the mouth of the mine letting my rifle hang down from its strap. I put my hands out to each side, away from my body and visible. The last thing I needed was someone outside with a case of nerves to shoot me. If I had to die, I wanted someone to do it on purpose. I'd have raised them over my head, but I didn't think I could get my left arm up if I tried.

More than thirty heat signatures surrounded the opening of the mine when I reached it.

"Raise your visor, sir."

I complied, and the remnants of the thermal view left purple spots in front of my eyes, leaving me blind for a minute. "I'm going to hold you to your word as an officer, Mallot. Everyone else goes."

"Yes, sir." His voice came from thirty or forty meters away. "Once we're clear of the area. I'm actually counting on your people to tell the incoming ships not to bomb us."

I grunted. "Yeah, that would be a shitty way to die. What now?"

In answer to my question, a group of Cappans came forward. One of them unclipped my rifle, another took the grenade off of my armor. He slammed his rifle butt into my back just under the bottom of my vest and I crumpled to my knees with a groan. They hauled me halfway back to my feet and started dragging me until my feet caught up and I started walking. One of them prodded me painfully in the back at random intervals for the first half kilometer.

Only footsteps and a few stumbles broke the silence, except for the occasional ship flying over in the distance. They set a brisk pace, and my legs burned with the effort, already worn down from our long run.

Even so, my mind had plenty of time to churn. I never considered trying to escape, but the others . . . I hoped they got clear. And I hoped they didn't do something stupid and try to come after me. Mallot wanted me alive, and I kind of supported that part of the plan. I needed to get close enough to talk to him.

I picked up my pace a little trying to get up toward the front, where I assumed Mallot walked. The Cappans didn't stop me until I reached a point with only four or five of them left in front of me and then one of them barred my way.

"Captain Mallot," I called.

Lights flashed in my eyes and I crashed to the ground. It took me a moment to realize that one of the Cappans had slammed his rifle into the side of my head. My helmet had absorbed most of the blow, but the force of the impact still left me stunned. I guess they didn't want me to talk.

Two of them grabbed me under each of my arms, making me cry out in pain from my shoulder injury. They dragged me, screaming, for at least fifty meters before I finally thrashed enough to force them to drop me. I lay there for a moment, not sure if I could still move.

One of them kicked at me, its boot glancing off my hip. Apparently I could move, because I instinctively curled into a protective ball to protect my face and my groin as more kicks rained down. The whole time I thought, *Why go through the trouble of calling me out only to let the Cappans kill me?*

"Sir!" Mallot yelled loudly enough that it startled everyone. At least the Cappans stopped kicking me. "You need to get up."

"I—"

"Don't talk. Get up and walk, or I won't be able to help you with the Cappans."

I pushed myself slowly to my feet, frustrated and in pain. I forced the negative thoughts down and concentrated on putting one foot in front of the other.

At one point we went underground and walked through a tunnel for half an hour or so before we stopped and they tossed me in a small cell with a stone floor and rough-hewn walls. After maybe an hour they pulled me back out and we started moving again, going above ground, then entering another tunnel after a kilometer or so. We stopped and started several times, nobody explaining anything or even speaking to me. What I did know was that anyone trying to follow us would have a tough time of it, even with air assets. We spent as much time underground as we did above.

I couldn't keep a perfect measurement, but I figured we had to have traveled twenty kilometers by the time we crested a low hill and finally stopped for good. Several generators whirred to our front, and I could barely make out the silhouette of a low, domed building. Two Cappans guided me inside and I winced as the one on my left grabbed my arm.

The building smelled like chemical disinfectant, and the darkness grew thicker inside until the door thunked shut and someone cut on blinding white lights. I scrunched my eyes but let in as much light as I could stand so they'd adjust. I wanted to take advantage of the first few moments to gain whatever information I could. You never knew what might prove helpful.

The large oval room had six beds, three on each side leaving an open space in the middle, all with fancy medical machines clustered around them. It gave the impression of a field hospital with much better equipment. A small portable X-ray unit sat against the wall beside a mobile scanner unit. The same kind of unit they *didn't* have in the spaceside hospital. We had to be in the building that showed a high-power signature on our scans. It made sense now. We were back near Karikov's base. It gave me hope that Stirling's people might find me, but only the slightest bit. They'd be reeling from the battle, and even if they recovered quickly they weren't designed for rescue operations. That would have been Karikov's job.

I didn't think he'd be coming to save me anytime soon.

Four Cappans stood in the room with two humans: Mallot and someone I didn't recognize. Mallot's pupils nearly filled his eyes, oval, like a Cappan's. I hoped he remained more lucid than the last man I met with eyes like that. Our interactions so far made him seem rational, but I wasn't ready to commit.

"So what now?" I asked.

"Sir, this is our medical facility. Where we get our treatments," said Mallot.

"Great. It's a nice rig. I approve. If there's nothing else, I'll be going." Two of the Cappans stepped forward before I even moved.

Mallot gave me a flat smile that didn't show his teeth. "People said you had a sense of humor, sir."

"Yeah. I'm a riot. So let's cut to the bottom line. Why am I here?" I desperately wanted to sit down, but I wasn't sure I'd be able to get back up again.

"Simple. We need your help, sir."

"I'm not . . . wait, what?" I almost took a step backward. I had mentally prepared for several possibilities. That wasn't one of them.

"We wouldn't ask, but we're pretty desperate," said Mallot. "Colonel Karikov is . . . no longer an option. And as much as I'd like to take charge, I recognize that I don't have the skill set required for the level of operations we need to conduct."

I stared at him. "So you lured me down to the planet so that you could kidnap me, in hopes that I'd take over as your leader?"

"No, sir. We didn't lure you down to the planet. We took advantage of an opportunity."

"And you let the Cappans beat the shit out of me. That's how you convince me?"

He stared at me for a moment before speaking. "That . . . was unfortunate. But it's a loose partnership. I'm not really in charge."

"You're not . . ." I paused. If he wasn't in charge, who was? The Cappans? "You're going to have to forgive me, Mallot, but you understand how ridiculous this all sounds, right?"

He took an aggressive step toward me, his nostrils flaring. "It's not ridiculous at all, sir. You just don't see it yet."

"Sure, sure," I said, holding my hands up. Never piss off a potentially dangerous guy with a gun. It's a rule that's served me well.

"Don't patronize me, sir."

I paused, considering my next move. I didn't know where the line was, and I had a feeling if I crossed it I might not survive the experience. "Okay. I'll be straight with you, Captain. I have no idea what you're talking about. What will I see?"

"You'll see the truth."

"The truth is a funny thing. Whose truth?"

He clenched his fists, but didn't come any closer. "*The* truth, sir! The only truth."

One of the Cappans raised a weapon at me. I'm not an expert at Cappan body language, but it gave the impression that it wouldn't hesitate to use it.

"Okay. Okay. How am I going to see it? Because I don't see it now."

Mallot smiled. "Once you get the treatment, everything becomes clear."

"What treatment?"

He shook his head.

"What, I don't get to know?"

"It will help you with your cybernetic appendage, sir. I've got two robot legs, and I'm functioning. It's revolutionary. We're better than other humans."

Two robot legs. That explained the ridiculous speed. It shouldn't have been possible, but it matched what Karikov had said. "I don't want the treatment."

"I'm afraid it's not optional, sir." He locked his creepy gaze with mine and held it there for several seconds. "Look, sir. You've got a few hours. Why don't you try to get some rest? It's going to be hard on your body."

I didn't drop my stare. I'm not sure if I meant to intimidate him or try to read him, but I failed either way. "Yeah. Sure."

"You want a painkiller for that arm? I'm sure we've got something here."

"No, I'm good." I walked over to one of the beds and tested the mattress. Too much had happened too quickly. I needed time to think.

"Suit yourself. But sir?"

"Yeah?"

"Please don't try anything stupid. As much as I might want you to join us, the Cappans will shoot you." He glanced over to the guards.

I swung my legs up onto the bed. "Thanks for the warning." I closed my eyes for a moment, trying to collect my thoughts. "Mallot."

"Yes, sir?" He hadn't moved.

"What is it that you need me to do? Why do you need me?" I didn't figure I'd get a straight answer, but it didn't hurt to ask.

"Can't tell you that yet, sir. We've got big plans, though. We need a strategic thinker."

I nodded. "Sure. When you say 'we,' do you mean you and the other humans, or do you mean the Cappans?"

"We're together, sir. We see the truth."

"The truth . . ."

"You'll see, sir. Rest now. You're going to need it."

"Okay." I closed my eyes and my mind spun. However unlikely it seemed that I'd help them, Mallot definitely believed it. That made me nervous.

I didn't sleep.

IT MAY HAVE been an hour, it may have been two. The lights came up and new voices brought me quickly to awareness. One of them was female. I knew that voice.

"Why aren't my follow-ups here?"

"We have a new patient, ma'am," said Mallot. "I knew that would take some time, so I scheduled the others for later."

"You need to let me know these things before I come, Captain. This isn't a simple procedure, and it's not easy for me to get down here when things are exploding all over the place. Luckily I have everything I need, and I brought Doctor Kwan, who can assist."

"Hello, Doctor Elliot," I said. I got some satisfaction as she stopped dead and almost dropped her medical bag. The other doctor stopped as well. Mallot kept walking toward me.

"What's he doing here?" Elliot's voice rose.

"He's the patient," said Mallot, oblivious to Elliot's angry glare.

"No, he's not." Elliot regained her composure quickly, and set her bag on a square polymer table.

"Ma'am—" Mallot tried to protest, but Elliot cut him off.

"No. I only work on volunteers." She looked at me. "Have you changed your mind since we talked spaceside?"

"No." I shook my head. "Fuck no."

"I didn't think so. What's the meaning of this, Mallot?"

"We need him," said Mallot.

"That's not how it works," said Elliot. "I'm a doctor. Patients have rights."

Mallot faced her, leaving his back to me. I thought about making a move, but my aching shoulder and the two Cappans on the other side of the room with rifles made me think better. The other two and the human had disappeared.

"It works that way now," he said. "There's no choice. Colonel Karikov isn't stable anymore."

"I'm aware of Colonel Karikov's condition," said Elliot. "That doesn't change anything."

"It changes everything!" Mallot stepped forward. His hand hovered a bit too near his sidearm for comfort.

"Not to me. I'm not treating him. So unless you've got some medical training I don't know about, that's that." Elliot turned to grab her bag.

Mallot drew his pistol. The small pulse weapon screamed, the sound strangely dull inside the facility.

Doctor Kwan looked down for a moment at the fist-sized smoking hole in his chest before he crumpled to the ground.

"Shit!" I started to jump down from the bed and one of the Cappans leveled a rifle at me. I raised my good arm and froze.

"What did you do?" yelled Elliot. She rushed over to Kwan, heedless that the second Cappan followed her with its weapon. She felt at Kwan's neck for a pulse, then looked back over her shoulder at Mallot. "You killed him!"

Mallot bounced from one foot to another, his weapon halfway raised and swinging slightly from side to side. "I didn't want to do it," he said softly.

"You shot him." Elliot stood and stormed toward him. She stopped quickly when he pointed his weapon at her chest.

"You made me!"

I glanced toward the Cappans, who still had their weapons raised. "Let's take it easy," I said, as calmly as I could manage. Elliot probably hadn't seen someone shot in cold blood before. I had. It didn't make it okay, but it lessened the impact and I recovered my wits quicker.

Mallot stepped back so that he could cover Elliot and me at the same time, keeping his weapon trained somewhere between us. Thankfully Elliot stopped going toward him. She stood, her eyes glazing over, her hands shaking.

"This is your fault too, sir," said Mallot.

"Sure. We've all got some responsibility." He had the gun. I wasn't going to argue. "What do we do now?"

"Now you get the treatment," said Mallot.

I nodded. "Okay. But I'm not sure Doctor Elliot is up for it right now." Her whole body trembled, and she appeared like she might collapse.

"She has to be!" shouted Mallot.

"Okay," I said quickly, my voice level despite my pounding heart. "Let me talk to her. There's no rush. Give me a minute."

Mallot pointed his pistol at me and took a step back as I walked over to Elliot.

"Elliot." I put one hand on each of her shoulders to steady her and to stop her from shaking. "Hey. It's me, Butler. Everything is fine."

"Doctor Kwan . . ."

"Doctor Kwan is gone. There's nothing we can do about that. Focus. Look at me."

She raised her eyes to mine.

"Can we get the Cappans out of here? I need to get her calmed down," I said to Mallot, without losing eye contact with Elliot.

"Don't try anything, sir." He lowered his voice, but it still held menace.

"I won't. But if you want this done, we need a doctor. You're going to have to work with me here."

After a long moment, the two Cappans headed for the door. I had no idea what I was going to do with an unstable superhuman pointing a gun at me, but whatever I did would go easier without two armed Cappans.

"Thanks," I said. "Doctor Elliot. I need you to focus. Can you hear me?"

She nodded.

"Good. I need you to perform the procedure on me. The one that helps amputees." I didn't dare turn to look at Mallot. "Can you do that?"

"It will help your shoulder heal, too," she said softly.

"Great. That's great. What do we need to get started?"

She gathered herself. “Okay. I can’t do it alone. Mallot, you’re going to have to help.”

“Ma’am—”

“Look, do you want this done or not?” Elliot’s voice bristled with authority. She was back.

Mallot paused, then gestured with his weapon. “Okay. Sir, over there, on the bed.”

I looked back to Elliot.

“Go,” she said, and started walking to her bag. “Mallot, we’re going to need heavy-duty straps to hold him down. They’re in the cabinet on the back wall.”

Mallot didn’t hesitate this time. I paused before climbing onto the bed. He had his back to me, but I had twelve or thirteen meters to cover and a bad shoulder. It might be my best chance.

A pulse weapon whined behind me and Mallot spun, slamming into the cabinet with a crash, then fell to one knee. The pistol skittered out of his hand and across the polished floor. I took three sprinting steps and dove for the weapon, knowing even before I hit how bad it would hurt.

But you had to be alive to feel pain.

My fingers clasped around the stock of the pulse weapon and I rolled up into a sitting position, my bad arm tucked into my side.

Mallot pushed at the floor with his hand, struggling to get up. His other arm hung limply, his shoulder charred and burned.

Elliot held a pulse weapon in shaking hands, still pointed in his general direction.

I stood. “You okay?”

Elliot nodded.

"You can lower your weapon." I pointed Mallot's weapon at him. He'd barely made it to his feet, so I risked a glance in Elliot's direction. She had her weapon pointed at the floor.

Mallot stumbled, and almost went back to a knee. He looked up at me with his strange eyes, almost pleading. "This doesn't change anything, sir. They won't stop, even without me. They're ruthless. They'll never stop, not until all of you are dead."

"Won't stop what? What are they planning?"

He shook his head.

"What are they going to do?"

He got all the way to his feet and met my eyes. He wasn't going to tell me.

I shot him in the face.

"Ah!" Elliot shouted. "What did you do that for? He was wounded!"

Mallot crumpled to the floor, what little remained of his head smoking.

"No choice," I said.

"What do you mean?" Elliot started quickly toward Mallot's corpse, then stopped.

"Exactly what I said. Come on, we need to move. The Cappans will have heard the shots. They'll be here any second." I glanced over at my armor in the corner. We didn't have much chance, but I'd go down fighting.

Elliot shook her head vigorously. "No. The building is soundproof."

I stopped. "You're sure?"

"It's bad medical practice to let people hear screams outside."

"I suppose it would be. We're still surrounded. We need a plan."

"You killed him," she said.

"I did."

"Why?"

I walked toward her. "He's High Councilor Mallot's son. When this story gets told, we don't want contradicting viewpoints."

"That's . . . that's cold blooded." I almost mentioned that she shot Mallot first.

"He killed Kwan," I said.

Elliot glanced toward her dead subordinate. "He did. Yeah. Fuck him."

"Exactly. Now we just have to figure out how to get by the Cappans guarding this place before they decide something is strange and come in to check."

"They won't come in," she said. "They can't. The door is coded."

"They could blow it down."

She shook her head. "We've made it well worth their while to protect this place."

"You've what?" I stared.

"We've traded technology for cooperation. We needed live Cappan volunteers for our work."

"You've traded . . . how long has this been going on?"

Elliot shrugged. "A while. Certainly since before my time here. There was a lot of research that went into this before we could put it into practice."

"Do you know what you've done?" My voice rose. "And for what?" I gestured at Mallot's body. "A bunch of unstable soldiers."

Elliot looked down at the floor. "We're going to have to adjust the procedure. Something isn't quite right."

"*Adjust the procedure?* There's no adjusting. Don't you see the problem here? You've given the Cappans technology and they're using it to kill people."

"I gave those soldiers their lives back! This is groundbreaking."

"You experimented on humans, Elliot."

"And it's working. I can figure this out. It's going to change medicine across the galaxy." She took a couple steps, then whirled and paced back.

I shook my head. "When word of this gets out . . . people are going to go berserk."

"They'll understand. The greater good. I'm not the only one, you know."

She still didn't get it. "Elliot. It's over. I don't care who else is involved. It's you who has to put a stop to it." I realized at that point she still had a weapon clutched in her hands. It didn't change the end result, but she was armed and I didn't know what she was thinking. "It's over."

She stood there, looking at the floor for at least half a minute, rocking slightly from foot to foot. "It can't be over. I can figure it out."

"Elliot . . ."

She raised her weapon and I took a step back. I had a weapon too, but something froze me in place.

I can't say why. I couldn't move. A hundred thoughts flashed through my mind. Did anyone else know what I knew?

"It's over," she said, softly.

It confused me, which also kept me paralyzed.

Before I could move she put the gun to her head and pulled the trigger.

I'm not the only one. I didn't know what she meant by that, but I didn't like the implication. Did she mean more people on Cappa Base, or was she referring to something broader? It wouldn't matter unless I could get off the planet.

Stepping over Elliot's body, I dug through her bag, looking for something I could use to call for help.

CHAPTER THIRTY-ONE

THE SEVEN MINUTES that I spent in decon dragged like an hour. No matter the situation, you didn't rush decontamination, so I waited. Scans, treatments, checks . . . everything you needed to make sure you didn't bring something alien back with you. The fact that I'd done it hundreds of times didn't make this one any easier.

The trip back spaceside had proved easy enough once I found the comm in Elliot's bag. Forty minutes later two companies of infantry dropped in with enough firepower to melt buildings while I hunkered down safe inside the medical facility.

Mac limped over to me as soon as I walked out of the decon facility.

Stirling stood back a couple paces, tapping his foot and looking like he had a stick up his ass.

I ignored him and shook Mac's hand. "You had that foot looked at?"

Mac hesitated, looking down at his damaged boot. "Not yet, sir."

"Get it done. I'll catch up with you after."

He nodded. "Yes, sir. Glad you made it, sir."

Stirling didn't even wait for Mac to get on the nearby cart. "What in the fu—what happened down there?"

I knew he didn't like to swear, but if there was ever a time for swearing, this had to be it.

"How many people made it back?" I asked, purposely lowering my voice since he'd raised his.

He paused. "Eight. Seven plus the pilot who ejected. Most of them are at the hospital."

I nodded.

"We need to debrief you. About what happened in the medical facility," he said.

"Nothing to debrief. Mallot shot Kwan, Elliot shot Mallot, then Elliot shot herself."

"I'd like to get you on a polygraph."

"Fuck you."

"Excuse me?" He stopped abruptly.

"You heard me. I have things to do." Serata gave me authority over the command, so I didn't have to do anything Stirling said unless I chose. I glanced around us at several soldiers staring. As mad as I was, we had nothing to gain by starting rumors about colonels arguing. "You want to talk, let's go somewhere private."

Stirling was about to say something more, but no matter what I thought of him, he hadn't gotten to where he was by being stupid. Spinning, he walked off and I followed, trying to ignore the throbbing pain in my shoulder.

"So what do you know?" He turned on me as soon as we made it through his office door.

"Close the door," I said.

He complied. "I need to know what you know."

"Shut the fuck up and listen to me," I said.

He stopped short.

"You want to know what I know? What I know is that there was a fucking high-tech anti-ship battery down there that you didn't know about, and it shot down several of our birds. What I know is that there's a rogue Special Ops unit on the surface, most of whom are working with the enemy. What do I know? I don't know fucking anything! And apparently, neither do you."

He clenched his fists. "I don't know anything? I'm on the hook for this entire war. And you wheel in here like you've got all the answers!"

"You think I asked for this? If you hadn't screwed this investigation to hell, I wouldn't even be here. And you know what? I'd be fine with that. Sixteen men and women are dead down on that planet. More if you count the pilots."

Stirling waited for a moment, as if seeing if I had anything else to say. "You done?"

I gnawed on my cheek and thought about it. "I think so. Sorry. Long day."

He nodded. "You want a drink?" He walked over to his desk and pulled out a bottle of something.

"Synthanol?" I frowned.

"It's all I've got."

Beggars and choosers. "Yeah, I'll have a belt," I said.

Stirling took a glass out of his drawer and poured two fingers into it, then held it out to me.

"Real glass for fake booze," I said. "You're not going to have one?"

He half smiled. "I've got a base to run and a war to fight. You might not have heard, but things went poorly planetside."

"Yeah." I tossed back half the liquor, cringing at the chemical aftertaste. I paused for a minute and threw down the rest of it, then sighed. "Thanks."

"Don't worry about it. Have a seat," he said.

I pulled a chair away from the table and flopped into it.

"How bad is the shoulder?"

I pursed my lips and breathed through my nose. "I don't know. Bad. Hurts inside. Something's not right."

"You should get it looked at," said Stirling.

"At Elliot's hospital? I don't think so."

He raised his eyebrows.

"Some of them are part of this. I don't know who, and I don't know how big a role they had."

Stirling's eyes left mine, losing their focus. "They're going to fry me for this," he said, almost caught between talking and a whisper.

"For what? You didn't do anything wrong."

"The enemy had a damned anti-ship battery. I didn't know about it."

"Nobody knew about it. It fooled everyone." Except that Karikov said that Stirling knew. He hadn't specifically mentioned the anti-ship battery, but he'd been clear about Stirling. I didn't know what to think. Even if I did, I'm not sure I'd have trusted my own judgment after the last two days. I needed rest.

"It wasn't everyone's job to know," he said.

"There are a lot of people whose job it was." I don't know why I tried to comfort him. I guess part of me felt bad for him. The part that didn't want to punch him in the face.

"And ninety-five percent of them work for me. I don't know what I'm going to do. I'm so screwed."

I wanted to grab him and shake him, but it wouldn't solve anything if I lost my shit again. "You're worrying about the wrong thing. There will be plenty of time for pointing fingers and assigning blame, later. Right now, you have to figure out what you do next."

He looked down at the floor for a moment. "Yeah. You're right."

"You've got to get your folks off of the surface." I don't know why that came to me, but as soon as I said the words, I knew I had it right.

He jerked his head up. "What? What are you talking about?"

"The report I got said that we've gravely misread the partisans, and that almost all of the Cappans are against us."

"That's impossible," said Stirling.

I raised my eyebrows. "Just like it's impossible that they hid a huge pulse weapon and a bunch of anti-air missiles?"

He stared at me, and for a minute I thought he might snap. "That would mean—"

"It would mean that there are a few million more enemy than you thought you had yesterday," I said.

Stirling sat silently for what seemed like a minute, but was probably less. "No way."

"I got the report myself," I said. "I saw military transport cases in a mine."

"Who gave you the report?"

"Karikov," I said.

"Karikov." He gave me a cold, flat smile. "And exactly how would you describe your interaction with Karikov? How was he?"

What did Stirling know? "He was . . . agitated."

"Agitated, or straight-up insane?" he asked. He *did* know. That pissed me off.

"You knew about him and you didn't tell me before now?" I started to stand, but fought the urge, tried to calm myself. "What else did you know?"

"I know he's an amputee living down on the surface that hasn't come up in a long, long time. And that any attempt to get in touch with him is blocked," said Stirling.

I paused. "But you asked if he was insane."

"Was he?" Stirling met my eyes and didn't blink.

"I'm getting sick of this game, Aaron." This time I did stand. I thought about ordering him to come clean, but that would give away information I wanted to hide a bit longer. I needed rest before I made that decision. "You know more than you're saying, and you've kept too many things from me."

"Was he crazy?" he asked, calmly.

I sighed. "I'm not sure he was all there. But he was lucid for a time."

"And you're basing your entire assessment of the enemy off of him. An assessment that is completely out of line with any other intelligence we've got. And you want me to run away," he said.

I paced, slamming my feet down into the cheap, industrial carpet. "I'm basing my assessment on more than that, including the bullets that kept getting shot at me. We got chased across a planet by hundreds of enemies that did things we didn't know they could do. Ask your pilots what they think."

"You're too close to the situation to see it clearly, Carl. I'm not running away because you have a hunch."

"Fuck, Aaron! It's not because I have a hunch, and you know it. And I'm not telling you to run away. Fall back until you've got a better picture. Pick your locations. Conduct assaults. Figure out where the Cappans might be hiding more surprises." I couldn't tell if he was spinning me up on purpose or not, but I'd pretty well lost it, either way. He needed to see the situation for what it was.

"We're working on the hidden weapons right now," he said. "I've got my intel focused on it. We'll find them and we'll destroy them."

"So why not get your people to safety while you do it?" I asked. "You have no idea when they might attack, and with how much."

Stirling started to pace, then turned back to me. "I'll have another brigade here in a couple of months. My guys can hold out for now, and when we get the added forces, then we can go on the offensive."

I started to respond but lost my words. A chill shot

through me. *Another brigade.* Serata mentioned adding a second brigade out here when I met him at his office months ago. Why was he rotating an additional brigade out here?

"Carl?"

"Yeah. Sorry, just thinking about something." I wondered if Stirling saw this as more than a coincidence. I wondered if he *knew.* Why did Serata have another brigade coming unless he knew they'd be needed?

"We'll monitor activity." His voice calmed measurably, like he was trying to pacify me. Asshole. "If we see anything out of the usual, anything we can't handle, we'll get our folks clear."

"Sure. I hope when you figure it out, it's not too late." It pissed me off that he couldn't see things clearly. Or that he wouldn't.

"It won't be. Even if they launched a full offensive, it would have to come from somewhere."

"They're hiding equipment in the mines. When you scan, you're going to pick up machinery, but you won't know if it's there to work the excavations or if it's something else."

Stirling frowned, lines forming on his forehead. "We'll get something in closer."

"You'll need to."

"We can work our biological assets. Folks on the ground. We've got some Cappan informers." He kept pacing, really thinking about it. He wasn't a good enough actor to fool me.

"If you can trust them," I said. His failure to see

the truth frustrated me more and more. It was as if he couldn't grasp the real meaning of my words. And he continued to miss the point.

"They're rated sources. Vetted. We've measured what they give us. Compared it to what we actually found," he said.

"Yeah, I get it." I just hoped that the Cappan sources hadn't been feeding known information in order to create a false sense of dependence. Even I thought that was too far, though. I was being paranoid.

Maybe.

"I need to get some sleep."

"Yeah, you do that," said Stirling. "Don't worry, we've got this."

"I know you do."

Maybe.

ALENDA MET ME outside the door to Stirling's outer office. "Heard things planetside went a little pear shaped."

I grunted. "A little."

"I should have been there, sir."

"And done what, Lex? What would it have changed?"

"I'd have been there, sir. I wouldn't have had to sit up here, wondering what the hell was going on when those ships went down."

"Then you'd either be dead, or wounded, or in the best case have a lot of souls to carry around in your brain for the rest of your life."

"Do you think it was better up here, sir? Powerless?" She turned away for a moment, but the angry twist of her lips remained when she faced me again.

"Yeah, you're right, Lex. I should have taken you," I lied. She didn't understand, and it was better that way. But she was mollified, and it was better than continuing to try to convince her about the horrors she'd missed.

"What do you need me to do, sir?"

"I'm going to sleep for eight hours. Don't let me go any longer than that. In eight hours and thirty minutes I want you to bring me the most up to date intelligence reports you can get about what's going on down on the surface."

She looked at me, then walked along beside me without speaking for a bit. "What am I looking for, sir?"

I looked at her.

"It will help me prioritize the most important reports, sir. It's a lot of data."

I breathed air out through my mouth. I had to decide once and for all if I trusted her to do what I needed instead of running to Stirling. I flipped a mental coin. She won. "Right. Any evidence of Cappan movement beyond a couple dozen. I don't care if they're friendly, enemy, armed, unarmed. Anything that moves."

"Yes, sir."

"I want to see everything intel gets on the mines, and anything that indicates any sort of weapon larger than a rifle," I added.

"Yes, sir. I know they've been gathering a lot on that since the fighters got shot down."

"Good," I said. "Anything else that looks like an attack, or a preparation for an attack."

"You really think there's going to be something, sir?"

"I'm not sure. I just think we don't know anything, and I know that's bad."

She pursed her lips, but if she wanted to say something, she decided against it. "Roger, sir."

We walked for a few minutes, then I stopped short of my door, where G One and G Two stood on guard. "What are you two doing here? I've been off base."

"We're guarding your quarters, sir," said G One, looking at me like I'd asked a ridiculous question.

I scrunched my face and rubbed my eyes with the heels of my hands. "Why?"

"Sergeant Mac told us to," she said. "Told us not to let anyone inside for any reason."

"Okay then, G. I'm going to sleep now. Don't let anyone in for eight hours. Nobody. Not even Sergeant Mac." I knew I'd have trouble sleeping, and if somehow I did manage to doze off, I couldn't afford someone waking me up.

"Yes, sir," the two Gs said.

Inside my room I went straight to the whiskey and poured myself three fingers, then I looked to see if I had any painkillers to dull the throbbing in my shoulder. You never thought about your shoulders until one of them hurt and you had to try to lie comfortably on a bed.

I was definitely thinking about it now.

I sipped my whiskey and savored it, so smooth after the horrible chemical burn of synth. I peeled my clothes off, struggling with my shirt because of the pain. My shoulder had already turned an ugly shade of purple and black that streaked down into my upper arm.

I'd finished half my drink before I stepped under the shower. My mind churned, even with the booze and the pulsing water. I kept coming back to the brigade. Serata had planned to send it before he even sent me out here. But he *still* sent me instead of sending a general. That was way out of the norm. Why would he do that? What did he expect me to do? He'd said that he wanted me because I didn't face any political pressure. I'd thought, at the time, that he meant from the senator. I wasn't so sure any longer.

Technically, I could wrap up my investigation. I had definitive evidence on Mallot and what happened to him. They'd already taken his body for transport home. I'd blasted his face, so they wouldn't see the eyes, but I couldn't rule out if some other test might discover the Cappan influence in his system. They'd certainly see he had two artificial legs, and that would raise suspicion.

In the end it wouldn't matter. I'd lied to Stirling about Mallot's death, but Baxter's people—what remained of them—they'd seen humans fighting beside the Cappans. They saw me captured. That story would get out, if it hadn't already, and when it did, somebody would start asking questions and draw the link back to Mallot. It might take weeks, it might even take months, but the truth always finds the light.

I padded out to the main room in my robe, whiskey still in my hand, almost empty. I needed to send Serata a note before I went to bed. I'd never sleep if I didn't.

I just had no idea what I was going to say.

Finally, though, the words came to me.

Sir—Found Mallot. He's dead. 100% confirmation. I saw the body, but there are complications I need to clean up with the investigation. We had issues with the Cappans that you have probably heard about. They've got more capability than I thought they did. Potentially dangerous situation. Not sure that Stirling appreciates it. He's counting on the additional brigade. What's the intent for that force?

Respectfully, Butler

I read it over, then went and poured another drink, came back, and read it again. I wanted to mention the brigade without directly questioning him about it. If he wanted to tell me something, he would. I took another swig of my liquor, then pushed send. I shut down the terminal. If I left it on, I'd be too tempted to get out of bed in half an hour and sit there, waiting for a response.

I shut down the rest of the room, poured a water to keep bedside, and lay down. I tried to push all the thoughts out of my head. Everything I'd seen the last two days. That part was easy. Easier, at least. I'd had a lifetime of practice of pushing dead people out of my thoughts. The future . . . that's where it got tricky. I could let go of the dead, but I couldn't let go of the living. The dead—nothing you did could change that. The living might soon be dead, though, unless someone did something. Unless *I* did something. I could hope for Serata to send me a magical solution, but in my heart I knew he wouldn't. I could hope for Stirling to get the right intel, to make the right decision. I didn't feel great about that, either.

My mind churned through all that until the exhaustion took me. At least for a while.

CHAPTER THIRTY-TWO

I WOKE UP SOME time later for no good reason I could explain. I don't know how long I slept, but it hadn't been eight hours. I'd have felt lucky if it were half that long. Once I lay there awake, though, I started to think that Serata would have answered by now, and once that thought took hold in my mind, I couldn't dig it out. It grew there like a weed.

I padded over to the terminal in bare feet wearing just my shorts. Sure enough, a message flashed as soon as I powered up and logged in.

Carl—Aware of the situation with the antiaircraft. Stirling says it's containable with little risk. Need you to put another set of eyes on it. We had intel that suggested they had more capability than we knew, but nothing like this. I can't transport anyone out there fast enough, and you're the guy I trust the most. Do whatever you need to do. Acknowledge on Mallot. Will organize a notification of the family within the next twenty-four hours and notify you when it's complete.

Serata

I sat in the dark room, bathed in the glow from the screen. I understood Serata to a point. He wanted my assessment and action, but he still didn't say *what* action. He had another brigade on the way, but if we expected a ground war against the entire Cappan population, we needed a lot more, and a lot heavier. And a lot of folks were going to die. Mostly Cappans, but a shitload of humans, too, both here and throughout the galaxy, if I believed Karikov. *Stirling says it's containable with little risk.* Idiot.

We could cut our own casualties if they authorized drones. If we put the big, mechanized killer bots down on the planet, it would be indiscriminate slaughter. That seemed unlikely given the political climate, however. The press would have a field day with that, and the politicians would lose their will soon after.

Shit.

ALENDA SHOWED UP exactly on time carrying a disposable container with mess-hall breakfast. "Eggs and fruit," she said, when I looked at it questioningly.

"Eggs and fruit? What kind of breakfast doesn't have meat in it?" I frowned.

"Yes, sir. I was messing with you. There's sausage."

"I've shot people for less." Sausage sounded perfect. It

had so much crap in it already that the mess hall couldn't screw it up. I took the container from her and pulled out a greasy patty, ignoring the rest of the fake food. "You want coffee?" I asked around a mouthful of meat.

She thought about it for longer than it required. "Yes, sir. I could drink a cup of coffee. Black."

I hit the button for coffee and gave her the first cup before returning to make one for myself. "Okay. What do you have for me?"

Alenda blew on her coffee. "Not much, sir. Activity planetside is consistent with normal patterns. Calmer, if anything. Less movement."

I stopped and turned to her. "So no attack imminent."

"Not that we can see, sir."

"What about the search for ground-to-air or ground-to-space weapons?" I asked.

"No trace yet, sir."

"Huh." I took a sip of coffee and snagged another sausage patty from my breakfast, which I'd set on the desk. "Well that's about useless."

"Can you give me a day, sir?"

I raised my eyebrows. "For what?"

"I have an idea. Had an idea, really. Last night."

She hid a smirk behind her coffee, as if thinking herself exceptionally clever. If I wasn't starving and focused on my sausage, I might have wondered why. "Sure. Take a day."

She knitted her eyebrows, probably surprised that I didn't ask about her idea. I was just messing with her. She'd tell me anyway. Kind of a dick move on my part.

"We didn't have anything to scan deep underground," she said, confirming my judgment about her patience.

She waited for me to comment, but I just took another bite of sausage. "So I thought about who might be able to do that sort of thing, and I checked with the mining companies. They have liaisons who work up here. It turns out they have commercial sensors that do deep planet scans."

"Makes sense. To look for minerals." I had to admit, she'd gotten my attention.

"Exactly, sir. Except they can do more than that. They can detect pretty much any anomaly in the ground up to five thousand meters down."

Wow. I had no idea. "That *would* help."

She nearly vibrated with energy. "Yes, sir. I asked them how long it would take to do a scan of the entire inhabited land area." She paused, waiting for me to ask how long.

"How long?" I gave up playing games. She'd done good work, and now I wanted to know the rest.

"Four months. So I narrowed the parameters of the search to the current mine locations, based on your conversation with Colonel Karikov."

Had I told her that? I couldn't remember. It didn't matter. "What did they say?"

"They thought it was silly, sir. They know what's in the mines, because those were the areas where they did their most in-depth studies."

"But the studies are old," I said.

"Yes, sir. Months. Even years in some cases. So I convinced them to do it."

"Nice. How'd you do that?"

"You don't want to know, sir. Contracts. Supplies. Access. Basically, we owe them some favors."

I chuckled. "You're right. I don't want to know."

"They can do it in two passes. Two days. But we'll get the first half of the data today."

I nodded and took a sip of my coffee. "Nice work, Lex." She deserved to be proud. But it left me wondering what I'd do while I waited. "How hard would it be to send a platoon over to apprehend Major Chu and bring her here?"

She scrunched her face up. "The Special Ops guys won't be pleased, sir."

"Obviously. But what are they going to do about it?" I asked.

"Complain to their bosses, probably," she said.

"And their boss is?"

She looked at me, as if wondering what I was getting at. "Colonel Karikov."

"Right. Karikov. Who's planetside, maybe dead, and even if he's not, he's unlikely to answer. They'll call down there and get some operations officer, who will claim to be speaking for Karikov."

"Sir . . . you lost me."

I smiled. "The only one who can chew me out is Karikov himself. Colonel to colonel. I'm betting he won't do it."

"So you're bluffing," she said. "I don't understand the game."

"Not exactly bluffing. More like confirming a theory. Plus I want to talk to Chu."

She still looked confused. "Yes, sir. I'll get some people over there."

"Tell them that if she doesn't come willingly, they can drag her," I said.

"Sir, you know that if you give that order to soldiers . . ." She spoke with caution in her voice, like I should know better. Which I did.

"That's why I gave it."

She nodded. "Yes, sir. I'll get on it."

"Thanks." I poked at the reconstituted eggs in my tray and decided against them. The fruit didn't look bad, but I let that sit too. Instead I pulled up a listing of combat assets in the theater and started to read. I needed to know what I had available.

CHU WALKED IN smiling, not nearly as pissed off as I expected. That disappointed me a little bit. Maybe she hid it well. Good trait to have. Probably one reason she was in Spec Ops in the first place. I gained a little respect for her, even though I should have known. Serata liked her, and the general didn't make many mistakes about people.

Chu wore full uniform, which told me that either she'd known something was coming or the people I sent gave her time to change. I'd bet on the latter.

"What's going on, sir?" Chu spoke like she'd popped in on her own for a chat.

"Needed to see you." I stood up and walked over to shake her hand.

"Yes, sir. The soldiers made that pretty clear. You could have called." She took my hand firmly, but not overly aggressive.

I met her eyes. "I could have. I wasn't sure you'd come."

"What are you talking about, sir? Of course I'd come."

"When was the last time you talked to Colonel Karikov?" I changed the direction of the conversation, purposely not answering her question to keep her a little off balance.

She furrowed her brow. "I don't know, sir. Yesterday, I guess."

"No. When was the last time you actually talked to Karikov himself, rather than someone speaking for him?"

"Sir, what are you getting at? I never talk to the colonel directly. I haven't since I've been here."

"So all his orders are relayed," I said.

"That's right, sir." She frowned, but I didn't care.

"You can sit if you want." I took the desk chair, faced it toward the sofa and plopped down in it. "What did they tell you yesterday? That there was a firefight?"

Chu sat on the right arm of the sofa. "Yes, sir. Minor firefight, everything under control."

I stared without speaking for a moment. "Minor firefight? So they didn't mention getting overrun by a couple hundred Cappans?"

Chu's eyes widened. It either legitimately surprised her or she was the best actor I'd ever met. "Sir . . . what are you talking about?"

Ignoring that, I said, "Chu, I'm not even sure that Colonel Karikov is still alive. He's sure as shit not in charge. Did anybody mention to you that half your guys were fighting for the other team?" I tried to keep the anger out of my voice, but failed.

"Sir, that's impossible." She stared, as if trying to read my face, figure out what I was playing at. I doubt she'd find anything. But it didn't matter, because I was telling her anyway.

"Screw impossible. I was there. I talked to Karikov, I got shelled by a few dozen rockets, and then chased by a bunch of pissed-off Cappans, aided by some of your people."

Chu didn't speak for a long moment. She nodded her head up and down slightly, but not enough to mean anything. "That explains a few things," she said, finally.

"It does? Like what?"

"Well the obvious one is why Colonel Karikov never speaks to me. If he's a hostage . . . but that can't be." She shifted herself off the arm onto the couch itself, then sagged back into it.

"It can be," I said. "Here's one thing I can guarantee: There are a lot of things that we think can't be, that absolutely can."

Chu nodded again. "Okay, sir. I'll make contact with them."

"You can put a call through?"

"No, sir. Only at specific times. The enemy jams their commo, and they have to . . ." Her voice trailed off.

"They can only contact you on their schedule, right?" I knew the answer, but I wanted to hear her say it.

"Yes, sir. But that's not unusual for our teams in the field." Her tone told me that she knew it sounded weak, even as she said it.

"Right. So nobody wondered why."

She nodded. "It's a little odd, sir, but not so far out that I thought to question it. I've got to get some people down there."

"Not going to happen. They've got hidden anti-air weapons. Until we find them, shuttles would be easy targets."

"I read that report, sir. I thought it had to be exaggerated. Pilots overreacting to shoulder-fired weapons."

I shook my head. "No overreaction. I saw the shoot-downs live."

"Fuuuck." Her face sagged.

"That sums it up," I said. "Even if you could get down there, who knows how many armed Cappans they have crawling around?"

"I have a pretty good guess at that, sir."

I paused. "How's that? You don't even know how many of your people are left alive."

"No. But I know how many weapons we shipped, sir."

I took a deep breath in through my nose. Of course she did. We'd been arming the Cappans who fought on our side. Not with our weapons. They used lighter rifles with different trigger mechanisms that fit their short, stumpy fingers. But we made them. "How many?"

"In the last six months, seven thousand. Give or take," she said.

"Okay, that's not so bad." Seven thousand we could

handle. Although they clearly had heavy weapons from another source, so we couldn't be sure they didn't have more rifles.

"We've been arming them for a lot longer than six months, though, sir."

I drew my lips into a flat line. "What's your total number? Best guess it for me."

"Forty, sir."

"Shit."

"What are we going to do, sir? I've got to call this in to my higher headquarters. Not Colonel Karikov. Higher."

"I've got a feeling they already know," I said.

Chu slumped deeper into the sofa. "They can't, sir."

I shrugged. I was done trying to convince her of what could or couldn't be. "I hope you're right. Do what you need to do." It didn't matter. Even the fastest reinforcements would be too late.

CHAPTER THIRTY-THREE

DONE WITH CHU, my next order of business was MEDCOM. I had to do something about Elliot's experiments before word got out on its own. I needed to send another message to Serata, though I almost didn't want to. Somewhere deep down I think maybe I still wanted to solve this without bringing the general too far into the details. At least that's what I told myself. I think that's why I didn't tell him in my previous message.

Once I told him everything . . . well, at that point it would no longer be airlock-tight. Hell, it already leaked out of a half dozen cracks, all of them getting wider by the minute. But formally reporting on the genetic research . . . that would blow the entire oxygen supply. I knew better—at least, subconsciously I did—I couldn't keep it quiet for long. It had to come out at some point. Too many people knew to keep it quiet.

And yet my orders were to close it up tight, and I didn't like to fail. I compromised and sent half a message. A piece of what I should have said earlier.

Sir—Acknowledge your guidance. Situation is worse than initially reported. Colonel Elliot, the Hospital Commander, was involved in illegal activity planetside that includes Cappans. She's KIA, but need MEDCOM to act immediately to give me access to the hospital in order to determine other involvement. Need authority to arrest MEDCOM personnel. Highest priority.

I might not have conveyed the severity of the issue, but I had to trust Serata to trust me. Which doesn't make a lot of sense. Except it did.

PLAZZ WAS WAITING outside my door, leaning against the far wall, when I exited. I'd planned to go to the gym and had dressed for it. She had dressed appropriately for stalking, apparently, in tan pants and a white shirt, her hair up in some sort of thing in back.

"Your guards wouldn't let me in," she said.

I glanced at G One. "Huh. Bad guards." G One gave no reaction at all. I kind of liked that about her. Sometimes you need a good straight man. Or woman.

Plazz rolled her eyes. "I'm sure. You've been avoiding me. But at least you dressed up for the occasion."

I looked down at my gym attire, then started walking, motioning for Plazz to come along. "Give us some space, guys." G One hustled a dozen meters to the front and G Two dropped back behind us. Mac hadn't returned. Probably recovering.

"I haven't been avoiding you. I just didn't seek you out," I said.

"You didn't answer your line, and your major told me you were too busy to talk."

"Odd." I hadn't told Alenda to do that, but I couldn't fault her judgment. Generally any opportunity to put off a reporter made sense. "Not my intention."

"You're going to the gym with an injured shoulder?" she asked.

"This?" I nodded to my shoulder. "It's not bad."

"Really? Can you raise your hand over your head?"

"That's doctor-patient privileged information," I said.

"That only applies to doctors giving information about their patients, not the other way around."

I looked over at her. "You sure?"

"Pretty sure."

"I'm going to take a ride. They've got a good holo bike here. Makes you feel like you're riding out in the real world."

"Which world?" she asked. "Cappa?"

"That would suck. They could probably program it, but not for me. I'm taking a nice ride down a shady path beside a lake. I can't just sit there in my room. I'll go stir crazy."

"So the investigation is complete?"

"I didn't say that," I said, a little too quickly.

"But if you had more to do, you wouldn't be sitting in your room." She made it hard to tell what she knew already and what she didn't. I guess that was the point.

"Still ongoing." I took a more formal tone. "I can't comment."

"Yeah, don't give me that bullshit."

I put my hand over my heart. "I'm hurt."

"I know," she said. "You're hurt from a daylong firefight down on the surface. What was that about?"

"Who'd you talk to?"

She smiled without showing her teeth. "Could have been any of a hundred people, now, couldn't it? It's hardly a secret."

"Still. Who told you?"

"I'm not going to re—"

Light blossomed in front of us and a wave of force flung me backward through the air. The sound followed, an earsplitting crack. It seemed to come an eternity after the flash, even though it had to be no more than a split second.

I crumpled in a heap after what might have been a full flip. My shoulder exploded into fire, a lesser pain ripped into my lower leg, hot but distant. I tried to roll over, find a target, grab my sidearm. The corridor filled with smoke and dust, obscuring the source of the explosion with haze. Plazz lay on the floor to my right, huddled up into herself, her head buried in her arms.

I continued to scan for targets. G One had been up there near the bomb, but the debris in the air obscured her. I forced myself to my knees, stumbled, then continued to my feet. I wobbled as I walked, staggering forward into the smoke. G Two rushed up to me.

"Sir, get down!" His voice sounded distant, like someone speaking underwater.

"We need to—"

"I got it, sir! Get down!" He put his hands on each of my shoulders, sending a new wave of agony through me, and I jerked away.

"Gaaah!"

"Sorry, sir. I need to go find Gute." He turned and shuffled forward into the smoke.

An alarm clanged somewhere that sounded far away but probably wasn't. I rubbed at my ears.

The smoke disappeared through vents, some kind of emergency system sucking it from the hall. When it cleared enough, I could see G Two bent over what was left of his partner. A red mess. She'd taken the blast too close. Her position walking well in front of us probably saved my life. It had to have been a proximity trigger. If it had been a remote, whoever set it off would have waited for me. It might have been ego, but I had to believe I was the primary target.

I tried to cut through the fog in my brain. I put my hand to my forehead to wipe away a bead of sweat and it came away smeared with blood. It hadn't even stung until I touched it, but afterward it burned. Maybe more of an abrasion than a cut. That was my expert diagnosis without a mirror. I did have some experience getting blown up though.

Plazz still lay on the floor. She'd untucked her head, but was still curled into a half ball.

"You okay?" I asked. My voice sounded funny, barely audible over the ringing in my ears. "Karen?" I tried to make eye contact, but she wasn't seeing me. "Karen!"

"Huh?" She turned her head.

"You okay?" I shouted.

People started arriving—a few at first—but the trickle quickly turned into a flood and swarmed around us. Plazz never did answer me before we got separated by emergency personnel.

I'm not sure when I sat back down, but I struggled to my feet again, ignoring the soldier who told me not to get up. I stumbled, which I'm sure made the soldier say *I told you so* in his head. I disregarded what was going on in his head and my own and forced my way through the gathering crowd back toward my quarters. I should have gone to check on G, but the MPs had started to cordon off the area and I couldn't focus enough to argue with them. They'd secure the site until explosive ordnance got there and did an assessment of the bomb, took forensics.

"Sir? You're bleeding from your head." Alenda accosted me as I cleared the majority of the crowd.

"True," I said.

"Are you okay, sir? You're wobbling. That explosion . . ."

"I'm okay. G didn't make it. Plazz . . . I think she's okay," I said.

"Sir, you need to go to the hospital," she insisted.

I kept walking toward my room, forcing Alenda to turn around to walk with me. "I'm fine."

"Sir, you probably have a concussion. You might be in shock."

"I'm not in shock."

"Sir, you have a piece of metal sticking out of the front of your leg."

I looked down. A finger-sized piece of jagged shrapnel had wedged itself on the inside of my shin, blood oozing around it. That explained the pain. Perhaps I was in shock after all. "What did you find from the mining company's scan?"

Alenda's face lit up, momentarily throwing her off of the topic of my injuries. "Eleven mines show significant anomalies, sir."

"Eleven. How significant?" I asked.

"Very significant," she said. "Dozens of unexplained pieces of machinery in some cases. I've asked them to expand their search to look at areas other than known mines as well."

I nodded. "Have our assets run an elemental spectrum scan over the eleven sites."

Alenda looked at me. "That's a good idea, sir. I should have thought of that."

"Pretty good for a guy with a concussion," I said.

"Sir, you really need to go to the hospital."

"Alenda, it might have been the hospital that tried to blow me up. No way am I going to make it easy for them. Just get me a medic to pull this shrapnel out of my leg and glue it up."

Alenda breathed out audibly in about the most outward sign of disrespect I'd seen from her. I probably deserved it. "Roger, sir. Will you at least get off your feet?"

"Sure." We reached my door and I put my hand on it to activate. "But bring me the results of the elemental spectrum as soon as you get it, I don't care what else is going on."

"Yes, sir. I'll send a medic and get you more security as well."

I stopped. "Yeah. Check on G Two, also. He's going to be in bad shape over his partner."

Alenda nodded. "Yes, sir."

THE MEDIC TOOK longer than I planned. I wouldn't let him give me anything for the pain because my head was fuzzy enough already, so he had to work a local anesthetic for my leg before he could pull out the metal. Then it stuck. Sometimes it's just one of those days. He finally worked it free without causing too much additional blood or screaming and got the wound closed, but by the time he finished I couldn't feel anything from the knee down. He said it would wear off in an hour or so, but the imaginary itching had already started.

Mac rushed in as the medic opened the door to leave, almost bowling him over. "Sir, what happened? I heard about an explosion!"

"Sit down, Mac." I didn't know if he knew about G yet, plus I didn't want to keep looking up from my position lying on the sofa.

"Are you okay?" He stared at the bandage around my leg and whatever the medic had done to my face. I had a new sling for my shoulder, too, but Mac knew about that injury already.

"I'm fine," I said. "I've had worse. Sit."

Mac took the desk chair and pulled it over. "I heard about G, sir."

I nodded. "It sucks. I'd pushed her farther ahead so

I could talk to the reporter. If not, the blast would have got me too."

"Yes, sir. I talked to the guys at the blast site."

"Are you okay?" I asked. "How bad were you beat up from planetside?"

"I'm good, sir. I mostly needed rest. Nothing broken."

I breathed out deeply. "Good. I'm going to need you."

"We're getting a squad for protection, sir."

I nodded slowly. "I need to see how Plazz is doing."

"They took her to the hospital. Her brain got rattled, but she's okay, I think. Treated and released. A little out of it."

"That could be the blast, or it could be the shock of the attack," I said. "You never know how somebody is going to react to something like that."

Mac nodded. "Yes, sir. Ain't that the truth?"

"You checked on Hardy lately?"

"Yes, sir. He's doing well. Chasing around some female doc, I think. Might be he plays hurt for a couple extra days."

"Get him released as quickly as you can. I don't want him hanging around there any longer than absolutely necessary."

Mac stared at me for a moment. "Sir, what the fuck is going on?"

I shook my head. "I wish I knew. But until I know who set that explosive, I'm not taking any chances."

"You think you know who it was, sir?"

I half shrugged. I didn't want to tell Mac too much.

I trusted him, but I also didn't want to drag him into the crosshairs.

"All I know is that there are people in the hospital who know things, and someone tried to blow me up." I didn't really think one of the doctors did it, but I couldn't rule it out and I was done taking chances.

Mac shifted his lips to one side. "Wow."

"Yeah."

"I'll see what I can do to spring the lieutenant, sir."

"Thanks. Now help me over to my terminal," I said.

Mac came over and I put my good arm over his shoulders so he could support my numb leg. I was running out of body parts that worked. We moved awkwardly over to the terminal and I sat down, taking a few deep breaths to relax after the strain.

"You going to be okay, sir?"

"I'm good. You get Hardy."

Mac nodded and disappeared. I punched up my messages, and Serata's flashed on the screen so I brought it up.

Butler—Contain the situation. Expect no help from MEDCOM.

What. The. Fuck.

One line, two sentences. I had a serious situation that could affect the entire galaxy if it got out of control, and he gave me two sentences and zero help. It didn't make sense.

I started to reply, but stopped myself. If I answered Serata, I'd just get myself in trouble. He'd put up with a lot from me, but not the vitriol I had boiling in me right then. I needed to let his message sit. On a whim, I wrote to Chu.

> *Chu—I need to talk to Karikov. No alternates acceptable. Get the man on the line to me. He's got four hours or I take action without his input.*
>
> *Butler*

I had no idea what I would do if he didn't answer in four hours. Hell, I had no idea what I'd do if he *did* answer. Maybe Serata's vague message inspired me. Maybe I was just being an asshole. Either way, I hoped my message might force something to happen. Anything, as long as it gave me a direction I could move. I had a feeling it would work. Someone tried to kill me and failed. A lot of men might take that personally, get angry. I wouldn't let it affect me, but nobody else knew that. They didn't know how I'd react, so they didn't know what I'd do in four hours. I was betting that they'd want to find out before it happened.

My door buzzed and I shut down my monitor before calling for it to open.

"Sir, you're not going to believe this." Alenda spoke before she even got in the room.

"I don't know, somebody attacked me in the corridor of a friendly base, and that's the second time that's happened since I've been here. I'd believe a lot right now," I said.

"I've got the elemental spectrum scans back."

"Damn. Already? That was fast."

"Yes, sir. I diverted the assets from all other missions."

I nodded. "Okay, what did you find?"

"Sir . . . three of the sites." She paused. "Tritium, deuterium, lithium."

"Oh fuck," I said.

"Yes, sir."

"Fusion engines."

"Yes, sir. Or at least, all the elements needed for one. And the tritium levels suggest that they're either testing or already working."

I spun my chair back and forth for a moment. If they had fusion engines that worked . . . I searched back through my memory for what space assets we had that might be able to blockade them. I'd just looked at it, but I couldn't remember clearly. I shook my head and recalled the information. We didn't have much. Not enough. Space was too big. Once they cleared the atmosphere, they could go anywhere.

Fusion engines. Shit.

"Sir, they could—"

"Yeah," I interrupted. "If they've got fusion engines, they could leave the planet. If they reached the nearest jump site, they could disappear and we'd never find them."

"But they're in a mine. The ships, if they are ships . . . they can't be that big. There's no way, right?"

I stopped rocking in my chair. "At this point, I'm not sure I'd bet on what they might or might not be able to do. Because if I was betting, I'd have lost a lot of money on 'There's no way the enemy has fusion fucking engines.'"

Alenda nodded. "Yes, sir. They might not be . . ." she stopped, perhaps sensing that I was going to continue my diatribe if she said anything else.

"Sorry," I said. "Go ahead. Say what's on your mind."

"Yes, sir. I was going to say that it might not be ships. It might not even be engines. We'd see a similar signature from—"

"From weapons." I finished her thought for her.

"Yes, sir."

"Fuck."

"Yes, sir."

Fusion weapons. Just one would be the end of Cappa Base. I hadn't checked our defense systems. We had them, but no base had ever been attacked from a planet, so I didn't know what they'd handle. We parked the base far enough from the planet so it wasn't supposed to need defense from it.

A fusion missile wouldn't even have to hit us to destroy us. I didn't know if that was worse or better than a ship powered with a fusion engine. Hell, they might have both. Launch at the base and use the chaos to provide cover for escaping ships. Not that they had anywhere to go. We knew all the habitable planets. They'd eventually have to land on one. Or slam a fusion bomb into it. They could hit us anywhere. If they picked the right targets they could kill tens of millions. Or they could smuggle themselves in somewhere. They had humans. Or mostly humans. I didn't know how far their network extended.

I tried to slow my breathing, control myself, concentrate. My head had started to hurt, though I don't know if it came from the earlier explosion or the situation Alenda alerted me to.

"Are you okay, sir?" asked Alenda.

I nodded without looking at her. "I'm good." My mind went back to Serata's message. *Contain.* Shit. How did I contain this? I sat there for I don't know how long, trying to figure it out. Alenda stood by without speaking. I don't know why. Maybe she sensed something. Maybe she thought she needed permission to leave.

"We've got to tell Stirling," I said, finally.

"Yes, sir." Her tone said she agreed. When people answer you with 'yes, sir' all the time, you learn to read more into it.

"I need to wait here in case Karikov messages. You go brief Colonel Stirling. Talk to him personally. I don't want this filtered through an analyst, or buried in some report. Tell him exactly what you told me, and if he doesn't understand the significance, tell him what I think it means," I said.

"Yes, sir," she said.

CHAPTER THIRTY-FOUR

THE DOOR WHOOSHED open and Stirling entered my quarters exactly seven minutes later. I hadn't moved from my spot in front of the monitor, but I minimized my messages. I didn't need to stand up and have him see me wobble.

"Are you okay, Carl? That blast—"

"Yeah. I'm good. How's Plazz?"

"She's okay. Mild concussion, no shrapnel."

"Huh. That's a miracle. Lucky woman."

"EOD says that Sergeant Gutierrez absorbed most of the blast."

"Sergeant?" G One had been a corporal.

"We had her promoted," he said. "It won't mean much, but it's a little more money for her family."

"Smart. Thanks," I said.

"Wish it was my idea. My XO came up with it."

I nodded. "Still. It's a good action."

"It's not enough."

"No." I paused. "It never is, though. Still, you can catch the asshole that did it. It wouldn't help her, but it would sure make *me* feel better."

"We're looking now. We've locked down the entire base. Nobody moves in the halls without explicit clearance. We're going room to room," he said. "We've shut down all travel off base, too."

I raised my eyebrows. That was a serious step that would piss off all the commercial entities that used Cappa Base. The situation warranted it, but I hadn't thought Stirling had it in him to make those kinds of waves. Perhaps he'd come to the same conclusion I had. That we couldn't contain this anymore. "Probably called for. Whoever it was killed a soldier."

Stirling nodded. "It's more than that, though. We got lucky that the bomb was in an interior corridor, but if someone can do that . . . what if next time it's against an exterior wall? Or in a crowded room? We've got to take every chance to stop it, and if that means inconveniencing everyone on the base . . . well they've had it easy for a while now. They'll survive."

Now it made sense. He took action because if someone breached the station—hard, but possible—it could kill dozens before the emergency systems sealed the breach. Maybe more, if the attacker set it up right. A commander's career wouldn't survive something like that. Good to know I could still count on Stirling's desire for self-preservation. It kept me from having to order him.

"But you're not here to give me an update on the search," I said.

"No."

"Alenda found you? Gave you the report."

"She did. I told her to wait outside." He walked over and sat on the arm of the sofa.

"What do you think?" I asked.

He sat silently for a moment. "I don't know. Tritium. Ship or weapon. Has to be, right? At least ninety percent."

I nodded. "Yeah. But which?"

He took a deep breath and blew it out. "Hard to say. I think we have to plan like it's both."

"I agree," I said. "And I think you've got to pull your people off the surface. Immediately."

He sat silently. "That's a big step. It changes the whole war forever."

I kept my voice level, kept the sarcasm out of it. "If they set off a fusion weapon near one of your camps, it changes the whole war forever too. And it's much more likely they can do that than to fire one up here successfully."

He rocked back and forth a bit before he spoke. "A ship is easier. I already ordered a temporary embargo. Nothing goes to the surface except military vessels, nothing comes up without being searched. If they want to get away, they'll have to run. We can't contain everything if they make a fast rush for a jump point, but at least we'll know."

I nodded. "If you search ships, they'll know you're onto them."

"Definitely. But what's the choice?"

I sat for a moment, thinking. What was the choice? I hadn't thought that part of it through. I'd been focused on the soldiers planetside. "Don't give them time."

Stirling started to speak, then stopped. He clasped his hands together. "What do you mean?"

"Force them to act. Order all ships off the surface in the next four hours, regardless of mission."

He sat, contemplating. "That would make it harder for us to search them all. Easier for one to get through."

"It would also give them no time to load something they didn't have planned without you being able to spot it," I said.

He started nodding slowly, then stood and clapped his hands once. "I like it. We know where the contract ships are. We can focus the collection assets before we give the order."

"Good." I liked that he added his own take to it. The more he thought it was his own idea, the better he'd execute. "Confiscate silver, too. That's what the contractors will try to get out."

"That will piss them off. Good call," he said.

"What about the forces planetside?" I asked.

He sat back down. "I hate to do it, but you're right. I'll send a note to SPACECOM asking for the authority."

"No!" I started to spring up out of my chair, got a head rush, and fell back into my seat.

"Easy, Carl."

"Don't worry about me. But you can't contact SPACECOM. If you wait to ask permission, they'll debate it, ask for more data, then debate it some more. Maybe you get an answer in a day. More likely two or three. And all that time your people sit down there, vulnerable."

He threw his hands up. "I know it. But I can't make that call. I can't end the war."

"Fine. If you won't make the decision, I will. I'm

giving you a direct order. Pull your people off the planet right now. You can notify SPACECOM after you've started." I waited for him to explode. He didn't know I had authority to give that order, and it would appear as me stepping way outside my authority.

He sat without speaking. I'd stunned him into silence. Or so I thought. "Okay, I'll give the order," he said.

I started to speak before it registered, ready to direct him to my authority, then I stopped, speechless. *He knew.* He knew before he ever came to see me that I had the authority. More important, he *wanted* me to give the order. He wanted me to cover his ass so he could do the right thing, but have someone to blame if it went wrong.

And it would go wrong. No matter what happened, it was the kind of decision that news people and politicians and even military leaders would second-guess. If only they'd considered this, if only they'd thought about these other factors. They'd armchair-general the decision to death, after they had more information than we'd ever see. They'd find something wrong with the decision, no matter what decision I made. It's what they always did. So . . .

Fuck them.

Part of me wanted to punch Stirling in his coward face. Another part of me wanted to slap myself for bailing him out and making it easy on him. But it didn't change anything. We had the information we had, and I made the decision I had to. But then, that's why Serata sent a dead-end colonel out here.

Someone who could make a decision without political pressure.

Then it hit me.

"How long have you known?" I asked.

"Known what?" he asked, but his voice caught. Still not good at lying.

I fixed his eyes with mine. "Aaron . . . you know exactly what I'm asking. How long have you known I had that authority?"

He looked down at the floor. "A while. I don't know. A few days, at least."

I took a deep breath and blew it out slowly through my nose. "Okay. This is important. How'd you find out?" I had a suspicion, but I needed him to confirm it. What he said could change my thinking.

He wouldn't meet my eyes. "I just know," he said, after a minute.

"Not good enough. I really need to know how." Even as I said it, I knew the harder I pushed the more he'd resist.

"Sorry," he said. "It doesn't matter."

I bit back my response, started to speak, then waited another few seconds to control myself. Asshole.

"Fine. Give the order to evacuate the planet. Let me know when it's done." I turned back to my monitor and pulled up a screen full of information. I didn't read it. I just didn't want to look at Stirling anymore.

I SAT THERE for a long time after Stirling left, staring at the same meaningless screen. Alenda didn't come in. Maybe she saw the look on Stirling's face and thought better of it. Maybe he said something, told her not to. I was fairly sure she'd been keeping my confidence recently, but it started to gnaw at me, the way things did when things got messed up and you had too much time to think. What could she have given away? I hadn't told her about the order. He got that from somewhere else. I knew where he had to have got it from, but my mind still wouldn't accept it.

Serata had to have told him. It could have been someone close to Serata, another senior leader. Stirling surely had connections. But my gut told me that Serata did it, or at least directed it. But why? I thought about it a bit longer then decided it didn't matter. Stirling knew, and even if he didn't, he'd have known once I gave the order. Nothing changed.

I couldn't sit still and think about it, so I got up, despite my balky leg, and limped to the door. Four soldiers I didn't know stood outside.

"Find Sergeant Mac," I said. "Tell him I want to go see Karen Plazz." Karikov might call, but I figured I had some time. I'd given him four hours, and I didn't expect him to rush.

It took them five minutes to get Mac and another five for me to convince him that I could walk. It took us ten minutes to walk to Plazz's room, which was five minutes longer than it would have taken if I'd been telling the truth and actually able to walk. I scuffled, dragging my feet on the no-slip flooring of the deck. To his credit, Mac didn't say "I told you so."

I was starting to appreciate how my rank kept me from hearing that recently.

The door opened into a room just big enough for a bed and a small desk. A half-packed bag sat on the floor, Plazz busy stuffing clothes into it.

"They sure don't give you a lot of space." I stepped inside, leaving my entourage of guards in the hall.

She looked up from her task. "You look like hell."

I chuckled. "Thanks. How are you feeling?"

"I've got a headache." She stood up. "Mind if I close the door?"

I glanced outside where two of my guards were looking in. "We're fine," I told them. "Go ahead."

She hit the button and the door zipped shut. She pulled the chair out from the desk and offered it to me, then sat on her bed.

"Going somewhere?" I nodded toward her bag.

She shrugged. "I think I'm going to hang it up here, yeah."

"How come? The attack?"

She thought about it. "The perspective. The attack just triggered it. I've been out here away from real life for a long time, and why? What's here?"

"You got attacked on a SPACECOM base. That's a story."

She shrugged again. "Sure. It's a story for a day. Maybe two. But it's not the kind of story I came to tell."

"What do you want to tell?"

She didn't answer immediately. "Why are you here, Carl? I mean . . . not here in this room. Here. At Cappa."

I met her eyes. "You know why. The investigation."

"Right. The investigation, I know that. But why *you*? Why send a guy who lost his daughter here? What about this investigation was *that* important?"

I looked down, thinking about the question. She'd given voice to the question that had been burning in the back of my mind. It was never about finding Mallot. When I looked back up, she was still staring at me.

"Did you think I didn't know about that?" she asked.

"That's not it," I said. In truth, I hadn't thought about it. Of course she knew.

"You got quiet there."

I nodded. "You're a good reporter."

"Why do you say that?" she asked.

"You ask a lot of really hard questions."

She sighed. "I'm sorry."

"No, don't be. People need to ask those kinds of questions." She'd asked the question I should have asked myself. I stood, using my good arm to help lever me out of the chair. "You should unpack your bag."

She stood as well. "Why's that?"

"There's a story here that you're going to want to tell."

"What—"

I waved my hand, cutting her off. "Don't ask, because I can't answer right now. Give it a day. I think you'll have your answers."

She stared at me for several seconds. "Okay. I can give it a day."

I nodded. She couldn't have left anyway, with Stirling's flight embargo, but I took it as a small victory that she made the decision on her own. "Hope you feel better."

I had Mac call for an electric cart to transport me back. I didn't need the additional strain on my leg, and more important, I needed to think. Serata had put me into an impossible situation, some of which he knew about and some of which he probably didn't. Serata didn't do anything by accident. He sent me for a reason, and he trusted me to decipher that reason and act. As I turned over what I needed to do in my brain, I shivered despite the uniform temperature of the processed space-station air.

CHAPTER THIRTY-FIVE

I FLIPPED OPEN THE feed on my monitor to operations and looked over recent actions to make sure that Stirling followed through on the decision to withdraw. He had.

Orders had already gone out, which made me think that Stirling had prepared ahead of time, which meant that he suspected that I'd give him the directive to evacuate. Asshole.

I wondered where else he might have predicted my response. I thought through my recent actions but didn't see anything obvious. Someone had predicted my path away from my room and planted a bomb, but that hadn't been Stirling. Not possible.

I watched the screen update, which it did at about the same rate that the sun crossed the sky in mid-afternoon. It served no purpose, but I couldn't pull myself away. I couldn't even extrapolate a timeline for the withdrawal. It would depend on how much they tried to take off the surface and what equipment they decided to abandon. We could pull people off easily. The years and years of built-up stuff . . . that would take time. I resisted the urge to call Stirling. He'd have made the decision on what to take and what to leave, and I could live with it, whatever he chose.

The Cappans hadn't moved against us, which was a good break. I didn't know how long I could count on that. They could fire anti-ship missiles at a departing ship, if they knew we were leaving. By now they had to know something was happening, but I couldn't predict their reaction. They wanted us gone, but they clearly weren't so naïve to think we couldn't come back at any time, so that wouldn't deter them. They'd be planning quickly. I had to assume that. I would have been in their situation, and I had to give them credit for having the same level of thought. Anything less was foolish. Never underestimate your enemy.

When the phone beeped I almost jumped out of my chair.

I let it beep a second time before I picked it up. "Butler here."

"Butler. It's Karikov."

"Karikov. Glad to hear you're alive."

"Ha! It will take more than a little firefight to knock me out."

"Yeah. Little firefight my ass." My mind raced. I hadn't thought it all the way through, what I'd do if he called. With Mallot dead, I needed to know if Karikov had regained control, or if there were more humans working with the Cappans. If anyone knew their plans, it would be Karikov or someone near him. "Are you alone?"

"Yeah, I'm alone. Hey, Butler . . . I meant to ask

you when you were down here. You know a guy from Polla Five named Kapinski? Short white guy."

"Kappy? Yeah, I knew Kappy." I also knew Kapinski was tall, thin, and black. A signal. Karikov wasn't alone, and what was more, he wanted me to know it.

"What ever happened to that bastard?" he asked.

"Kappy's on Ferra Three. He retired. Works as a contractor, sucking money off the government."

"Ha!" He answered. "Sounds about right. Anyway, they told me you needed to talk to me. Said it couldn't wait."

"Yeah. Stirling is pulling all his forces off the surface. Thought you should know. With no conventional forces for support, you probably should think about pulling out too. Just for a while." I wasn't giving anything away. If the people listening didn't know about the withdrawal, they'd have figured it out soon enough.

"That's good to know. We'll take a look at it," he said.

"Which way do you think the Cappans will go? You think they'll try to hit us as we pull out, or do they have other plans?" On the surface it was exactly the kind of question a conventional commander would ask a Special Operator. They knew the locals best. But I used it to give him a chance to tell me something else, if he could. I wanted him to give me a reason not to do what I had already, in my head, started planning to do. Anything at all.

The line stayed silent for several seconds. "Fuck that," Karikov said, in a muffled voice away from the comm. "We're probably not pulling out," he said, clearer. A thud came across the line and a moment later it went dead.

I didn't know what made the noise, but it sounded like a rifle butt striking a man's head. Karikov had paid the price for giving me that answer. It didn't sound important on the surface, but it had clearly meant something to him. It gave me the answer I needed, as much as I didn't want to hear it. Karikov wasn't in control planetside, and whoever was wasn't going to let him tell me anything else.

I pushed myself up out of the chair and got a plastic tumbler, then filled it half full of whiskey. I added four ice cubes for good measure. I swirled them so they tapped against the side. I missed glass. The sound of ice clacking against plastic didn't have the same effect. I was down to a bottle and a third left. I needed to wrap this thing up. I'm sure a doctor would have said something about drinking after a possible concussion. Good thing there were no doctors present.

I searched in a drawer for something to write with. All I could find was a crappy pen, but it worked. I got some paper and sat down to write. I needed to put some things down, and I didn't want it on the network.

I WOKE UP several hours later, the lights still on, but at least I'd made it to the bed. I didn't know what time it was, but my gut said probably the middle of the night. I'd ignored two buzzes at my door that I knew of, and who knew how many more while I laid there passed out. The visitors had clearly given up and left.

The pressure behind my eyes told me a hangover

draped over my future, so I got a big cup of water and drained it to lessen the effect. I went over to shut down the monitor and checked my messages. Nothing new. I didn't pull up the operations feed, because I didn't want to head back down that black hole. I planned to go back to sleep, and that would wreck it for sure. On a whim, I opened a new message to Serata.

Sir—No matter what happens, take care of Sharon.

Butler

I hit send and shut the system down. I stopped by the counter and took the last swallow out of my next-to-last bottle, then called for lights out.

THE BUZZER AT my door sent shards of pain into my pounding brain. As expected, mixing a bunch of booze and not enough water with a potential concussion had been a poor idea. The inside of my mouth reminded me of a sweaty sock that had dried in the sun.

"Open," I croaked. I didn't bother sitting up in bed. "Lights."

"Sir . . . you're still in bed. And there's half a battalion outside your door."

"Hardy. You're right. You're also out of the hospital. How's the hip?" I asked.

"Still stiff, sir. But I'm going to continue therapy on an outpatient basis."

I nodded, then thought better of it as it started my head throbbing. "Be careful at the hospital."

"Yes, sir. Mac mentioned that to me when he told me to get out of there, but I didn't understand. What's going on?"

"They've been doing genetic experiments using humans and Cappans. I know about it. They might not be happy that I know about it. Of course, now you know about it too," I said.

"Holy shit. Sorry, sir, I meant—"

"No, it's okay," I said. "'Holy shit' is about right."

"What are you going to do about it, sir?"

I half smiled at the innocence of being a lieutenant and thinking that the colonel could do something about it. I wish I shared that feeling. "Unfortunately, we've probably got bigger problems."

Hardy stood there, looking at me expectantly.

"You missed a lot," I said. "Get an ops brief. That will give you most of what you need to know."

"Yes, sir. You want me to turn the light off as I leave?"

"No, leave it on," I said. "I'm getting up."

I lay there for a few more minutes after he left, but eventually I did force myself out of bed and over to the coffeemaker, then turned on my monitor. A message from Serata flashed in the upper corner, and I touched it open. His response to my drunken message to take care of Sharon. One word.

Always.

I knew the answer before I ever asked the question, but seeing it on the screen still gave me chills. We'd promised each other a long time ago that if something ever happened to one of us, we'd look out for family. That was back in times when the chance of something happening seemed higher. With the recent events and the lack of direct guidance, it was good to confirm.

After a moment I flipped open the ops feed to see what progress Stirling had made, and more important, if there'd been any interference from the enemy. It took me a moment to fight through my fuzzy head and digest everything, but when I pieced it together, it looked good. Stirling had moved fast, shuttling troops up throughout the night. He had more than half the force off the surface, and the rate would only pick up from there. They'd be removing support stuff first, leaving lighter combat troops to secure the area for the transports to continue their mission.

I flipped it off and stared at the blank screen, sipping my coffee. I really wished at that moment that I had someone I could bounce my thoughts around with, but I didn't fully trust anyone. Alenda had proven herself, but the fate of a planet—that was beyond her. Stirling was definitely out. Hardy . . . his head would explode. I had Mac, but I couldn't put that kind of burden on him.

What made it worse was I had hours. Hours until the surface cleared, hours until I could take any sort of action at all. Hours where I had nothing to do but think about the most horrible act in a century. I couldn't sugarcoat it with myself. It was easy to blame the Cappans, but it really wasn't their fault. They hadn't asked us to show up and take over their planet. We were the invaders, and it would have been hypocritical to blame them for wanting to fight back.

That's why he'd sent me. He knew I'd do the job, despite my misgivings, despite my conscience. I'd live with it. There was too much risk to do anything else. If the Cappans got off planet with fusion weapons, there was no telling how many people would die because of it. That didn't make it right for us to attack them. But there was more than one right, and I always picked the right that helped our side.

I considered one more message to Serata, but decided against it. He'd said what he was going to say. I considered sending a message to Sharon, but decided against that, too. She'd only worry at the change in routine.

I looked around the room for anything else I might need to do. I pulled up the map and checked the recon reports that Alenda had provided for the fourth or fifth time, just in case I'd find something different. I didn't. The door buzzed and Alenda entered.

"Hello, Lex. Any news?"

"Nothing that's not in your feed, sir. What do we do now?" she asked.

"We go to the gym," I said. It was a stupid thought, given my badly beat up body, but habits die hard. I didn't know what I'd do there, but I'd find something.

"Excuse me, sir?" she said. "You want me to come?"

I smiled. "No, Lex. I don't. Your part in this mission is done. It's time for you to go back to your regular duties."

Hurt washed across her face, but she composed herself quickly. "What do you mean, sir? There's still work to do."

"There is. But only I can do it."

"I can help, sir."

I shook my head. "You've done great work. I couldn't have done this without you." I paused. "But right now I need you to give me some space. It's important."

She looked like she expected me to elaborate further, but I didn't trust myself to keep talking. She went over and made herself a coffee, then took a seat on the sofa, leaning back into the cushions.

"That's bullshit, sir." She sipped her coffee.

"Excuse me?"

"I'm part of this. You can't push me away like that." She looked at me over her mug. "Whatever you're doing, I want in."

"You . . ." I started to snap at her, but caught myself. I nodded, slowly, so my head didn't hurt as much. I needed to help her understand. It would have been easier if I could tell her everything. But I couldn't. "Lex, I trust you. But now I need you to trust me when I tell you that you can't be part of this."

"I can help!" I'm not sure if it was anger or frustration that crept into her voice.

I sighed. "Watch after Lieutenant Hardy for me. Make sure he's got a good mission."

She held my eyes for a time without speaking. "Sir,

what are you going to do? If you need me to take care of Hardy . . ." Her voice tailed off.

I sat silently, letting her think things through.

After a minute she nodded, set her cup down, and stood. "Sir, it's been an honor serving with you."

I struggled to my feet. I put my hand out and waited for her to take it in her firm grip. "The honor has been mine."

CHAPTER THIRTY-SIX

I STOOD IN THE hangar after dinner, watching the last ship arrive with troops from the surface. A big transport, long and narrow, it carried sixty soldiers. I waited patiently for them to come through decon, standing back so they wouldn't notice me. I wanted to gauge their mood, try to get a feel for what the last soldiers from planetside thought about pulling out.

I think I expected to see disappointment, but they didn't show any. They smiled and joked among themselves, but I guess that didn't mean much. They could simply be happy to be out of the miserable planetside existence and back to the relative comfort of a base station. Their real feelings wouldn't set in until later, and that made me feel a bit silly for thinking I'd learn something.

I gathered my funeral procession of guards and headed back to my quarters. When we arrived, I told a soldier whose name I hadn't learned to get Mac, and one of the other soldiers scurried off.

I looked over at the one unopened bottle of whiskey and thought about it. I thought about it hard. But

I didn't touch it. That was a long five minutes, waiting for Mac to buzz at the door and come in.

"You wanted to see me, sir?"

"Yeah." I took two envelopes off the desk. "Take these. In twenty-four hours, no matter what happens, I want you to hand this one to Plazz."

"Yes, sir." Mac had to have questions. Where I'd be, why Plazz. But he didn't ask. I knew he wouldn't, and I loved him for it.

"The second one, have it sent to Sharon," I said.

"Sir, that will take months," he said.

"I know. I have my reasons."

Mac stood silently, looking at me. "Yes, sir," he said, finally. "Sir . . . is everything okay?"

I forced a smile. "It's okay. Just cleaning some things up, that's all."

I stood there, unmoving, and watched him leave. Once he'd gone I sat down in front of my terminal and opened up a comm link to the operations floor.

"Operations." A woman's voice, the hum of activity around her. Things always moved and buzzed in ops.

"This is Colonel Butler. Let me talk to fire control," I said.

"Yes, sir." The line went silent for a few seconds.

"Fire control, sir. This is Major Salcedo."

"This is Colonel Butler. I want you to port a link to the fire-control program to my terminal."

The line stayed quiet for a few seconds, but I knew he was there from the noise around him. "Are you sure, sir?"

"Check my authorities. I'll send a bio confirmation."

I tapped to open the box on my screen, then placed my thumb against it.

"Got it, sir. I acknowledge your authorities."

"Okay. Good. Send me the link," I said.

"Sir, if you have targets, I can execute them for you."

"Salcedo."

"Yes, sir?"

"Do you know who I am?" I asked.

"Yes, sir."

"Okay. If you know who I am, then you know that I'm perfectly capable of managing the interface with a fire-control computer. Right?" I'd spent a lot of time with fire control. It wasn't a secret, and as a fire-control officer himself, Salcedo would know.

Silence. "Link is open, sir."

"Thank you." I cut the voice connection, then opened the link. I didn't have long. Right now Salcedo was panicking, trying to decide if he should monitor my activity or report it. He'd be calling for the ops chief, who would take less than a minute to decide whether or not to call Stirling. Stirling would take longer, though. He'd think about it, wonder if he could stop me. Wonder if he should. I'd have enough time.

I gave a last second thought to how I'd reached this point. If any one of half a dozen things had gone differently, it may have ended another way. If I'd managed my relationship with Elliot better. Or Stirling.

Or Serata.

I took a handwritten page of notes out of my drawer and typed in eleven sets of coordinates from the paper. I left the munitions field on the fire order blank, until it was the only thing left to complete, in case Salcedo was watching.

XB25

The comm beeped almost instantly. I didn't wait for it to beep a second time. "Butler here."

"Sir, this is Major Salcedo. You entered XB25 in the fire order."

I smiled to myself without joy. I knew he'd be watching. "I know what I entered."

"Sir, with that munition and that firing solution, the result will—"

"I'm completely aware of the result. Thank you." I hung up.

I looked at the screen for perhaps two more seconds, then hit execute. I couldn't see the result, but within a couple of seconds missiles launched from ships in orbit around the planet. They'd have been on blockade duty, but their fire systems were still active and the remote order would trigger them. I stood up, walked over and picked up the unopened bottle of whiskey, then opened the door.

"Sir!" The team outside snapped to attention.

"Let's go," I said. "Colonel Stirling's office."

We didn't quite get to Stirling's office. Stirling met us in the hall, doing some sort of funky run where he tried to make it look like he was walking. He pulled up short when he saw me. "What did you do?" he asked.

"Let's talk in your office."

He stared at me for a moment, then he looked at

the soldiers around me. He turned and headed toward the office. My protection detail danced to get out of his way. I followed behind, not hurrying. My leg throbbed. Neither of us spoke until we reached his inner office and he'd shut the door.

"XB25s! What the fuck did you do?"

"I brought you my last bottle of whiskey." I held it out to him.

He looked at the bottle in my hand for at least four or five seconds. "Carl . . ."

"You're going to need to arrest me," I said.

"Arrest you? For what?"

"Probably genocide," I said. "They'll figure out the charge."

His shoulders slumped for a moment, his normally rigid posture shrinking in on itself. He reached out and took the bottle from my hand. "Carl . . ."

"I know what I'm doing with fire control, Aaron. I picked the targets carefully."

"Fusion weapons. Planet busters . . ." He walked over and got two glasses out of a drawer in his desk. Real glass, heavy and perfect. He popped open the bottle and poured us each two fingers, then got ice from a dispenser and put two cubes in each glass. He walked back to me and handed me one, then held his up.

I clinked my drink against his, then swirled the brown liquid, listening to the ice tinkle against the glass. "The situation is contained."

He took a drink, then nodded. "At a heavy price."

I sipped my drink, savored it. I wouldn't have another for a long time. "A heavy one indeed. But I paid it. I acted alone. I had the authorities. Nobody could have stopped me."

He stood silently, looking into his cup, probably trying to think it through, see if it would come back to him. "So what now?"

"Now—after I finish my drink—you arrest me. You put me in cryo, put me on a ship, and send me back to SPACECOM. By the time I get there in six months or so, they'll have figured out what comes after that."

He blew air out through his nose. "Yeah. Okay."

"Take care of Mac. Sergeant McCann. I mean it. Whatever he needs, you make it happen."

He nodded. "Sure. Of course."

"One more thing I need you to do," I said. "I can put it in a written order if you need me to."

"Not sure a written order would matter after I arrest you. At that point an order would be a pretty flimsy cover."

"Yeah," I said.

"What do you need?" He picked up the bottle and poured more of the liquid into my glass.

"You need to go into the hospital. Find the geneticist and arrest him. Elliot and her people conducted genetic experiments on Cappans and humans. I don't care if you have to burn down the hospital. Send him back on the same ship as me."

Stirling smiled. "I'd be happy to execute *that* order."

"It will piss some people off," I said.

He shrugged. “Fuck ’em. Are you okay?”

I thought about it for a moment, but I didn’t know. It didn’t matter. I nodded and gave him a fake half smile, then finished my drink in a big swallow.

“You ready?” he asked.

I set down my glass. “Yeah. I’m ready.”

ACKNOWLEDGMENTS

A novel is not a solo endeavor. Many, many people had a hand in this.

I could not have done this without my agent, Lisa Rodgers. She believed in the book, sold it, and answered my ridiculous debut author questions, but more than that she provided absolutely brilliant editorial advice that refined the story into what it is today.

Thank you to David Pomerico and the entire team at Harper Voyager for their belief in my book and their hard work to make it a reality. Thank you to Sebastian Hue for the art, and anybody else who had a hand in the awesome cover.

I owe a debt of thanks to Dan Koboldt and the entire Pitch Wars crew. Dan has been a huge help to me through more than just the Pitch Wars contest. He's taught me a ton about what it means to be a professional writer, and he continues to mentor me to this day.

Thank you to my brother, Steve Mammay, who was the first one to read any of this. His advice and confidence gave me the initial push I needed to turn it into something better. Thanks to my sister-in-law, Melissa

Mammay, for her excellent feedback. Thank you to my early readers David Kristoph, Jessica Bloczynski, Tahani Nelson, and several others who read smaller portions of the book and offered advice.

Three critique partners have been with me before, during, and after I wrote this book. I learned more than I can express from each of them. Morgan Levine does beautiful things with words to which I can only aspire. Her fingerprints are on this book in a dozen subtle ways. Rebecca Enzor kept me sane during the trying times that come with any book, and continues to do so.

I cannot possibly overstate the importance of the support and advice of Colleen Halverson. Her work on this book, and more significantly, helping me to develop as a writer, defies words. I appreciate her attitude, her work ethic, and her friendship.

Most important, I would like to thank my wife, Melody. Her unwavering support and belief is amazing. Her sacrifices for me and our family, not just with this project but in all things, are humbling. Without her love, none of this would matter.